DEAD WOLF FALLING

BAD MOON ACADEMY TWO

RORY MILES

AUTHOR'S NOTE

Hello and welcome back.

Bad Moon Academy is about to get a little darker, a little creepier, and a little more perilous.
You forgot to tell them about all the peen...
NOT NOW, JOAN!

This is the second installment of Bad Moon Academy, and as such, there will be a cliffhanger. Book three will mark the final book and end with a happily-ever-after.

Please note: There are triggers for substance abuse and self-harm. Take care of yourself.

Copyright © 2021 by Rory Miles

All rights reserved.

No part of this book may be reproduced in any form or by any electronic or mechanical means, including information storage and retrieval systems, without written permission from the author, except for the use of brief quotations in a book review.

***

Editing by Bookends Editing

Cover design by Design by Definition

❦ Created with Vellum

Walls have ears.
Doors have eyes.
Trees have voices.
Beasts tell lies.
Beware the rain.
Beware the snow.
Beware the man
You think you know.

Catherine Fisher

PROLOGUE

RAVEN

"Happy birthday to me!" I sing to myself like a lunatic. But hey, who wants to be sane when you can be insane? What does it take to be free of memories? If I try hard enough, maybe I can forget. Opening my mouth, I tip the cheap plastic bottle of vodka up, scowling when only a few drops make it to my mouth. It's gone.

Dammit.

I shouldn't have shared with Tracy, but she was in desperate need of a drink after her boyfriend broke up with her. Jacking the convenience store was easy, especially when she kept the clerk busy by leaning on the counter and pushing up her cleavage. I swear I could have set the place on fire and he wouldn't have been able to rip his eyes from her boobs. We're new friends, and I didn't tell her it was my birthday, so we spent the whole night cursing Zach's name instead of pretending to be excited about me turning seventeen. Who cares about birthdays when your parents are dead?

Sighing, I toss the bottle into a shrub, stumbling slightly on the gravel road that leads to Aunt Lou's.

"Tracy's lucky I like her," I say to the country road. My new home is about a mile closer to town than hers, and I make a point to walk when I'm drinking, saving all the destruction for myself.

Rocks crunch and wobble under my chucks. I run my hands through my hair, shoving it out of my face as I stagger on. A strong summer's night breeze caresses my skin, cooling down my overheated body. The familiar buzzing sensation in my stomach makes me giggle, and despite being out of alcohol, I smile.

The best part of being drunk is when my head fills with bubbles and I feel like I'm floating. Spreading my arms out, I toss my head back and howl at the sky like an animal, gasping when I trip over my own feet.

"Oh shit," I say when I drop to my knees, hissing in pain when a sharp rock bites into my skin.

That'll leave a mark.

Sitting back on my heels, I clutch my stomach and laugh, rocking side to side as the stars above spin and swivel. My stomach cramps, warning me I'm about to heave. Crawling on my knees toward the ditch, I spew the seven-dollar Ice Castle and whatever food is left in my stomach from dinner onto the wildflowers. My eyes fill with tears as the burn of bile stings my throat and the sharp tang of vomit fills my nostrils.

Ugh. I hate throwing up.

A wolf or coyote howls in the distance, a mockery of my attempted one, and I scowl over my shoulder.

"I get it, okay. I'm not one of you." I shake my head and shove to my feet, continuing home. I'm well past curfew, but I have to make it home or Aunt Lou will have my ass.

Something massive and covered in dark fur leaps from

the other side of the road, landing in a slight crouch in front of me. Bright yellow eyes study me, and gleaming white teeth threaten to eat me up, like the nursery rhyme. I touch a lock of hair, wondering if it's a coincidence or if I'm hallucinating.

I didn't take any shrooms this time, but with enough alcohol, things can get weird. It's so big it has to be a male. Aren't most males bigger than females?

Tell me nature isn't sexist. Why do they get to be large and in charge? Well, female lions run the show, so I guess not all of nature is sexist. Either way, I'm pretty sure this pup is a boy.

A bubble of gas works its way up my throat, and I burp, smacking my hand over my mouth in horror. Where are my manners?

"'Scuse me, Mr. Wolf." I curtsey, or do my best wobbling version of one. "I'm Little Red. Have you come to eat me?"

The wolf tips his head to the side and licks his lips, like he understands what I'm saying.

"You're going to be disappointed." I step toward him. "I'm all rotten inside. You'd be better off finding a bunny."

With a shrug, I squat a few feet away from him and click my tongue at him, then frown. That's for cats. What do you do to get a wolf to come over?

"Here boy!" I pat my thigh and suck in a sharp breath when he moves toward me. There's no way this is real. "I'm so drunk," I tell my new friend, extending my hand so he can sniff it.

His nose is wet and cold, breath hot against my fingers, and if I were sober, I'd already be running home screaming for help. A smarter version of me would listen to the little voice in my head telling me I'm being incredibly stupid.

But this wolf is nice. Maybe he wants someone to pet him. Biting my lip, I tip to the side and reach for him, falling on my ass in the process and making him growl. The hair on my arms rises, and shivers race down my spine.

That's not friendly at all.

"Here I thought we were going to be buddies. Ow," I say, getting off the rocks which are poking my butt.

The wolf has stopped growling, and his glowing gaze is pinned on me. I hold his stare, trying to figure out what he's thinking.

Poor thing stumbled upon a lame human.

Jerking my thumb toward the trees, I say, "There's a little path in there. Want to walk with me?"

He doesn't answer. Of course he doesn't, he's a wolf. They don't talk. Rolling my eyes at myself, I stand up and grin at the midnight-black animal, holding my arms out to keep my balance.

"I run," I tell him like we're good old pals.

God, I'm pathetic.

"You like to run too, right?" I ask, starting toward the trees.

He chuffs.

I spin on my heel, eyebrows hitting my hairline. "Was that a yes?"

Silence. He blinks and prowls closer, keeping his steady gaze on me.

"I'll race you." I run, pathetically so in my drunken state, tripping and weaving, but I run all the same.

A sharp yip sounds behind me, and a flash of black races past.

"Show off!" I shout after him as he lopes ahead of me with ease.

After about a minute, I have to stop. I bend over and put my hands on my knees, breathing way too hard for the distance I just jogged. The ground spins, and I tip over, rolling onto my back with a groan when my body hits the earth.

A mouth full of sharp teeth appears above me. The wolf stands over me, squinting at me. He's probably wondering what's wrong with me. To be honest, so am I.

"It's my birthday." I reach up and brush my fingers over the fur covering his chest. Impossibly soft and silky. This is definitely a dream. Dream wolves can't bite, right? "You're so pretty." Sitting up, I wrap my arms around his neck and hug him despite the deep growl rumbling out of his mouth. "Yeah, yeah. I get it. You're a tough guy."

With a heavy sigh, I lean against him and hold on, soaking up his warmth and forest scent. He smells like midnight runs, earth, and pine. For some reason, it makes my chest pang, and I long for home. Not Aunt Lou's house, but my childhood home, where on any given weekend my parents and I would explore the forest and hills surrounding our countryside home. Breathing him in, I hold a little tighter. *Home.*

"I think you and I are going to be good friends," I tell the imaginary creature, rubbing my hand over the top of his head. I start to doze off, fingers still pressed against the wolf, his steady breathing providing me a sense of security. That is until he pulls out of my arms. My eyes snap open, and I stare at him.

He blinks, releases a small chuff, then turns away.

"Wait!" I scramble to my feet.

The wolf is trotting away now.

"You're going to leave me too?" I scream, starting off in a jog after him. "Don't leave, please."

He picks up speed, so I do, too, ignoring my stomach which cramps in protest.

"Take me with you! Hey! Wolf!" I pant. "Don't fucking leave me," I whisper.

Casting a glance over his shoulder, he bares his teeth like he's trying to warn me off.

"You don't scare me," I say with a laugh, tripping over my own feet. Shooting my hand out and grabbing a nearby tree branch, I groan.

I'm way too drunk to be chasing after an imaginary wolf.

He tips his head up and howls; the eerie sound should terrify me, but if anything, it draws me closer.

Throwing my head back, I join in, but my ridiculous attempt cuts his short. Looking at him, I shrug to say *sorry for interrupting.*

He growls again; this time it's deeper and draws a sliver of fear down my back. When he runs off, I don't try to follow.

"Stupid wolf." I wipe my hand over my damp cheek, cursing myself for being sad about something my imagination created.

CHAPTER 1

DRACO

Raven races out of the room before any of us can stop her. By the time the three of us make it to the hallway, she's already jumping over the rope blocking off this wing. Everett shouts her name, but she doesn't slow down. We stop at the top of the stairs, watching as she dashes through the front door. I don't even know if she got Joan back. She fled before answering Everett's question.

"Fuck, who was that?" Carter asks, running his hands through his hair.

"I don't know." My wolf growls, and Everett shoots me a look which reads *control yourself*. How can I control myself when she left us behind to race toward two men? Two men means one of us is out.

As much as these guys annoy me sometimes, I can't imagine myself getting along with anyone else. It only works if Raven is with us.

"Let's go; she'll have a few moments before we catch up." Everett rushes down the stairs, but the door snaps shut and the lights switch off.

"Where are you going?" a pouting feminine voice asks.

I grind my jaw. Should have fucking known she'd show up. Jinx walks out of the west wing of the first floor. Her black hair is piled high on her head in some ridiculous hairdo and she's wearing a corset-bodice gown. When her glowing white eyes lift to take us in, my wolf snarls in my head. He doesn't like her, and I can't blame him. Jinx is bad news.

The three of us pause on the stairs. Carter glances at Everett who shakes his head. I roll my eyes. Why must I always be the one to engage the fucking demon?

"Jinx, I didn't expect to see you for another week."

The grin splitting her lips is vicious and half-cocked, like she's waiting for a reason to lose her shit. She's always dangerous, but this version of Jinx is the deadly one. She's like a mass of clouds swirling above the landscape, waiting for the perfect dip in pressure to drop to the ground in a cyclone of destruction.

"Shall we go get our friend?" she asks, moving toward the door.

"Jinx, don't." Everett's voice cracks through the air, filled with alpha power which sucker punches me in the gut. He'd do anything to protect Raven, including enraging this bitch.

I slam my elbow into his stomach, and he growls. The idiot is going to make things worse.

"Why don't we leave Raven? Maybe we can get some tea?" Carter asks, trying to sound friendly. The vein on his forehead tells another story though, and he shoves his hands into his pants to keep her from seeing his fingers have curled into fists.

Jinx pauses with her hand on the door, tilting her head to gaze at us with those milky eyes.

"You think you can protect her from me? You know your

power can't touch me." Jinx tsks. "What did I tell you about trying to keep my presents from me?"

Carter takes a step down. "Jinx—"

The demon spirit gasps and clutches her chest, sneering at the door. "Fae." She hisses the word like a snake about to strike.

A rush of air slams into the academy, rocking the walls. I stumble slightly but grab the railing to steady myself. Everything creaks, like the foundation is suddenly unstable.

"What was that?" Carter asks, eyes swinging to me like he thinks I'll know what happened. Or like I'm the one who caused it.

Narrowing my gaze, I scoff. Why do I always get blamed? Sure, sometimes I do bad things, but I'm not all bad. Sometimes I do good things.

Everett lets out a whoop of joy. "Can you feel it? The ward is gone! Let's fucking leave." He sprints down the stairs, but Jinx shoves her hand into the air, catching him in a wave of magic and holding him suspended above the ground.

"Silly fool. You are *mine*." Then she swings her arm toward the floor and Everett crashes into the marble hard enough to break it.

He groans and curls into a ball, clutching the back of his head which is turning red, the buzz cut doing nothing to hide the blood from the cut. Judging by the way he's taking shallow breaths, he may have cracked a few ribs.

"What's happening?" Morris, one of the newer wolves asks from the third floor. He rubs his eyes and yawns. "Did you guys feel the earthquake?"

Stretching my senses, I search for the familiar darkness that is our cage. Invisible magic which holds us prisoner. Nothing is there. The wards fell. Jinx can't keep us here any longer.

Carter and I share a look then rush down the stairs. Jinx

opens her mouth and screams, the sound reverberates through my skull, and I trip, losing my focus due to the vicious sound slicing through my mind.

"Jinx." Carter wheezes her name. He's a step ahead of me, and he crashes to his knees, clutching his throat and gasping for air. She can hurt us, but thanks to the bracelets she gave us, she can't feast on our souls or wolves. Remembering this, she stops screaming and snarls. Carter collapses, forearms slamming onto the marble as he sucks in a ragged breath.

A shout of pain rises behind me, and a series of thuds follow the sound as Morris tumbles down the steps. Jinx's lips split in an evil grin, and she races around us toward Morris, distracted by the easy prey. My heart is slamming against my rib cage, and I set my hand on the wall to keep from crashing to the floor like Carter. The demon magic she released with her scream is still rolling over me, making it hard to breathe.

Raven. I need to get to Raven to stop her from leaving without us. A violent wave of nausea washes over me. I lean my head against the wall, eyes catching on a little girl standing at the end of the hall which leads to the headmaster's office. Bea, Raven's friend. Her eyes are round with fear. I grimace and stagger forward, reaching for the doorknob. Jinx's hand is covering Morris's chest; his body is shriveling the longer she pulls from his essence. The once strong shifter is slowly being reduced to nothing more than a husk of a being. I reach the door and stare at the girl, using the fingers dangling at my side to gesture her closer.

Her eyes flit to Jinx, and her chin trembles at the sight of the demon spirit sucking Morris's soul from his body.

Hurry, I mouth the word to her, hoping she'll see the plea in my eyes. If we can't escape, I have to make sure she has a chance.

Bea shifts on her feet, and her sneakers give a soft squeak.

Fuck.

"Now!" I shout.

Dashing toward me, she squeals when Jinx whirls around and screams. With the last dredges of my strength and sanity, I wrench the door open in time for Bea to slip through.

She yells Raven's name as she runs toward the gate. Jinx hisses, starting toward the door, mouth pressed in a firm line. I stagger into her path and slam my hand into her chest to try and keep her back, though it's more of a fumbling touch than anything.

"You've been a naughty boy, Draco. My snack has escaped." Her eyes light with malice, and she drags her finger over my neck. "You're lucky you'd make a better meal."

"No," I rasp, trying to shove away from her, but it's too late. A vile smelling, oil like substance spills from her lips, and she spits a glob of it at me.

"Sleep well, dear. We're going to have so much fun."

I'm a fool. Jinx has kept us for years without feeding on us. I assumed we were safe since she marked us as hers and gave us protection. The jade stone wrapped in leather has been our safeguard ever since the incident with Brayden, but now it seems our time has run out. We're no longer playthings to her but the enemy.

There's a shift in the air, and the demon's eyes glow even brighter than before, lighting up like beacons as darkness surges around her. Dozens of specters materialize around her—Morris included. Tiny threads shoot from their bodies and wrap around Jinx as they nearly form into tangible beings. There is only one person who can make her this powerful.

Licking her lips, Jinx tosses her head back and cackles, the sound booming around the room and out into the night. "Welcome home, Raven."

CHAPTER 2

❦

RAVEN

A frigid breeze sweeps around me as the cackle floats through the air. A trickle of fear spreads through my body as a shiver races down my spine. Four wolves howl from inside the academy. I recognize three of them. Draco, Carter, and Everett. The other one is unfamiliar, but something in me stirs when the howl brushes over my skin.

"No! Raven? Raven! Where is she?" Aunt Lou's voice rises with every word she utters, and her panic steals my breath.

Spinning on my heel, I race toward the gate, forgetting all about the wolves. I grip the bars and try to yank the gate open. The lock doesn't move. A sharp sting zaps my palm, but I grit my teeth and tug on the iron, not caring that the pain intensifies the longer I hang on or that my hand is growing slick with blood.

"Aunt Lou! I'm here." I groan and pull on the gate again. It doesn't budge. Why can't Aunt Lou see me? I don't understand. Maybe the pack magic makes it hard for her to see through?

Adler's strong hand grips my wrist and peels it off of the bar, saving me from further injury.

"I can see you, little wolf." Adler's fae friend stares at me, making me feel less crazy.

"She's there? Where is she? Get her out of there!" Aunt Lou pulls a pistol from underneath her shirt and points it at the fae.

"Aunt Lou, no." I glance at Adler's friend. "She won't shoot you. She's scared."

At least, I hope she won't shoot him.

Maybe she should, Joan says.

He's not the one who put us in here, I remind her.

She harrumphs and quiets, so I return my attention to the gun Aunt Lou is holding.

"Tell her... tell her I kept my promise."

He murmurs the words to her, and her eyes widen and search the space where I'm standing, but she still can't see me. The pistol wobbles as her hand begins to shake, and the fae spins, snatching the gun from her hand and hurling it into the forest.

Aunt Lou gasps. "Why can't I see her?"

"I don't know," the fae says. "Adler is with her, can you see Adler?"

"Lou," Adler says, arm brushing against mine as he steps in front of me.

She furrows her brow. "No."

Adler waves his hands around. "Lou!"

A heavy stone drops to the pit of my stomach. *Oh no.* I swing my gaze to Adler's. Is he stuck in here because of me?

"Can you shift and fly out?" I ask, reaching for his forearm and giving it a quick squeeze. "Try."

Heavy lines crease his forehead, but he dips his head and shifts, taking to the sky and flapping toward the gate. When he reaches the top, he screeches, his eagle form seizing and plummeting toward the ground. Moving with supe speed, I reach both of my hands out and catch the bird. His eyes are closed, but his body expands when he breathes in. He's okay. Knocked out, but alive.

Adler's friend is cursing in a foreign language, and Aunt Lou keeps asking what's happening.

"Raaaveeennn," the voice says again, taunting me. "You can't leave this time. You're meant to be part of the academy."

Like fuck I am.

When we find this chick, I'm going to rip her fucking throat out, Joan says on a growl.

At least we're on the same page.

But first, I have to do something I don't want to do. Even though I know sending Aunt Lou home, where she's safe, is the right thing to do, part of me wants her here with me. Swallowing all my selfish desires, I swing my gaze to Adler's friend.

"What's your name?" I ask the fae.

"That creature can't help you!" the voice says, growing louder.

Glancing over my shoulder, I check for any sign of life. My eyes land on Bea, still crumpled on the ground. Other than her and the lights blazing from inside the academy, there's nothing out here.

"Lucien," the fae says.

"Will you make sure my aunt gets home safe, Lucien?"

His attention strays to Adler who is still asleep in my arms. His eagle form may be smaller than his human one, but he's still heavy. My biceps begin to burn the longer Lucien stares at his friend.

"I will take your aunt home, but you must promise me no harm will fall on Adler."

Aunt Lou gasps. "I'm not leaving, you fairy *freak*."

Recalling changeling's sordid history in Faerie, I don't

understand why this obviously powerful fae cares what happens to the discarded low fae. Still, he makes me an offer I can't refuse.

"Please don't hurt her."

He grimaces. "I will have to remove her memories. Otherwise, she will find a way to return."

"Excuse me?" Aunt Lou lashes out at him with her palm, but he catches her wrist and hisses at her, much like a cat would an enemy.

"You can do that?" I ask.

What sorcery is this? Joan's suspicion mirrors my own.

With a final glare at Aunt Lou to make sure she doesn't try to hit him again, he turns to me and dips his head.

"I have to."

Wavering with indecision, my stomach churns and threatens to turn at any moment. To strip someone of their memories has to be crossing a moral line. I'm not sure knowing it was for her own protection will be enough to make me feel less guilty. I'd be asking him to take something from her she'll never get back. Surely she wouldn't want to keep this memory though, right? He has to do it, especially if I want her to stay safe and far away from the academy.

"Okay," I say, tears pricking my eyes. "I will make sure nothing happens to Adler." A bold promise I'm not even sure I can keep, but I will fight with my life to keep him protected from whatever darkness waits for us.

His eyes grow cloudy, and he grabs her other arm, holding her still. Aunt Lou releases a soft breath. Her face smooths, and the fight in her eyes slowly fades until all that's left is confusion. He whispers something to her, and her eyelids flutter closed, legs giving out. Lucien catches her around the waist before she can fall to the ground.

"It is done. When you get out, tell Adler he knows where to find me."

Not if. When. His confidence in my ability to make it out of here is overwhelming, but he doesn't give me a chance to voice my worries. He sweeps Aunt Lou into his arms and disappears into thin air.

Another freezing rush of air swirls around me, reminding me my business with Bad Moon Academy is far from over. I adjust Adler in my arms, not getting much relief from the strain, and turn. Bea is stirring, so I rush to her side, shooting my gaze around for any hidden threats.

Whoever is keeping us here is part of the darkness: the spirit who attacked me and stole my wolf in the ballroom. The thing that thinks I belong here.

"Raven?" Bea's voice is as frail as she looks, her body sickly thin. "She has them."

"Has who?" I ask, gently placing Adler on the grass to rest my arms. He's still knocked out cold, but his chest is rising and falling in a consistent pattern, so I know he's okay. The pack magic didn't keep him here before. I'm not sure what's changed, but the ward shocked him when he tried to leave.

"Carter, Draco, Everett, and the dark one." Bea kneels, and I take her hand, flipping it over and feeling for her pulse. Her heart is beating so slow.

"The dark one?" I ask, trying to figure out if I should be worried about her heart rate.

The little one will heal. Her wolf is a delta, so her power is not as strong as ours.

Strength impacts healing? I ask.

Yes. The stronger the wolf the faster the healing.

Another bit of shifter information I store away for later. This world is so complicated compared to the one I'm used to. Humans don't have super healing. While there are some people who are master manipulators with an odd aura which seems to draw people to them like magnets, they can't control people with their words like I can. At least, not without abuse and conditioning. The toxic gravity of a narcissist is hard to resist, but it's nothing compared to shifter power dynamics.

If I told Bea to eat the grass beneath her, she would. She may try to fight me, but she'd succumb to my luna power. If only spirits listened in the same way.

Speaking of ghosts, the voice from earlier is gone, and the silence is almost too quiet. The hair on the nape of my neck rises, and I help Bea stand before scooping Adler up in my arms and climbing to my feet. The grass is soft, so at odds with how dead it was when the pack wards broke. I eye the academy.

Why would the wards breaking kill the grass? Why was the academy broken and desolate when the gate finally opened? What type of spirit am I dealing with?

Frowning, I glance at the little shifter. "Bea, can you take me to the guys?"

She whimpers and shakes her head.

"Can you tell me where they are at least?" I hold up Adler. "You can watch my friend to make sure nothing bad happens to him?"

Her eyes fall on the eagle and widen as though she's seeing him for the first time.

"Okay," she whispers.

"Follow me." I set off at a clipped pace toward the school.

Bea jogs to keep up with me, and when we reach the front door, which is standing wide open from Bea's exit, we pause. I crane my neck to look inside. There's no one in sight. The lights are blazing brighter than I've ever seen them burn, and the cold grows more intense, seeping into my bones like a winter's chill.

"I'm scared," Bea says on a whine.

Facing her, I take in the tears tracking down her cheeks and the tremble of her chin. Poor thing. She's only fourteen.

Sure, I'm four years older, but the years between fourteen and eighteen are more than just years. It's the transition from child to young adult, and Bea has yet to go through the hardest parts of it.

"It'll be okay," I say because what else do I tell her? *Yeah, me too. I'm pretty sure we both might die?* No. I can't give her a reason to panic. The best thing I can do for her now is to help her feel safe, so I lie. "I think I have a way to save everyone, but I need you to be strong. Can you do that?" I want to reach out and wrap my arms around her, but I can't because of Adler.

Her light brown eyes search my face, and whatever she sees there must fill her with confidence because she wipes the tears away and nods.

"Okay, we're going to go to my room. Whatever you do, no matter what you hear or see, don't stop until you get there."

Who knows what sort of shenanigans this spirit has in store for us?

This is a bad idea.

We don't have a choice, Joan. We have to help the guys.

Oh, now you want a harem. Joan scoffs.

Do you want them to die? I ask. *Because that's what will happen if we don't find a way to get them back from. . . this thing.*

No, she admits.

I check on Bea again to make sure she's still okay. Her jaw is set in determination and there's a fierceness about her gaze which warms my heart. She's a strong kid. I whisper count to three and we rush inside, making a beeline for the stairs. If I were human, the dash up three flights of stairs would affect me more, but as it is, I'm hardly winded by the time we reach the third floor.

Bea is right behind me as I sprint down the hallway toward my room. She surges in front of me when we reach it, opening the door and letting me in before pulling it closed. My heart is pounding in my chest. The lamp on my bedside table flickers a few times. I squint at it, wondering how every light suddenly got turned on when the wards slammed back in place, and then I set Adler's bird form on the bed. I wish he would shift so I could put clothes on him. Hopefully, he'll stay unconscious while I go to find the men; Bea doesn't need to see him in all his naked glory.

I toss a shirt over the lower half of his body, hoping it'll be enough to save them both the embarrassment. Bea's carefully walking around my room, hovering her hand over the globe and the raven on my desk but not actually touching anything.

"Where are the guys?" I ask her, pulling on a sweater over my shirt—which is damp with sweat. The academy is so cold I'm shivering.

Or maybe that's the nerves.

"She probably has them in the basement."

"Which one?" I run my fingers through my messy hair and twist it into a bun, not caring when a few stray pieces fall out of place. "The gym or the crypt?"

"Neither. They're in the dungeon."

The dungeon?

I frown. "Where is that?"

"The stairwell is on the opposite side of the first floor from where Headmaster Erron's office is."

"Past the cafeteria?" I raise my eyebrows. All my visits there and I didn't even think about there being more on the other side of the buffet line aside from a kitchen.

"Yes. Through the kitchen door and into the supply closet. There's a door there."

Chewing on my lip, I search her face. "Bea, how do you know where the dungeon is?" I cross my arms over my chest.

Is she the bad guy?

"I've been down there before. It doesn't feel right." Her eyes widen, and she blinks at me.

I cringe when her lip begins to tremble.

"Are you mad at me?" Her voice breaks, and I officially feel like the world's worst human, I mean shifter, being.

"No, Bea. I'm not mad." I cross the space between us and hug her, chest tightening when she releases a soft sob. "I'm sorry, sweet girl. I'll fix this, I promise."

I know better than anyone how soul crushing broken promises can feel, but I can't seem to stop the words from tumbling out of my mouth. She sucks in a hard breath, and I pull away and look at her.

"Take care of my friend, okay? He's important."

She rubs her arm under her nose. "Okay."

Shall we go save our men? Joan asks.

Hell yes. This spirit is going to wish they'd never messed with us.

～

THE ACADEMY IS QUIET AS I MAKE MY WAY TO THE CAFETERIA. Not a soul—alive or dead—in sight. The door leading to the kitchen stands ominously at the end of the buffet line, and my stomach churns the closer I get. I don't know what waits for me in the dungeon. I've never experienced a spirit like this, filled with such malevolence and obvious insanity. Who else keeps students here and slowly eats away at them?

Glancing down at my body, I'm once again amazed by the power it displays. When the ward—if that's even what it was—broke, I was bone thin and my skin was shriveled as though I'd sat in a bath for too long. Now my skin is healthy and my weight has gone back to what it was before I was turned into a shifter. Now I know why Joan is always so hungry; the spell over the academy made me oblivious to the fact that I was fading away.

I place my hand on the door, the hinges making it swing back and forth with ease, and then give it a shove. I shoot my gaze around the kitchen until it swings back and I catch it with my palm. Empty as far as I can tell. With a deep, steadying breath, I pull my shoulders back and push into the kitchen. The tile is a muted brown, and the appliances are all outdated and covered in layers of dust. Almost like they haven't been used in years.

I search for any hidden threats before I explore. Satisfied there are no boogie men lurking in the corners, I walk over to the stove. It's at least fifty years old. I run my finger over the grime, grimacing when I stare at my now black fingertip. This kitchen hasn't been used for a long time.

This doesn't make sense. Where did all the food come from? Where's the smoker for the brisket? Was it all a manifestation of the ghost? My eyes land on a large fridge. I rush to it, yanking the doors open and immediately covering my nose.

If you try to feed me that, I'll throw up all over you, Joan whispers.

Trust me, I have no inclination to eat. . . whatever that is. The only thing in this refrigerator is an awkward, almost oval shaped blob sitting on a shelf. It's black and moist. Congealed liquid pools around it. My stomach heaves and bile fills my throat. I slam the doors shut and lean my back against them, breathing through my nose to keep from throwing up. After a few moments, I recover and decide my time exploring this place is done.

Way to delay the inevitable with a disgusting detour.

Excuse me for being curious, Joan. Aren't you the least bit concerned about how our body is even functioning right now?

Our priority is saving the men, then we can deal with how we will find real sustenance.

Fine, I grumble in my head.

The door which I assume leads to the supply closet is shorter than an average sized one. I peek through the cloudy window. There are a few good potatoes, a box of pasta, and crackers sitting on one shelf, but the rest are empty. Entering the room, I walk around one of the shelves and see a small, worn door. White mist curls from the gap between the wood and floor, reaching for me. Cold seeps into my veins, and my breath fogs in front of my face. This is definitely what Bea was talking about. With one last steadying inhale, I open the door and start down the cement stairs. Wrinkling my nose and taking short breaths, I try not to gag on the mildew filling the stairwell.

I place my hand on the brick wall, cringing when something slick coats my skin. It almost feels like moss. Wiping my hands on my pants, I take slow, measured steps to avoid tripping to my death.

Something feels wrong about this place.

How observant of Joan. I don't respond to her because while I want to be a smartass, she's right. Something does feel wrong. There is no light, but my eyes have adjusted to the endless dark. I duck under a row of bricks which hangs down to frame the bottom of the stairwell.

Thank you, supernatural eyesight.

The sharp tang of copper fills my nostrils as I round the corner and my jaw drops. An old kerosene lantern sits in the middle of the floor. Morris is lying on the ground, body withered and void of life. A trickle of blood runs down his jaw. I wrap an arm around my middle and smack my hand over my mouth to keep from gagging.

Morris is dead.

How?

Raven, we have to get them out, Joan says, drawing my attention to the others.

Behind his fallen body kneel Draco, Carter, Everett, and Layla. Their mouths are gagged and their hands are tied behind their backs. On light feet, I move around Morris, avoiding looking at him because if I let myself stare for too long, I'm afraid I won't be able to focus on the mission. I bend to start figuring out how to undo the wrist restraints. Draco tries to say something, but the gag muffles the words.

Metal scrapes against concrete, a long, drawn-out sound that sends a shudder through me. My fingers pause on Draco's ropes, and I slowly lift my gaze to stare over his shoulder. A woman in a scarlet ball gown, black hair piled high on her head, holds a long, rusted pipe and stands next to Morris. She tips her head, nudging the toe of her shoe into his arm and tsks.

"Oh my, little bird, what have you done?" The woman's milky eyes swirl, and her form flickers slightly, like a picture cutting out on a television, before it solidifies and she seems as real as me. Her cheeks even flush, like there's actual blood rushing to her face.

"You killed him," I say, standing from my crouch and curling my fingers into fists at my sides.

All the more reason to kill her, Joan growls and pushes against me, trying to force a shift.

Gritting my teeth, I force her back down. She hasn't tried to break free of my hold for a while now.

The woman's lips curl back like a Cheshire cat, and she raises her eyebrows. "I did, didn't I?"

"Why?" I flick my gaze to Morris. "How?"

It shouldn't be possible. Ghosts can't kill people, can they?

She steps around him and moves toward me, the pipe dragging along the stone floor in an eerie screech. Everyone in line growls in warning, but whatever she's using to hold them in place is strong enough to keep them from shifting and breaking free.

More pack magic?

"Oh, dear. I'm afraid your friends don't like me, little bird." She places her hand on her chest.

I narrow my eyes. "Gee, I wonder why. Maybe it's the shifters you've been killing?"

"They're not all dead. Well, not entirely," she says with a wink. "You know a little something about that though, now don't you? The living dead."

Fucking witch. She saw those memories of my mother trying to raise my father when I saved Joan.

"And how long have you been the living dead?" I place my hand on the back of Draco's neck, right where the gag is tied, and try to wiggle my fingers through the knot.

She chuckles. "I'm not living, little bird. I'm dead as a doornail, just a bit shinier." She grabs the edges of her skirt and swishes it back and forth. "I think I look pretty good for being dead, don't you?"

How is she here if she's not alive? Joan asks.

Some spirits are strong enough to take shape like this; to be able to kill, though. . . she has to be incredibly strong. I'm not even sure how it's possible, I confess.

Talk about being out of my element.

"What do you want?" I ask as I slip my ring finger between the knot and start to work it loose.

"If you undo that gag, I'll have no choice but to kill him next." She sighs and gazes at Draco. "He is too handsome to die."

I drop my hand and step away from him. "What do you want?"

She exhales. "You're persistent, aren't you? You know, since I've met you, I've been wondering something. . ."

Not giving her a reaction, I blink and swallow my emotions.

"How is it that you managed to kill not one, but two parents?"

A deep growl rumbles in my chest thanks to Joan, and I bite the inside of my cheek to keep from gasping. Sometimes people are assholes to you because they're too afraid to deal with their own damage. I guess the same goes for ghosts. She obviously wants to hurt me, though I'm not sure why or what I've done to her.

"You don't know what you're talking about."

She purses her lips. "Hm. Raven, the beautiful young shifter. She's always *so* strong. I think you'll be the most fun to break, though Everett seems like he'll put up a good fight."

Everett snarls around the gag, saliva dripping down his chin. The light of the lantern reflects off of his yellow eyes, his wolf close to the surface.

"What do you want? Why do you need them if you had Morris?" I ask.

The woman—whose name I still haven't learned—scoffs. "Morris was an appetizer, hardly one at that." Her form flickers, and she sighs. "That's your fault, you know. You broke my ward. I had to recharge and he"—she points to Morris—"didn't give me nearly enough."

She uses their souls as energy. That's why shifters have been going missing over the past two years. She said they're not all dead though. Meaning this bitch is using them, keeping their souls alive somehow?

"You're going to take their souls too?" I ask, hoping to confirm my theory.

With a quick nod, she advances, flicking out of sight and reappearing next to me. Draco tries to turn around, but she shoves the pipe into his back hard enough he grunts and stops moving.

"Move and you die." Her gaze sweeps over Carter, Everett, and Layla who are all looking over their shoulders, torn between helping me and becoming her next meal. The men both look ready to lose it all to help me, so I shake my head at them.

No one else needs to get hurt. Not if I can help it.

A cool finger brushes over my cheek, and I jerk my eyes toward the woman, but her hands are still firmly wrapped around the pipe. Cool air, more frigid than the air already surrounding me, presses into my back before shifting around me.

My phantom friend.

I fight against the smile threatening to tug at my lips, but the woman sees my struggle and scowls at me.

"I don't know why you're laughing, little bird. You're the main course."

Like fuck we are.

You know, I agree with Joan. Reaching down into the well of forbidden power, pulling on the darkness I know better than to play with, I clutch it tight and send it through my body, channeling the ichor into my palms.

"Hasn't anyone ever told you not to play with your food?" I ask, shoving my hand through the cold, pressing my palm against her. In her mostly solid form, my fingers sink into her chest and she gasps in surprise.

Her eyes go wild, and she mutters in what sounds like Latin, but it could be another language for all I know. The freezing cold air around me grows even colder, and my teeth start to chatter. The woman wraps her hands around my forearm and electricity zaps from her to me, stunting my connection with my power.

I gasp when the electric power slices through my body like an invisible saw.

"You're a fool." She hisses the words, and a chorus of growls answers her insult.

Unable to pull my gaze from her, but feeling the others fighting to free themselves to try and help gives me strength to reach into the dark abyss of Death's power once more. Harnessing more than I ever have before, I grind my teeth, holding on until I have enough to light this bitch up like a Christmas tree.

Only one of us is going to die today, and it won't be me.

As if sensing my intentions, she amps up her powers, making me cry out when another bout of pain lances through me. She's so strong.

So are you. Send this vile creature to the other side.

Joan sounds so confident. I have nothing to lose, so I drag another ounce of Death's power into me and send it through my arm and to my hand. Just before the power blasts from my palm, a freezing cold chest replaces hers. My phantom.

"No," I say and try to pull my hand away, but it's too late. The dark power fuses my skin to my phantom's body, and my necromantic power pours into him. Trying again to pull away, I gasp when the dungeon grows even colder. I can't move my hand, can't stop what I've started. There's no controlling this now. My nose aches from the chill, and the air escaping my lips turns into a thick cloud of fog. The oily essence of death thrums through me in an uncontrollable river, drowning the phantom.

He'll be gone forever.

Tears sting my eyes, and I pinch them shut when the air begins to warm around me. He's fading from this realm, taking his chill with him.

I'm killing him, and I can't do a damn thing to stop it because I foolishly took too much of Death's power. This is what happens when you mess with necromancy. Nothing good ever comes from it.

How is it you managed to kill both of your parents? Those words bounce around my mind, the toxicity of them bleeding into my heart and turning it black.

No, Raven. That's what she wanted. Don't let her win.

I'm killing him, I whisper to Joan.

How can you kill something that was already dead?

Semantics. You know what I mean.

The spirit screeches, but the sound is cut off, and she gags. My eyes snap open, widening when I see Draco standing in front of me, holding her throat in his hand. My palm is flush with his chest, and I blink at where our skin is connected.

He's not wearing a shirt.

Wasn't he wearing a shirt?

I open my mouth to say his name, but he flexes his forearm, squeezing the spirit's neck harder. Her form flickers, fading in and out until she has entirely disappeared.

Draco turns around to face me and runs his hands through his long black hair, the light of the lantern illuminating his features.

"Hello, Little Red." His voice is deep, deeper than I'm used to, and when he stares at me, I see his eyes are almost electric blue. "Thanks for the level-up." He smirks and glances over my shoulder. "Hello, Brother."

CHAPTER 3

BRAYDEN

I turn around as soon as the demon spirit vanishes. The restraints holding the others in place dissolve with her disappearance. The woman bends forward, clutching her stomach, but the guys shoot to their feet, and my brother presses into Raven's back, crowding her space. She doesn't notice though, because she's too busy staring at me with a cute little furrow of her brow.

"Hello, Little Red. Thanks for the level-up." I smirk at the widening of her green eyes as she takes me in. I glance over her shoulder, meeting Draco's squinting glare. "Hello, Brother."

"Brayden," he says on a growl.

Raven gasps and spins around, jaw dropping open when she sees him. Her gaze bounces between the two of us and Draco scowls at me as though it's my fault she's slow on the uptake. He was the one who came up with the plan, not that anything has gone the way it was supposed to, but still. She's clueless because he's decided to keep my existence a secret, hoping she'd help him once she fell for him.

Idiot.

He's angry at me, I suppose, but I was tired of waiting. I saw my shot and I took it; even he can't fault me for trying. As soon as I knew Raven could sense me, I knew she might be able to bring me back. I just hadn't expected it to work out so beautifully.

"How?" she asks, stepping away from him and toward Carter and Everett.

I advance, but Draco lifts his arm to stop me. I press my chest into his forearm, relishing in the touch. How long has it been since I last saw him in the flesh and not through the lens of the other world? Showing myself to him and actually being here are two entirely different things. Before when I touched things, it was like wearing a pair of latex gloves. I could feel what I was touching, but there was no warmth. No energy. I felt none of the life which fills Earth. It fucking sucked.

Until Raven. Touching her was like being struck by lightning.

What are you waiting for? My wolf snarls in my head, making me chuckle in surprise.

So you're not dead after all, I say to him. It's been two years since I last heard him, and he's pissed.

Hardly. Shift so we can claim the luna.

I tsk. *Such a barbarian. Patience is key, my little friend.*

He growls at my insult, but I slam a mental wall up to focus on whatever Carter's murmuring to her.

"—brother. It's okay."

"How did this happen?" she asks, shooting me a look. Confusion lines her face, but there's a fire in her gaze, kindled by my sudden appearance.

Does she miss my phantom form?

"Your little demon friend likes to play with her food. Unfortunately for her, Death is stronger." I reach up and brush my fingers over my hair, loving that I can actually feel the softness of it.

"Demon friend?" Her gaze skates around the room. "She's not a spirit?"

"Oh, she is," I reassure her. "A demon spirit though."

"She's—gah." Everett bends over and places his hands on his thighs, sucking in a sharp breath like someone sucker punched him.

Raven reaches for him, rubbing his back as he composes himself. A low rumble of appreciation sounds from his chest. I narrow my eyes at the contact and ignore my wolf who is screaming for me to claim her.

Lunas are not meant for one, but many. My wolf has yet to accept his fate since Raven somehow brought him back not but two minutes ago. Draco steps closer and yanks me into a hug, taking a deep breath.

I awkwardly pat his back. "We spoke a few days ago."

He shoves me. "It's not the same. You were dead."

Knowing he's right about the first part, I place my hand on his shoulder and squeeze it. Time to correct him about the second part.

"In a sense," I say, sighing. "Like I said, unfortunately for our little demon spirit, Death is stronger."

And he's a bit of an asshole.

Raven snaps her head in our direction. Her bright red hair is tied up in a bun, and I want nothing more than to reach up and rip out the hair tie so I can watch it tumble down her shoulders.

"Death? As in... *Death*?"

"Precisely." I remove my hand from Draco and step toward her.

"I think I'm going to throw up," the other woman says before bending over and hurling on my shoes.

"Fuck," I mutter. "I already miss pretending to be a phantom."

"Pretending?" Raven asks with a bite. "Who the fuck are you?"

I glance up from where Layla's still retching and meet her angry gaze. "I'm Brayden. We've danced together, or do you not remember?"

"We've danced. . ." She trails off, flicking her gaze to Draco who is glaring at me like his annoyance will somehow make me shut up.

With a dark chuckle, I nod. "That was me." I side-eye my brother. "Oh, he didn't tell you?"

"What the fuck is he talking about?" Everett asks, finally recovered from his go with Jinx. The injury from earlier in the foyer is fully healed, but he's still covered in blood. Taking a deep drag of the delectable coppery scent, I grin.

"Your blood smells wonderful," I tell him.

Draco begins to growl at me. He's always trying to keep me down, so I roll my eyes and ignore him. He's so dramatic.

Carter pinches the bridge of his nose. "Can we please take this upstairs? Morris is dead, the demon spir—ugh—*thing* will come back, and I'd rather not be where she's most powerful when she does."

I see Jinx still has him under her spell. He can't even call her what she is without being attacked by her magic. There are some benefits to almost dying, I guess. At least she can't keep me from speaking.

"Oh, Morris," Layla whispers.

The color and spark of fire drains from Raven's face as she goes to help her friend. "I'm so sorry," she says, grabbing the woman around the middle before she can fall to her knees.

"Come on, let's get everyone upstairs."

Everett helps Raven and Layla to the stairs and goes with them.

"What happened?" Draco hisses. "This wasn't the plan."

I shrug. "No, but it worked, didn't it?"

"Yes, but at what cost?" He growls and shoves into me hard enough my shoulder jerks back.

My wolf rages in my head, but I excel at ignoring him. He's a bit blood thirsty.

"She'll come around," I say. "Trust me."

"The last time I did that you ended up dead." He shakes his head and storms out of the dungeon, leaving me with Carter.

The professor stares at Morris's body with a severe frown. "I don't know what you two have been planning, but if you screw this up for me and Everett, I'll kill you myself."

I pout and place my hands on my cheeks. "Are you sending me to detention?"

Not expecting a reaction, I laugh in surprise when he plows into me and my back slams into the brick wall. He punches the brick, breaking it, and bares his teeth at me. His eyes flash yellow, and I can't help but stare at his beast to rile him up. He's only a delta, so if I wanted to, I could make him submit, but it's been too long since I toyed with him.

My wolf howls, begging me to use my beta power.

Not yet, I tell him.

Carter's pinning my chest, so I lean my head forward. "So touchy," I say quietly. "Calm down, Carter. Our luna has already chosen us. Raven will come around."

Carter punches the brick again, this time with a partially shifted hand. His claws gouge the mortar. "You'll only get one warning," he says before stepping away and retracting his claws. Straightening his shirt and concealing his every emotion behind a calm facade, he glances over me and points up the stairs. "Go fix the mess you've made."

CHAPTER 4

RAVEN

Once we get to the first floor, I help Layla to the stairs, and she sits down, dropping her head onto her knees. I join her and watch Everett pace in front of the door.

"What is going on?" She doesn't lift her head, so the question is muffled.

"I'm not exactly sure," I say. "Whatever we're dealing with is dangerous."

Layla sobs, and I rub her back, unsure of what to do to help her. I hardly know Layla, but she's always been nice to me. She doesn't ignore me like everyone else.

"That's the first dead body I've ever seen," she confesses in a soft voice. "What happened to him?"

So many questions and so few answers. I bite my cheek and shake my head, though she can't see it since she's still curled into a ball.

"We'll figure this out," is all I can say.

I don't want to scare her with what might be. The spirit, or demon spirit if Brayden is to be believed, was stronger than before. She's the same thing that tried to attack me in the ballroom. This time she appeared almost human after what she did to Morris.

Layla sobs. Rubbing my hand on her back, I try to say something reassuring, but everything I think of sounds superficial. There are some deaths which leave a permanent scar on your soul, an invisible reminder that life can be cruel and violent. I've seen too many of those in my short life. Morris is another nightmare to contend with.

Something flickers in my peripheral, drawing my attention to the corner near the front door. Mom is standing with her head tipped to the side, studying me and my friends with a small frown. Her wrists are seeping blood. I pinch my eyes shut and will her away. I hate when she shows up. When I first started seeing her ghost, I was happy. Now though, her presence pisses me off. A reminder of what she did and how she left me.

"Raven," Carter says.

I open my eyes. He's squatting in front of me, forehead wrinkled with frustration or confusion. Maybe both. Still, his gentle gaze pulls me from the depths of my anger and misery and brings me to the present. Brayden, Draco, and Everett stand behind him, whispering. Everett's mad at Brayden, and Draco's trying to defend him.

Twins.

Identical twins. Brayden is a carbon copy of Draco. If it weren't for the slight eye color variation and deep timbre of his voice, I'd never know the difference between the two.

I look at Carter. "Can you explain?"

He pinches his eyebrows together. "Not as well as Brayden."

"He's not bound by pack magic?"

"No. His death must have broken the hold it had."

I shake my head. "He wasn't dead."

"What do you mean?" Carter places his hand on my knee.

Layla lifts her head, swiping at her damp cheeks and sniffing. "I don't understand any of this. How do you know he wasn't dead?" Her voice is shaky. She's still in shock.

"I can see the dead." Pressing my lips together, I wait for Layla to freak out. Much to my surprise, she doesn't.

"Brayden can't have died, because if he had, the person I brought back would have been a shell," I answer Carter's question. "He's been gone for over a year?"

He nods. "Close to two years."

I furrow my brow. "He wasn't dead." There's no way. He wouldn't have come back with this much consciousness. Mom's little experiment with Dad showed me how messed up and void of life Brayden should be if he had died. I glance at the man. He's watching me with slanted eyes. His teeth sink into his lower lip, and I scowl.

He's *too* alive.

"What does she mean brought him back?" Layla asks Carter, voice rising to a squeak. "What is happening?"

Carter searches my face, and I nod, giving him permission. "Raven can bring the dead to life."

"What?" she screeches the question.

Apparently, seeing the dead is okay, but reanimating them is a no-no. Go figure.

"Layla," I begin, but she stands, stumbling away from me.

"You're a freak," she whispers. "All of you are. None of this is normal. Morris is *dead*. Why are you all so calm?" She turns and runs down the wing with the headmaster's office.

I sigh and rub my temples. Telling Morg and the guys went so smoothly, I guess I expected Layla to be all right with it too. She's only been here a week longer than me though, so she's been through a lot of shock in the last month. Adding the fact that I'm a necromancer on top of everything else, well, I can understand her reaction. At least she's an adult and I don't have to worry about leaving her alone while she deals with the trauma. I'm so relieved Bea stayed with Adler.

"Crap," I say before hopping to my feet. "Bea's in my room with Adler."

"Who's Adler?" Everett asks, breaking away from his pow-wow with Draco and Brayden.

"My. . ." I trail off, thinking of the right word for him. "Friend," I say, finally settling on the simplest explanation. How would I explain what Adler means to me without making them upset?

Adler has been in my life for a few years, and over the last few weeks, he's gone from coworker and friend to something more, but not quite definable.

He's part of our harem, Raven. Get it right.
Not now, Joan.

"I have to go check on them." I turn and head to my room.

No need to give the men more of a reason to get defensive. Wolves are territorial by nature, and seeing as now a fae is within their territory, I'm certain there's going to be a confrontation, or at the very least, some grumpy growling. I hear and feel the men following after me. I'm keenly aware of the new energy behind me. Brayden's presence is stronger, almost like there's a string tying us together which sways with each subtle movement he makes.

A side-effect of bringing him back from wherever he was? Maybe.

There's no time to get information out of him now, though, because we've reached the third floor. I head down the hallway leading to my room, growing more concerned with every step because the door is cracked open, and I distinctly remember shutting it. The light inside my room shorts out.

"Something's wrong," I whisper before sprinting the rest of the way to my room.

"Raven, wait!" Everett shouts, but I don't stop.

Shoving the door open, I glance around my empty room. Bea and Adler are nowhere in sight. I go to the bathroom, wrenching the door open and checking in the shower and cabinets.

"No. No, no, no!" I say, returning to the bedroom. I drop to my knees and check under the bed. There's no one hiding under there. "They were here." I sit back on my heels and glance around; three of the men press in, forming a protective half-circle behind me.

"Uh, Raven?" Everett asks from where he stands at my window, glancing over his shoulder at me. "I think your friends are outside. The little one is running toward the woods... carrying an eagle?"

"An eagle?" Carter murmurs. "The one from her first day. Of course, that bird was so strange." He's talking to himself.

I get to my feet and turn, smashing into a wall of muscle. The three men before me have their arms crossed over their chests and none of them look entertained. I'll be damned if they keep me from getting Bea and Adler back inside where it's safe.

"Move," I say, filling my voice with luna power so it cracks like a whip.

They split apart and drop their gazes in unison. I glance them over, shaking my head at their weirdness in response to my command, and run out of the room.

Why are Bea and Adler outside?

∼

"Bea!" I scream, searching the grounds once I go out the back door.

The sky is still pitch black in the early morning hour, but

the nearly full moon gives me plenty of light. Bea was heading toward the woods.

Let me help, Joan says. *I can find our little wolf.*

Okay.

Releasing control of myself to Joan, we shift, shredding our clothes and landing on four paws then race into the tree line as soon as we catch a whiff of Bea and Adler. Joan's better at tracking than I am, so I sit back and watch the world race by.

Up ahead we see a flash of brown hair.

Don't scare her, I say.

I'm not scary. Joan huffs.

Bea is already frightened, having a wolf jump out and surprise her probably isn't the best plan.

We can let her know we are near, Joan says.

Lifting our head, we release a soft howl, saying *we're here, little one*. Bea stops when she hears it, and we close the distance between us, slowing to a trot when we reach her. She's holding Adler in his eagle form in her little arms and blinking back tears. Strands of brown hair stick out at odd angles, like she ran through brush and snagged them on small twigs.

"Raven?"

We chuff.

She cries. "It tried to take him, but I wouldn't let it." She holds Adler up. "I kept him safe like I promised."

We nudge her hands with our nose and brush against her, trying to calm her down. When none of this works, we shift.

"Bea, it's okay," I say, dropping to my knees so she doesn't feel threatened. She's short for a fourteen-year-old, probably a few inches shorter than five feet. Maybe it's why she seems so frail to me.

Her eyes widen at my sudden shift and nakedness. "I was trying to keep him safe."

"You did a good job, Bea." I squeeze her shoulders, and she blinks back more tears. I wipe away one that escapes her control and jerk my head toward the academy. "I got the others back. What do you say we go back inside so I can get dressed?"

"Okay," she says with a nod.

"All right." I shift, and we set off toward the academy at a slow walk, trotting next to Bea. For how terrified she is, she carries Adler like he's made of porcelain.

"It's okay. It's okay," she says. Bea's nervous energy is making me wary of returning, but I do need clothes and there's the matter of figuring out how to help everyone escape before someone else dies.

Something tells me we won't escape unscathed. The demon spirit doesn't strike me as someone who gives up easily.

Too bad for her I don't either.

I'll find a way to protect everyone. I have to.

CHAPTER 5

EVERETT

"Let's go make sure nothing happens to our luna." I tap the pane of glass and head to the door.

Brayden smirks. "So it's decided then? She's ours?"

"We will be hers if she chooses us," Carter says, shooting him a pointed look. "Lunas are not taken, Brayden. You know this."

He lifts a shoulder and rolls his eyes. "Relax, Carter. No one is going to force her into anything."

"Shut up, let's go." Draco storms from the room, shooting a sneer at his brother on the way out.

"Trouble in paradise?" I ask Brayden with a smile.

Flipping me the bird, he heads out of the bedroom, followed by Carter. Going to Raven's dresser, I grab a shirt and shorts for her in case she shifts and doesn't take off her other clothes. I know how she gets about being naked in front of other people. She's still new to shifting and it embarrasses her.

Before I leave, I glance around the room once more, checking for any sign of Jinx. Satisfied the vile creature isn't in here, I head after everyone, knowing soon enough Jinx will make her appearance.

I can only hope we'll be ready for her this time.

∼

RAVEN

We make it back to the school. The guys are waiting for us, each wearing their own version of a displeased frown. Everett tosses clothes in front of me, so I shift, landing in a crouch and quickly pulling on the shirt and shorts. Not that it matters. None of them are paying any attention to me since their eyes are all transfixed on the eagle.

I glance at Adler in Bea's arms and grimace. He still hasn't woken, and I'm not entirely sure how to go about explaining what he is and how I know him. I mean, obviously he's an eagle shifter, but his other form presents some issues since the only shifters from Earth are wolves. Bea presses into my side, and I wrap my arm around her shoulder.

"It's okay; I'll deal with the men." Shooting my gaze around them, I sigh and shake my head. "Let's go inside, and I'll explain."

Carter's eyes narrow. "How do you know a fae?"

With a shrug, I steer Bea around them and start inside. "I didn't know he was a fae until about three weeks ago."

We walk through the foyer and up the stairs to my bedroom. I glance over my shoulder on the way, taking in the way they eye Adler's eagle form like he might attack at any second. This is going to be one of the longest days of my life.

Everett closes the bedroom door once we all filter inside and leans against it, crossing his arms and lifting one eyebrow. "How do you know we can trust him?"

Bea lays Adler on the bed and carefully sits next to him,

taking care to make sure he doesn't roll off. I run my hand over the soft feathers covering the eagle's chest.

"Adler's my friend. We can trust him." I set my jaw in a firm line. There will be no debate about this. Adler is like family.

Draco and Brayden share a look which seems so inherently twin-like that I stare at them a moment before clearing my throat to continue.

"He works at Aunt Lou's bar. He's a fae, like Carter pointed out, and he's the one who helped break the pack magic."

Brayden snorts. "Pack magic? Is that the song we're singing?"

"It was the easiest way to explain—you know what? We don't have to defend ourselves to you." Carter pinches the bridge of his nose and turns away from Brayden. "Why did he help you?"

I furrow my brow and sit next to Bea. "Because he wanted to save me from being held prisoner? What does he mean by *the song we're singing*?"

Scrubbing his hand over his face, Everett bangs his head against the door. "You're in such a talkative mood, Brayden, why don't you explain since none of us can." Holding up his wrist, he flicks the bracelet.

Ah. More pack magic weirdness.

Brayden's piercing gaze sweeps over me and a flush rises up my neck when I remember he's the one who got me off in the ballroom. Not Draco, who I know, albeit a little bit, but Brayden, a virtual stranger. My stomach flutters at the memory, and the men inhale.

"My, my, Little Red, whatever are you thinking about?"

I flip Brayden off, and he smirks. Draco squints at his brother before focusing on me. The way his eyes light with desire makes me wonder if perhaps Brayden had been lying. Maybe it truly was Draco in the ballroom and not his twin?

"Pack magic is not what's keeping you prisoner, Raven. It's the demon and the alpha."

Pulling my attention from Draco, I clasp my hands together and stare at the wall. "The demon spirit is keeping me here?"

"The demon spirit *and* the alpha. You shouldn't forget his role in all of this." Brayden steps closer and my eyes snap to his. His face contorts with annoyance, though the emotion isn't directed at me. "You see, without abusing changed wolves, he wouldn't be as powerful, nor would our little friend Jinx."

"The missing shifters," I conclude. "They're using them for power, right?" I figured as much earlier.

Brayden nods. "Bad Moon Academy doesn't run without Jinx, and Jinx doesn't run without food, and you, my dear, have been slowly devoured by her. Jinx's little illusion makes a functioning academy out of what would otherwise be a dilapidated mansion with broken doors and lights. Filthy, but functioning all the same."

"How did you figure this out?" Draco asks, stepping in line with Brayden so their arms brush against one another.

I volley my gaze between the two, searching for any distinguishing feature which keeps me from being fooled by twin switching. Or if Brayden wants to pretend to be Draco again; though I guess he wasn't entirely pretending... I never called him Draco, and he never told me he was. Still, he knew what he was doing, letting me believe it was his twin all along to get close to me. But, then again, I let the phantom get close too, and I didn't mind that.

You're conflicted about him.

Obviously, Joan. He isn't who I thought he was... or, he isn't who I expected him to be.

She hums. *If he were a phantom, would you still long for his touch?*

I don't long for the phantom's touch, I respond with a huff.

Sure you don't.

Whatever. Sometimes I hate having her in my head. It means she knows way too much about my reactions and desires.

"Being sort of dead comes with its perks, Draco." Brayden flicks his hair out of his eyes.

Everett grunts. "Speaking of sort of dead—" He cuts off, and his eyes widen.

A small whoosh is the only sound I hear as Adler shifts. He doesn't have enough room on the bed though, and he slides off the mattress, landing on his bare ass on the floor. Bea squeaks and scoots to the middle of the bed.

Hopping up from the bed, I grab a towel from the bathroom and hand it to him, smiling when he looks at it then down at his naked body. His fingers brush against mine when he reaches for it. Once he wraps it around his waist, he stands, earning a growl from each of the men. I scowl at them all before pulling Adler into a hug.

"Are you okay?"

He keeps one hand on the towel but wraps his other arm around me, squeezing me tight.

"A little tired, but alive."

"Well, that counts for something, right?" I ask and pull away to meet his amber gaze. "Your friend took Aunt Lou home."

The arm around my back slides away, and he adjusts the towel, tucking it tight against his body. "He'll take care of her."

"I'm Draco." A hand shoots between us, causing me to take a step back. "You are?"

I dig my elbow into his stomach, but Draco simply grabs

it and yanks me against his body, wrapping a possessive arm around my shoulders.

Adler tracks each movement he makes, narrowing his eyes at the shifter.

"I'm Adler."

Draco tsks. "I must have misspoken. What type of fae are you and which court are you from?"

"I'm not from a court."

"Lying already? Is this why you like him?" Draco whispers the question into my ear, and I roll my eyes.

"He's not lying." I glance at Adler. "Right?"

Adler's mouth twitches. "I'm not lying. I'm not from a court, and I'm a changeling."

"That explains your interest," Carter mutters to himself, remembering the day I wanted more details about Adler's particular brand of fae.

I look at him and lift my shoulders in apology.

"A changeling from Faerie with sights on our luna. What do you want with Raven?" Brayden asks, placing his arm on top of Draco's and caging me between them.

Someone call the doctor, I feel faint.

Joan, really? I ask.

Normally, I'm more of a charcuterie type of wolf, but I can get down on a twin sandwich.

You are one thirsty bitch, you know that, right? Also, pun intended. I can't judge her too much because she's not the only one picturing being pinned between the two bad boys.

Bad boys, bad boys, whatcha gonna do.

How do you even know that song? I chuckle inside my head.

Unlimited access to your memories has its perks. Though I'm not sure I enjoy years sixteen through eighteen much.

Sighing, I say, *Yeah, me neither. Okay, I have to focus, the guys are going to start thinking I'm crazy.*

More like they want a snack.

Putting up the mental shield, I block her out, shifting my attention to the guys who are all glaring at Adler like he's enemy number one.

"I want whatever she's willing to give," Adler says, dropping his gaze to mine. "Whatever she wants. However I can help. I'm hers."

Heat crawls up my neck, and the twins growl. I scoff and shove out of their hold. "Adler came to help me. Be nice to him."

Draco and Brayden's eyes pierce into mine, and I don't know which twin to focus on. Adler moves into my space, cupping my elbows with his hands.

"Do you need my help now?" he asks.

Being subtle isn't something Adler is known for. I crane my neck and glance at him, seeing his stoic gaze set on the twins. He's almost a foot taller than me, so my forehead brushes against his scruff. Adler glances at me, his irises darkening when they meet mine, promising to hurt them if I ask.

"They're harmless, Adler. Troublemakers for sure, but they're okay."

His face softens, and he nods. "This one is from the bar."

Draco hums and runs his hand through his black hair, pushing the longer strands out of his eyes. "You're the bartender." His lips curl into a cruel smile. "You stopped me from beating the creep to a pulp."

Adler's fingers tighten around my arms. "I would have stopped you from hurting him at all had I known you were a shifter."

I knew Adler went out to run interference the night the skeeze at the bar tried to hit on me and shoved Draco, but I didn't realize Draco had actually started beating the guy once he dragged him outside.

A loud boom shakes the academy. The shifters in the

room release growls at the same time, and Adler bands his arm around my chest. Bea whimpers from the bed and points at the desk. The globe starts to spin. The black and white sphere moves slowly at first before spinning faster and faster, making the metal rod whine.

The raven statue rattles, and Bea screams. The casted wings break free, pieces of black clay falling to the floor. Opening its beak, it releases a shrill shriek before shaking its head and flapping into the air. Shards of clay tumble to the floor as it screeches and flaps overhead.

Bea drops her forehead to the mattress. The bird swoops toward me, so I lift my hand and swat at it, hitting the soft feathers of its underbelly.

"Grab it!" Carter shouts, reaching for the bird.

Snapping its beak at his fingers, the bird dodges his hand and circles close to the ceiling, evading the other men as well.

The globe stops spinning, toppling over with the force of its abrupt stop. Another explosion rocks the building, and the bird drops mid flight. Falling to the floor with a thud. Everett scoops it up and grimaces.

"There's no heartbeat."

"Doesn't mean it's dead," Carter says, grimacing. "Jinx is up to something."

"Maybe I need to have a word with our little demon nemesis." Brayden turns toward the door.

"Wait," I say, stepping out of Adler's hold and grabbing his arm. His body is cold, much like the chill I feel when the phantom touches me, and he cuts his gaze to where my skin rests against his. "What if she hurts you?"

His grin makes me regret the question immediately. "Scared for me, Little Red?"

With a scoff, I drop his arm and back away. "No—"

Two screams, both distinctly feminine, echo down the hallway.

Growls rise around me, and I release one of my own, not liking the situation one bit.

Where's Morg? Joan asks.

I glance over my shoulder, realizing I haven't seen her. Aside from Bea, Morris, and Layla, I haven't seen any of the other students. Are they hurt? Does Jinx have them all?

I don't know but something tells me we're about to find out.

The screams ring out again, and I exchange a look with Brayden. His lips pull into a grim line.

"I think we all know what this means," he says, opening the door and looking back at us. "Jinx wants to play."

"I'll stay with the child," Adler says, sitting on the bed and holding the towel tight around his waist. Bea is curled into a ball on the bed, still terrified from the bird.

"Are you sure?" I ask. "The last time I left you alone. . ." I trail off, letting him fill in the rest.

He gives me a reassuring nod. "I can protect her and myself from this Jinx person now that I'm awake."

"Okay. There are shirts in the dresser. They probably won't fit, but we'll get clothes for you in a bit."

"I'll be all right."

I don't like it, but we don't exactly have time to argue because a pained cry fills the hallway. The other men crowd around me, and we move through the threshold. I glance at Adler one more time before Everett pulls the door shut.

"The screams are coming from the ballroom." Draco pulls ahead of everyone and leads us to where Jinx is likely to be.

We reach the second-floor landing, all of us stopping in front of the velvet rope which sections off the west wing. Carter places his hand at the small of my back.

"To stay safe, we stay together."

Brayden dips his head in agreement. "She'll try to separate us at some point. Picking off the weakest link first." His eyes flit to Carter, who bares his teeth at him. "You *are* the delta, are you not?"

"Yes," Carter grits out between clenched teeth.

"Then you better make sure you're not separated from the rest of us. It's either you or the eagle, and no offense, my money is on the fae being stronger."

Carter's chest rumbles. I place my hand on it to calm him down.

"Now isn't the time for a dick measuring contest."

I wholeheartedly disagree, Joan says, pushing past the mental shield.

Did you not hear the screams?

With a haughty huff, she says, *Fine, but soon.*

Yeah, yeah.

"Let's go," I say, starting down the hall and dragging Carter along with me.

Everett, Draco, and Brayden fall in behind us. A sweep of cool air washes over me and an icy finger traces down my neck. I toss a glare at Brayden, but his hands are at his sides. The curious smile he's wearing makes me uneasy. Can he use both forms, or is he stuck to the one now?

I focus on the ballroom doors again, fighting off a wave of nerves when the cackle from earlier—Jinx's maniacal laugh—reverberates through the air.

"You know what makes you all so soft, don't you?" she asks as we enter the ballroom.

Morg and Layla are lying on the floor. Neither are moving. My stomach cramps and churns with unease. I rush toward them but stop when Jinx steps in my path, blocking me. The woman's eyes are so white it's creepy, and the skirt on her ridiculous gown is so big it brushes against my legs even though she's a few steps away.

"Hello, my pretty."

I squint at her. "You chose to play the ugly witch." Despite her crazy eye color and being an insane demon, Jinx is pretty.

She grins. "Perhaps, but underneath all the green skin and warts, I have a feeling she was more beautiful than Glinda, the dunce." Leaning closer, Jinx whispers, "Besides, I quite like being wicked."

Stepping toward her, I clench my hands into fists. "If you hurt them—"

"Relax, your friends are asleep. For now." Her eyes stray over my shoulder, taking in the men. "I see you've found your harem."

She knows about Adler, Joan says.

Of course she does, she locked him in here with us.

"Do you know the answer?" she asks, grabbing my arm in a firm grasp. Her fingers are freezing and my skin goes numb where she's touching me.

"What?" I try to tug out of her hold.

She yanks me closer, bringing the scent of dead roses with her. I gag on the heady smell filling my nostrils.

"The heart makes you soft." Her nails dig into my biceps hard enough to draw blood. "Where do you think you're going?" she asks with a growl, flinging her other hand up and blasting the men with some sort of power.

They fly back and hit the wall. Each landing in crouches, ready to launch themselves at Jinx.

"Morg will die if you take another step." She tips her head and tsks at Draco's growling. "Do you think Raven will forgive you for getting her friend killed?"

Everett's fingers curl into fists, but heeds her warning. Carter glances around the room, probably trying to figure out how we can get out of this. I already have a plan.

Going limp, my body starts to drop toward the floor, forcing Jinx to let go or follow me down. As soon as her hand is off of me, I kick at her legs, connecting with her freezing form.

"You little witch." She grabs my hair, yanking on it hard enough to make me grunt in pain.

Before she pulls me all the way to my feet, I punch her right in the vagina, making her scream in rage. I may not be a warrior, but I know a few things. The self-defense moves Aunt Lou taught me have never been more appreciated. Her grip on my hair loosens, and I duck, grinding my teeth as a few strands are ripped out with the maneuver, but I'm out of her hold and that's all that matters. Crouching on the ground, I kick at her but miss when she spins away.

"Bad decision." Jinx disappears and reappears next to Morg. Her hand turns transparent, and she plunges it into Morg's back.

Morg's shrill cry is immediate and filled with agony. Her body curls into a ball, trying to hide from the pain.

"No!" I scramble to my feet. "Leave her alone."

Jinx lifts her gaze to meet mine. "Soft," she whispers, withdrawing her hand and making it solid once more.

Morg's fingers press into the marble, and her arms shake as she tries to crawl away.

"No you don't." Jinx lifts her skirt and presses her high heel into the side of Morg's throat. "Move and I'll jam it into your neck." When Morg stills, Jinx's lips curl into a nasty smile. "Good girl."

"Don't trust her, Raven. What do you want?" Brayden asks the demon.

Jinx slides her gaze in his direction. "So many things."

I scoff when her gaze drops, not so subtly checking him out.

"Jealousy is an ugly color on you, Raven."

"I'm not jealous," I say. "Why are you here? Do you need help going back to Hell?"

"Oh, you think you can save me?" She throws her head back and cackles.

"I think I can help you, if you let me."

Everyone can be helped, but only if they want to be.

She glances at me and shakes her head like I'm a fool, and maybe I am, but I know better than anyone what it feels like to be a lost cause. Aunt Lou taught me how second chances, or even third and fourth, can change a person. She helped me when I was too far gone in my grief, patiently waiting for me to see the light at the end of the tunnel. If it weren't for her, I'd probably have died from alcohol poisoning a long time ago.

"Tell you what, here's what you can do with your help." She shoves her heel into Morg's throat.

Morg gurgles, and blood spills from the wound, quickly coating Jinx's shoe and pooling on the floor.

"No!" I move toward Morg, but Jinx tsks, holding up her hand and using magic to make a black sword appear. She points it at Layla, lifting an eyebrow.

"You choose how many die, or haven't you realized that yet?"

I sink to my knees, staring at the blood covering Morg's neck. Her eyes are filled to the brim with tears and crimson liquid leaks from her mouth, trickling down her jaw as she tries to say something.

Pressing my fingers to my mouth, I shake my head. "Stop. Please, you're killing her."

Jinx extracts her shoe from Morg's skin, and my stomach turns at the sound of its release. I lean to the side and vomit up bile, thankful I haven't eaten recently. Swiping my arm over my mouth, I scowl at Jinx.

If you shift, I promise I'll kill her, Joan's growled words fill my head.

If we attack, she'll kill Layla too.

Joan snarls. I understand her frustration, but I won't be responsible for more deaths tonight. Morg whimpers and coughs, blood splattering the ground in front of her, landing in globs of scarlet. Her body goes unnaturally still. I dig my fingernails into my palms and shake my head. Her shifter healing hasn't kicked in.

"Oh, dear me." Jinx places her hand on her chest. "I think she's already dead."

"Fuck you," I snarl.

Her white eyes flash brighter. "Oh, I forgot, you're a luna. I'll have to do better if I want you properly broken." She struts to Layla, tapping the tip of the sword on the wooden dance floor with every step. "What's one more death?" She swings the sword up with both hands, preparing to strike.

"Stop! Stop it!" I scream so loud she snaps her head in my direction, face contorting with sadistic pleasure.

"There we go." She places the sword over her shoulder. "Now, let's talk about what I want."

CHAPTER 6

CARTER

Raven's head is bowed, and her hair creates a curtain around her, but the red strands don't block the sobs. Jinx watches her with wide eyes, excitement flaring over her face. This is what she does. She breaks shifters before feasting on them. Raven is just another meal to Jinx. She doesn't know who she's dealing with though. Raven conceals it well, and her soul may be a little splintered, but in spite of it all, she loves fiercely, and she'll do anything to protect her friends. I knew the moment she befriended Bea.

The poor child who's too young to be taken into a place like this. A house of horrors for a spurned demon. Jinx, the human with demon blood was turned into a shifter. Our asshole alpha uses her to gain more power, and in turn, she gets to take as many changed shifters within our territory as she wants. Sometimes she plays with her food, like with the guys and me, slowly dragging it out across the years. Other times she doesn't hesitate to steal the wolves from the shifters and suck their souls from their bodies.

What she did was purely to fuck with Raven, and I've

never hated her more than I do now. Her oil-like power still holds me in place, so I can't go to Raven no matter how much I want to. Neither can the others. We're helpless to her power.

Damn it all.

"Here's what I need from you." Jinx leaves Layla's side and squats in front of Raven, holding the black sword in front of her like a staff.

Raven lifts her head, glaring at her. "Go to Hell."

Jinx snickers. "Bold of you to assume I'm not already there. Earth is sort of like the Underworld, you know? More green plants, but honestly, the two places aren't so different." She reaches out to brush a lock of hair from Raven's face.

"Don't touch me." Raven swats her hand away.

With a slight frown, Jinx pouts her lower lip. "Fine, but you'll still have to play along."

"Play along?" Raven asks, sliding her eyes to me.

"You play my game, and I won't kill your friends." Jinx grins like she's delivering good news.

I press my lips into a line and shake my head, trying to tell Raven not to agree. Nothing good can come from making deals with this demon.

"What do I have to do?" Raven asks, tucking her hair behind her ears and straightening her shoulders.

She's so ready to do whatever Jinx wants to keep others safe.

"Well," Jinx says, adjusting the top of her corset dress. "The first part is easy; you keep doing what you've been doing all along."

Raven's eyebrows press together much to Jinx's delight.

"All you have to do is continue going to class."

"What's the catch?" she asks.

Jinx tilts her head to the side. "You promise to come to my party next weekend."

The full moon ritual. The entire reason she was brought here in the first place. If Jinx is willing to bind Raven in a deal, she's afraid the wards will be broken again. I'm sure the fae's magic breaking her little spell pissed her off.

Raven squints and glances at Draco.

"Don't," he says.

Jinx taps her nails on the blade of the sword, drawing Raven's attention. "Draco's never been a good team player, but you will be, won't you?"

Layla moves on the ground, slow and painful. Raven's face pinches in frustration. She doesn't want to agree, but she clearly isn't selfish enough to let Layla die.

"Fine, I promise to come to your stupid party."

Shoving her hand out, Jinx winks at her. "Shake on it?"

Eyeing the demon's hand like it might bite, Raven slowly places her palm against Jinx's. Jinx wraps her fingers around hers, and her eyes turn from white to black, a startling transition, as she channels her demon power. When she starts whispering in her demon tongue, Raven tries to pull away, but it's too late. The deed is done. Her fate is sealed.

"Good," Jinx whispers in English when she finishes her chanting. "Now, if you'll excuse me, I need to finish my dessert.

The vile creature disappears, taking Morg's body with her. The magic holding me in place lifts and I stumble forward. Raven gasps and crawls forward, her fingers slipping in the blood.

"No. Where did she go?"

I drop to my knees, reaching her before the others, and wrap my arm around her shoulder.

"I'm sorry."

Raven shakes her head. "She's not dead. She can't be."

I shush her, lifting my gaze to meet Draco's, then Brayden's, and finally Everett's.

"We can find where she's hiding and try to take her down." Everett rubs his hand over his head. "She can't hide forever."

Brayden scoffs. "What do you propose we do? Bite her?"

"Shut up," Draco says, slamming his elbow into his brother's side and pointing at Raven with his other hand. Brayden's eyes darken, but he listens and closes his mouth.

"I'll do some research. Maybe there's something in the witch's texts about this. A banishing spell perhaps." I run my hand over Raven's hair.

"Books won't fucking solve the problem, Carter." Everett walks to the nearest table and flips it over. "What did your books tell you about this? Huh?" He flips another, throwing it hard enough it crashes into the wall and makes a hole in the wood.

I close my eyes and grind my teeth together, doing my best not to snap back at him. He's mad our luna is hurting, and his wolf is probably wild with rage. He's not in control of himself. Fur ripples down his arms, and his hand shifts, sharp claws appearing in place of fingers. Being held against my will was annoying, but to an alpha, it would be demeaning. They're not keen on being seen as weak or unable to protect their pack. As far as Everett's concerned, the people in this room are his pack.

"God. Dammit." He punches a vase off a table, snarling at it.

Raven pulls out of my arms, patting my chest and slowly climbing to her feet as Everett attacks another table. A glass vase smashes against the floor, shattering into pieces as he releases an angry growl.

Draco and Brayden move to stop Raven, but she scowls at them, halting their interference.

"Raven, he's not in control," Draco says.

She scoffs. "Can you blame him?" Then she turns around

and runs straight to Everett, slamming her hand on the table he's lifting and shoving it down. He growls, and she narrows her eyes on him.

"Calm down." The words are a command, and my spine tingles, my body desperate to comply. "Breathe."

I take three deep breaths, hearing Draco and Brayden do the same. Only Everett fights against her dominance. His wolf is battling for control. Raven uses her supe strength to push him away from the table.

"Settle. Down. Now." Each word is like a slap in the face.

He growls, but the fur covering his arms recedes, and his heavy breathing begins to slow with each huffed breath. Raven steps closer, placing her hand on his chest.

"Don't let her win." Raven stares into his eyes with fierce determination. "We'll find a way to beat her at her own game, but losing your shit won't help anything."

"I couldn't save you."

Her eyes soften at his whispered words. "You're not responsible for saving me, Everett."

He shakes his head, and I do too. She's wrong. We're all responsible for her. She's our luna.

"I don't need a savior."

With a deep rumble in his chest, Everett grabs her arm. "You reject me?"

She gives him a sad smile. "No, Everett." Placing her hand on the back of his neck, she pulls his forehead against her own. "I don't need a savior, but I could use a partner."

Draco growls, and she glares at him.

"I could use a few partners."

Her words cut off his growls, and she shakes her head at him.

"But if we're doing this, I won't tolerate being lied to." Her eyes stray to Brayden. "Or tricked."

The fool is smart enough to look at the floor. He's not as ashamed as he should be, but it's a start.

Raven's electric green gaze finds mine. "As far as I'm concerned, you can solve almost any problem you have with the right book."

∽

RAVEN

I go into my room first, eyes connecting with Adler who is wearing my shirt—which is way too tight on him—and the towel around his waist. None of my shorts or pants would have come even close to fitting him. He's sitting next to a sleeping Bea. She's been up for a long time, and she's probably exhausted. We all are. Layla groans, and I turn around to check on her. Her arm is draped over Carter and Everett's shoulders, and she sags in their hold like a ragdoll.

Everett frowns. "She needs to rest." He glances around my room.

"We need to come up with a plan," Draco says, sliding past him and walking toward me. His icy blue gaze searches my face. "Brayden, go get the cots."

"There's a magic word missing in there somewhere," his twin teases.

Draco's face darkens, and he cuts a scowl in his direction, but Brayden isn't fazed. I thought Draco was a lot to handle, but my instincts are telling me where Draco is like a wave of chaos, Brayden is a tsunami. Between the two of them, I'm liable to drown.

Only problem is, I'm not sure I'd mind getting swept away in their currents, which is a dangerous thought. I don't need them, but damn if I don't want them.

"Go. Now."

Brayden rolls his eyes and releases a dramatic sigh. "Fine."

Then he pins me with a serious look. "Don't disappear on me, Little Red, we need to talk soon."

I flip him off because, of the two of us, he's the one who likes to disappear into thin air. His responding chuckle warms my insides, but I keep my face closed off, not letting him in.

It's a little late for that, Raven. You told them you needed partners. You may as well have banged them all. Their wolves won't let them walk away now.

I growl, drawing a curious stare from Carter who shifts on his feet and leans against the door, still propping Layla up.

I didn't accept them into a harem.

Joan snorts. *You already have, Raven... you say one thing but every action you've made in the past few hours tells an entirely different story. These men, they're ours.*

Crap. I know part of what she says is true, but for some stubborn reason I'm not quite ready to admit defeat. Jinx ripped away some of my defenses, exposing the weakest part of me. My heart. She killed Morg, knowing full well it would make me agree to do whatever she wanted.

Accepting these men means exposing more vulnerabilities, giving Jinx more to bargain with, and I'm not ready to be their downfall because while I've only known them for a few weeks, I like them and I don't want anyone else to die.

"I'll go get Adler an outfit." Draco leaves and returns a few minutes later, handing Adler a pair of shorts and a shirt. They're almost the same height, but Adler's a bit bulkier. At least Draco's clothes won't look ridiculous on him.

He glances at Bea, and I move to the bed.

"I'll stay with her while you change." I run my hand over his shoulder.

"All right." Scrubbing his palm over his face, he stands. His chest brushes against mine and he stares down at me.

"Are you okay?"

With all the chaos of the last twenty minutes, the simple question nearly sets me off in tears, but I swallow them, hating how weak they make me, and nod my head.

"I'm okay."

His gaze narrows on me, and he looks ready to say something else, but he decides not to. Instead, he places a hand at the back of my neck and presses his lips to my forehead.

"At some point, you're going to have to stop lying to yourself." He goes to the bathroom to change, leaving me out of sorts.

Draco, Everett, and Carter are staring at the wall when I look over to see if they notice I'm about to cry, saving me the embarrassment of making an excuse. Clearing my throat, I sit on the bed and force every ounce of sadness deep inside of me and lock it away the same way I did after rehab. Your feelings can only hurt you if you let them.

Adler returns after a minute, looking more like himself in the new clothes, and sits next to me on the bed. A bit later, after an awkward silence fills the room and we all stare at each other like we don't know how to behave in social settings, Brayden returns with a cart which holds six cots with pathetically thin mattresses. No one is going to be comfortable, but I'd rather know they're all here than worry about whether Jinx has returned to feed on them.

After helping get Layla tucked into my bed next to Bea, I climb onto one of the cots with a grim face. Any mattress, no matter how uncomfortable or thin, is better than sleeping on the floor.

Adler squats near my bed, dropping down low enough that we're eye to eye.

"I'm sorry, Raven." His face pinches, and I can practically hear him berating himself inside his head.

Reaching out and grabbing his hand, I give it a hard squeeze. "You tried, Adler. You came back like you promised. That's all that matters. It's not your fault I rushed back in."

He sighs and tosses a glance over his shoulder, taking in the shifters who all peer at us with unabashed curiosity. When he turns back to me, his amber eyes are filled with sadness. I wrap my arms around his neck and yank him toward me. He inhales, and I can't keep a little smile from tugging at my lips.

"I hate to say it, because it's selfish, but there's no other fae I'd rather be imprisoned with." I make sure to stress the word fae so as not to upset the other guys.

Adler chuckles, and his hands cup my cheeks, tilting my head so I'm forced to meet his gaze. One of his thumbs brushes over my bottom lip, and he sighs.

"I knew you were trouble when you walked in."

I frown, and his lips twitch. He drops his hands from my face, stands, and heads to his cot.

Everett takes in Adler like a man who realized there's someone else the woman he's after might be interested in, and the look has me on edge.

Didn't you say there were five?

Joan hums. *Oh, so you were listening.*

Of course I was. Are we going to have a problem here?

No. She chuffs. *The eagle is your nurturer. The harem will not work without him.*

I volley my gaze between the men who are supposedly mine. Draco gives me a cruel smirk and runs a knuckle over his lip. Brayden side-eyes his twin, watching my reaction before giving me a smile which manages to be more inviting and all the more vicious than Draco's at the same time. His eyebrows draw down over his eyes, hiding what he's thinking from me, but his thumb gently traces over his cheek. A reminder of who and what he is.

Unable to stare at him longer without feeling thoroughly

unsettled, I swing my attention to Everett who nods and yanks his shirt over his head, revealing his ripped stomach and chest before crawling under the sheet on his cot. Carter scoffs and shakes his head, meeting my gaze with a steady intensity which worries me most of all.

Truly accepting them means opening myself to the possibility of heartbreak.

Then again, how can they break something that's already shattered?

CHAPTER 7

RAVEN

I wake with a start a few hours later, a soft whisper near my face making my heart skip a beat. Bea is kneeling in front of my cot, eyes wide with fear. I reach for her and lift the sheet, scooting over so she can climb in next to me. When she settles on her side, I smile at her.

"Good morning."

"Morning," she whispers. "What happened to Layla?"

Blowing out a breath, I brush my hair from my face. "Remember the bad spirit?"

She nods.

"The bad spirit took her and Morg. Layla's tired, but she should be okay. Morg is gone." I swallow around the lump in my throat.

Her brown eyes bounce between mine. "I don't like her."

"Me either, sweetie." I smooth her hair, trying to think of something to say that will reassure her. I come up with nothing useful, so we lie in silence, staring at one another until the men begin to stir.

Layla is the last to rise, and she jolts up with a gasp,

fisting the blanket in her hands and snapping her head back and forth. I leave Bea on the cot and go to the bed, climbing on and sitting next to her.

"It's okay," I say, squeezing her arm. "You're okay."

Her face screws up in confusion. "What's going on?" she asks in a shaky voice.

"Well—"

"Basically, Jinx is going to feast on our souls unless we find a way to stop her."

I glare at Brayden, who's leaning against the desk.

He lifts a shoulder. "Better to rip the band-aid off."

Shaking my head, I sigh. "He's right. Jinx is dangerous, so until we figure out how to stop her, we should stay in groups."

"You agreed to keep playing school," Everett reminds me. "That means everyone else needs to play along too. I don't trust her not to call foul if one of us decides not to keep up the charade."

Layla scoffs. "I'm *not* going to class on Monday and pretending like there's not something trying to eat me."

Draco steps to the edge of the bed, placing his palms on the mattress. "I understand some of what you're feeling, but you don't have a choice."

Mmm. Moons he's so hot when he's angry.

Joan, I groan her name. It's too early for her to be this thirsty. I haven't even had coffee.

She opens her mouth to argue, but Carter clears his throat.

"What Draco is trying to say is that we need your help making sure Jinx doesn't come for Raven. If we all play pretend, there's less of a chance of Raven being attacked by the demon spirit."

Layla presses her lips into a thin line and shoots her eyes to mine.

"I won't ask you to pretend everything is okay, but I agree with the guys. We need to continue going to class to keep Jinx pacified so we can come up with a plan. If she thinks we're listening and afraid, she's less likely to suspect we're up to something."

"You're insane," she says, launching from the bed and running into the bathroom.

Placing my head in my hands, I release a hard breath.

Adler sits next to me, wrapping his arm around me. "We have a day to convince her."

"Key word being *we*, fae boy," Draco growls.

I throw my hands into the air. "There are more important things happening right now!"

Brayden clicks his tongue, and I glare at him.

"I disagree," he says. "Solidifying your position as luna, with the power of a five strong bond, will increase the odds of our survival."

Bea sucks in a sharp breath. "You're going to have a harem?"

"What do you know about harems?" I ask, unable to keep the curiosity from my voice.

"Carter taught me about them."

The shifter in question gives me a bashful smile when I cut my gaze in his direction.

"It's part of the required curriculum."

"I'm not questioning you," I say. Then I glance at Brayden. His dark hair is messed up from sleep, and he has a wrinkle on his face from his pillow. "You really think making us a thing is the best idea?"

Everett snorts. "Of course he does, he wants to appear out of nowhere and act like he knows you."

"I know Raven. We've met on many occasions while she's been at Bad Moon Academy, right, Little Red?"

When Carter and Everett look to me for confirmation, I

nod and note that Draco didn't seem surprised by this. He knew.

Bastard.

When I scowl, Draco moves away from the bed and leans on the other end of the desk, crossing his arms over his chest and becoming a mirror image of Brayden. My attention shifts between the two, and I can't decide who I'm more upset with. Brayden for toying with me or Draco for keeping his brother's presence a secret.

"Raven?" Adler asks, smashing me against his side.

With the simple touch, I feel grounded, and it's as if he's the post holding up a falling tree. If I let them, the other guys will be my anchors too. Keeping my roots from ripping free. I think of all the times my phantom friend came to visit, how I looked forward to his arrival, and how his icy cold touch sent shivers down my spine. My skin ripples with gooseflesh at the memory, and I stare at the man I brought back from another realm.

"Yeah, I know Brayden."

"How?" Everett asks.

"He came to see me as a phantom, but you never were a spirit to begin with, were you?"

Brayden's eyebrows lower. "It's complicated."

"So explain."

His gaze strays to Bea. "Later."

I purse my lips, not happy with the brush off. "Fine." I get off the bed, patting Adler's leg and going to the bathroom door, rapping my knuckles on it a few times.

"Go away."

Leaning my forehead against the door, I say, "Come on, Layla. We're all stuck here. We can work as a team, or you can go off on your own, but I don't think you want to do that."

Silence.

"I don't want you to do that."

Her feet pad closer. "I don't know why this is happening," she says so softly I almost can't hear it.

I roll my neck and meet Carter's eyes. They're shadowed with his own emotions. I hold his gaze.

"Sometimes there isn't a good answer to why bad things happen, Layla. Life is a fucking hurricane of misery sometimes, but if you find the right people, they can be your life raft."

Aunt Lou was mine after Mom died.

Carter opens his mouth to say something, but the bathroom door opens. I stumble and Layla catches me in a hug, her tears soaking through my shirt in a matter of seconds. I pat her back awkwardly until she sniffs and pulls away.

'I'm sorry," she whispers, eyes red from crying.

"You shouldn't apologize for having emotions," Carter cuts in, stepping closer. "There's no shame in crying."

She glances at him, forehead wrinkling and a fresh wave of tears filling her eyes, but she blows out a hard breath and blinks them back.

"I'm okay, I promise." Her smile doesn't reach her eyes. "So, how are we taking this bitch down?"

I laugh. "That's more like it." Sliding my gaze to Carter, I lift an eyebrow. "Well, professor? I seem to remember you mentioning research. How can we help?"

His lips curl. "I have a few books in mind."

Draco groans. "Great, we'll just banish the demons with a book."

"It works for the Catholics," Brayden says with a sigh. "May as well give it a try."

∽

After finding a good fiction book for Bea to read and making sure she's comfortable, I head to one of the oversized chairs on the first floor of the staff library; picking up one of the books Carter set down, I start leafing through the pages.

"We're looking for anything demon related. I don't know a lot about them, but once we read about the various types which have been cataloged and researched, we can narrow down the list from there," Carter says.

Everett grumbles something about finding a needle in a haystack, and Adler chuckles, grabbing a book for himself.

"If Adler can do it without complaining, so can you." The corner of Carter's mouth quirks.

With a heavy groan, Everett scowls at his friend then slides his gaze to Adler. "You and he can't get along, I'll be the fifth wheel."

Adler and Carter share amused looks, and I clear my throat. "Technically, there are six of us. So you can't be a fifth wheel unless I'm the sixth wheel."

"Touché," Everett says, picking up a book at random and flipping it open. "It's still a bad idea for them to be friends, but I'll allow it," he says, winking at me.

Carter chuckles and shakes his head. "It's almost like he thinks he's the one in charge."

"Are all alphas this controlling or just him?" Adler asks with a small smile.

"You say controlling; I say practical." Everett looks at him over the book. "Now shh. I'm trying to focus."

I watch Adler as he begins to read again, there's a little bit of hope written across his face. It's not obvious if you don't know the man, but it's the same look he got when the night would begin to slow at the bar and there was a good chance we'd get out of there early.

Draco and Brayden are sitting next to each other, both leaning forward and resting their forearms on their legs as they scour through their books. They haven't even looked up, so I'm not sure if they're still feeling conflicted about Adler's presence.

As if sensing my attention, Brayden lifts his eyes from the page he's reading and smirks. "Slacking already?"

Squinting at him, I settle back into the chair and start at the beginning of my book. After a few minutes of reading, my eyes stray to the stack of books. There are a lot, and I've only made it a few pages. If only there were coffee. Mornings are never the same without bean brew.

I hear a throat clear, and I slide my gaze to Brayden, whose eyes are alight with laughter.

Slacker, he mouths the word, and I roll my eyes. Whatever. Determined to prove him wrong, I stick my nose back in the tome and read. A few hours and fifteen microbreaks later, I slam the book shut with a growl. Carter places his finger on the page he's reading and gives me a pointed look.

"The book didn't do anything to you, Raven." He sounds like a professor so much right now.

It's kind of cute.

Mmhmm. I told you.

I never said he wasn't cute, I say to Joan before focusing on Carter again.

"Do you know how many demons were listed in that book?"

He shakes his head. "I pulled it because it talks about the Underworld."

"Right. The Underworld, the place most people call Hell. Well, guess what, this freaking three-hundred-page book only had three demons listed in it. Samael, Lilith, and their daughter Mazzikin."

"Should we add them to the list?" Everett asks, picking up the pad he's been jotting notes on whenever someone finds something useful.

"No." I sigh and set the book down with exaggerated care. "I doubt the rulers of the Underworld care about Jinx."

Carter snickers and goes back to reading. "Walk around for a few then get back to work."

I huff but waste no time taking the break he's offering me. I head up the stairs, going to the third floor, and lose myself in the rows of shelves, running my fingers over the spines of several books. Even if I'm not excited about reading research material, being around so many books makes my nerd heart happy. I'd be a hell of a lot more enthusiastic about my reading if there were some romance sprinkled throughout the pages upon pages of facts. But alas, *History of the Underworld* had zero romance, unless you count the dry fact that Samael and Lilith had a daughter. No steam or tension, just *they had a child*.

"Boo," Brayden whispers, brushing his mouth against my ear. I know it's him and not Draco because the vibrato of his voice is deeper and fuller, even when he whispers.

I spin and slap his chest, shooting daggers at him with my eyes. He chuckles and presses into me, backing me against a shelf and laying his hands on either side of my head. He's so tall I have to crane my head to maintain eye contact, and this only serves to make his smile widen.

"What do you want?" I ask.

"I said we had to talk, remember?"

I blink, not giving him an inch.

With a heavy sigh, he searches my face. "You can't trust your friends, Raven—"

"Like I can trust you?" I spit the question out, pressing my lips together in a firm line.

He moves his hand to my face and slowly traces my cheek bone with his thumb. My breath hitches at the contact, and my stomach flutters. Cheeky fuck.

"You're mad at me," he finally says, pulling his hand away and putting it back on the shelf next to my head.

"Am I?"

He narrows his eyes. "I didn't lie to you."

I shrug. "Omission is almost as bad. You knew who I thought you were."

"I'm sorry."

His apology is so unexpected I don't know what to say for a few moments. I expected him to deny it, to argue his innocence, but he didn't.

A shifter who knows how to communicate? Yum. Joan purrs like a cat in my head.

She's ridiculous.

With a sigh, I glance away. "It's fine."

"Raven," he says, pulling on my chin so I'm forced to meet his eyes.

His skin is so cold, almost like he's still from another realm, but that's impossible, right? I brought him back.

He leans closer. "I regret earning your anger, not our interactions." His eyes drop to my lips, and the memory of him pressing against me in his phantom form and kissing me just after Draco had flashes through my mind.

Kiss him, Joan whispers, completely ruining the moment.

Well, now I'm not going to, you freaking creep.

She scoffs. *Wimp.*

I growl, and Brayden's brow furrows and a funny smile tugs at his lips.

"Are you arguing with your wolf?"

"Yes," I confess, putting my hand on his chest and easing him back a few inches. "She's annoying."

Joan curses at me, but I studiously ignore her. Brayden searches my face again, gaze dropping to my mouth again for a millisecond before he turns and starts to walk away.

"Come on, Little Red, Carter wants us to study," he calls over his shoulder.

I nod and follow him down the stairs, feeling the curious looks the others send our way once we reach the second floor.

"They're staring," Brayden whispers. "What do you think they think we were doing?"

"Seeing as they were probably eavesdropping, they know exactly what happened up there."

Thanks to the enhanced hearing which comes with being a shifter, I have exactly zero privacy if someone really wants to listen in on my every conversation within the academy. I haven't tested the full range of my hearing, but I know if I focus, I can hear Headmaster Erron moving around in his office.

I stop halfway back to my chair and laugh because I'm an *idiot*. "Oh my god. Why didn't I think of it before?"

"What's she talking about?" Adler glances at the others like they might be able to clue him in.

"Your guess is as good as mine," Carter says with a shake of his head.

Rushing to the door, I yank it open, ignoring the men calling my name as I rush to the headmaster's office. He's in charge, right? Surely he knows of a way to stop her.

Isn't he an omega?

Yeah.

Joan hums. *Perhaps you are overestimating his abilities, Raven. He is here to keep the peace. I doubt he knows anything useful.*

I have to ask.

When I turn down the hall leading to Headmaster Erron's office, I see a flash of familiar curls disappearing down the stairwell which leads to the crypt.

Morg?

"Raven?" Everett calls my name from the foyer.

I sprint down the hall, using the wall to turn and run down the stairs. The light is flickering like the last time I was here, and I don't have a flashlight, so by the time I get down to the creepy brick corridor, I'm engulfed in the darkness.

My ears tune into the drip, drip, dripping of whatever busted pipe is leaking and my eyes adjust enough that I can make out the vague shapes of the objects in the room.

"Morg?" I whisper her name, but there's no reply.

"Raven?" Everett's voice sounds far away, and I turn toward the stairs with a frown.

I swear I saw her. Glancing around again, I foolishly hope I'll see her face, but my stomach sinks. If she were here, she would have said something. Morg is gone. Her spirit form hasn't come to me though. Her death was traumatic. Souls take time to process trauma. Being the only medium in Bad Moon Academy has its perks.

"She's not dead."

You're talking to yourself.

Shut it. Morg's not dead.

You're sure about that? Joan's skepticism is overshadowed by the new hope filling my chest.

Morg can't be dead.

Heading back to the stairs, I turn over everything Jinx did and said in my mind. I'm so lost in my thoughts that I don't notice the ghost standing in front of me until I pass through her.

The cockroach ghost from the locker room is even colder than Brayden's phantom form. Passing through her is like diving into the coldest part of the Arctic Ocean. As I trudge through her spiritual form, a voice whispers through my mind, *Aliceeeeee.*

My vision flickers, and images flash through my head at rapid speed. A woman with bright eyes and a big smile. Long, healthy brunette hair flying behind her as she swings back and forth at a playground. Gasps as a handsome man slams her into a wall and ravishes her mouth. Betrayal at his hands when she finds him with her sister. So many memories assault me, but it's the last one which leaves me haunted.

Alice wearing a maid's uniform, screaming at the base of the stairs in the foyer. A dozen ghosts float around her in the memory, pressing closer and closer. She's digging her fingers into her hair, pulling it out as they grow near. Her screams begin to soften, almost like the spirits are stealing her fear away until all that's left is a shell of a woman kneeling on the ground. The ghosts don't stop until a white mist curls out of her mouth and her body thuds to the ground.

A woman appears out of thin air. Jinx is wearing a pair of shorts and a T-shirt, but there's no mistaking the eyes and cruel twist of her smile. Waving her hand through the misting air, she pulls it toward her and sucks it in, eyes seeming to grow brighter when she finishes.

My foot hits the first step, and I rub my arms to try to ease the chill which came with my collision with Alice. I turn to face her, surprised to see she's watching me. If I were to put a word to what I see in her eyes, I'd use concern.

"Alice?" I ask, wondering if she can actually talk. The first time I saw her all she did was her fun little cockroach trick.

I swear if I see one bug, I'm going to scream, Joan says.

Can wolves scream?

Alice opens her mouth, and three of those nasty critters scuttle out. Holding back a squeal, I reach for one of the bugs, letting out a sigh of relief when my fingers pass through it. Not that ghost cockroaches are any less disgusting than real cockroaches, but at least they can't breed. Or at least I hope not. Four more race out of her mouth, and I jump back, scowling at her.

"Ugh, they're not even real, Alice."

Her head cocks at an unnatural angle, and I wrinkle my nose.

"Blink twice if you can understand me."

Alice's eyelids flutter, and I lose count of how many times she actually blinks.

I think this one has a few too many screws loose, babe.

Joan is always *so* helpful.

"Let's try again. One cockroach if you can understand me."

One bug crawls out of her mouth. I wait, seeing if it was just a coincidence but no more follow the first. Okay, I can work with this.

"You were a shifter? One cockroach for yes, two for no."

One creepy crawler escapes her cracked lips.

I think I'm going to throw up, Joan whines.

You and me both.

"Jinx killed you? Same number of roaches."

She blinks, a lock of scraggly hair falling off her shoulder and dangling toward the floor. Her current body position screams *Exorcist,* but I think Alice has developed this form for a reason. I don't know why, but she's obviously cognizant.

"Your last memory with the woman. She's Jinx."

One lone roach.

I shiver, unable to fight the repulsion. What? They're fucking gross.

"Raven?" Everett asks from the top of the stairs.

"I'll be right up," I say over my shoulder then turn back to Alice. "Do you want to meet again?"

One cockroach.

"Okay. Maybe later this week?"

Another disgusting bug means yes.

"Who are you talking to?" Everett takes a few steps down,

so I leave her and dash up to meet him, tugging him back to the first floor.

"A ghost named Alice." There's no point in lying. We're in this together, and I have nothing to hide from them anymore, especially not after telling everyone about my abilities.

"It's not safe to run off by yourself like that." His face lines with concern.

I smile and link my arm with his. "You being worried about me is kind of cute, you know."

He wrinkles his nose. "Cute?"

"Hot, incredibly sexy? Macho?"

This gets a laugh from him. "Yeah, yeah. You're okay though?"

"I'm good, but I need to stop here."

The little plaque marking the headmaster's office makes me unreasonably angry. I want to rip it off and find a way to shatter it. Headmaster? What kind of headmaster sits back and watches his students die? Cowers in his office? I tune into my supe hearing. His heartbeat is erratic. He's scared. Too bad, so is everyone else and not one but two of his students have died in the last forty-eight hours.

I open the door and head in. The secretary is nowhere in sight, so I march straight to his door and wrench it open. His heart is pumping so hard now it sounds like a kick drum. He's not sitting at his desk, so I walk around it and squat, glaring at Erron who's curled beneath it. His eyes widen.

Omega fear, but his cowardice is all his own. A good omega wouldn't hide, Joan's voice is laced with disgust.

"Raven," he says in a breathy voice. "You're all right."

"No thanks to you," I growl.

"Is it over?"

What is he talking about? Then I remember all the other missing shifters the guys mentioned. He knows what's happening every year too? Worse yet, he lets it happen. I've never been much for violence, but I grab him by the shirt collar and drag him out from under his desk. Everett takes a step forward, eyes darkening when he realizes how angry I am.

"You don't get to hide from this Erron." I release his shirt, and he thuds to the ground.

"Please, you have to know I can't stop this." He moves to his knees, scooting toward me.

I step back. "How do you know you can't stop it? Have you even tried? Or have you just been cowering in your office like a good little boy?"

Everett presses into my back. He doesn't intervene, nor does he try to take charge. I'm his luna, as they say, and he's only showing me he supports me. I don't need to lean on him, and frankly, I've never wanted to be that girl, but knowing he's here to support but not take charge softens some of my heart, and I lightly shift my weight toward him.

"I. I. You don't understand, the alpha ordered me to—"

"The alpha isn't here, and innocent people are dying. Are you so weak you can't break those orders when he's not around?"

Every type of shifter maintains free will when the alpha is not present. A good alpha commands respect. The pack knows he will take care of them, so they follow his orders. A bad alpha demands respect, so people usually follow out of fear. Either way, he had a choice to make as the alpha wasn't present.

"He chose wrong," I respond to Joan out loud.

The color drains from Erron's face. "Please, Raven."

"Quiet." I send a wave of luna power with the word, and he whimpers, dropping his forehead to the ground.

"Luna?" His voice is shaky.

"Yes, Erron. You don't get to hide behind the alpha's orders anymore. Now get up."

He stands, eyes rounding. "What are you going to do?"

"Taking you out of here and forcing you to live life the way you've made your students do."

Everett squeezes my arm, so I step aside so he can grab Erron by the back of his neck. Hauling the headmaster into the hallway, he shoves him toward the foyer.

"Start walking."

I glance around the office. Soft whispering fills the air, making my spine tingle with unease. Jinx is near. Taking off after Everett, I use my supe hearing to make sure she's not attacking him. All I hear is his and Erron's footsteps. No condescending demon voice. I'll take that as a good sign.

By the time I reach the end of the hall, they've stopped walking. A light feminine laugh fills the air, and I grimace. I round the corner to find Jinx standing on the first step. The tight bodice and flowing skirt of her dress screams regency romance.

"Well, well, well. Wherever are you going with my headmaster?"

Scowling and looking at Erron, I shake my head. *Her headmaster.* She's no alpha. Regardless, she's here and this works perfectly. He can now stare down the demon he's made countless shifters face.

"Jinx, Erron. Erron, Jinx. She's the one stealing souls."

A small whine leaves his lips.

"What are you up to, Raven?" Those white eyes sweep over me, narrowing slightly. "The omega is off limits."

I scoff. "Says who?"

Trailing her hand along the handrail, she steps off the stairs and onto the floor. "The alpha and I have an agreement. The omega is not to be harmed."

Fine by me. My intention isn't to get Erron hurt. He needs to witness what he's doing. There will be no hiding beneath desks while his students die.

"That's okay. He's going to hang out with us though."

Footsteps sound from the hallway upstairs. Jinx spins around and claps.

"Oh goodie. Our friends are awake, Raven."

Everett and I exchange frowns. I didn't even think about gathering the others. Jackson, the guy who brought me the clothes when I first arrived, bounds down the stairs, slowing when he sees us.

"I thought we had another week," he says in a wary voice. His gaze bounces between all of us. "The full moon isn't until Friday."

"There's been a change of plans, Jackson." Jinx takes a step up. "Your time is up today."

"No!" I shove luna power at the demon, but it doesn't faze her. I should have known, but I had to try.

Jackson turns and hightails it, racing away from the soul sucking bitch.

"I do love it when they run," she says on a wistful sigh. Tossing a glance over her shoulder, she winks. "Aside from you and your friends, there are fifteen other shifters in this building. Guess what happens once I take their shifter power?"

I'm guessing it'll be a level up for her. That's a lot of energy to consume, and judging by how much she had to take to get this form, she'll be able to do a hell of a lot more than physically appear. I've never heard of a poltergeist demon, but Jinx is heading toward that. The more power she consumes, the more she'll be able to mess with us. I don't want her to get any more because she's already a pain in the ass.

How exactly are you planning to stop her? Joan asks.

I'll make her an offer she can't refuse.

"Wait. Take from me. Leave him alone."

Pausing on the stairs, Jinx slowly turns and eyes me curiously, tipping her head to the side.

"Please, leave him alone. You can take some from me." And in the process, I'll try to use the necromantic power to light her up.

Darkness shrouds her features, and she huffs. "Don't worry, Raven. Your time will come. Try not to be a hero." Then she disappears into thin air.

I look behind me, expecting her to appear where Everett stands, but she doesn't. Erron is shaking, a pathetic hunch to his shoulders. If she's not coming for them, she's gone after Jackson. Running up the stairs, I use my supe hearing and try to find him. It takes me a moment because I haven't been around him much, but I hear panting coming from the third-floor west wing.

A throaty scream fills the air, but there is no pleasure in the cry. Fuck. I reach the third-floor landing and careen down the west hall, racing toward the sound. Sliding to a stop in front of a door to what I assume is his room, I shove it open. Jackson's body is contorted on the ground, like he thrashed back to escape her reach but didn't make it in time. His face is ashen. Placing my trembling fingers on my mouth, I shoot my gaze around the room, searching for Jinx.

"Boo," she whispers from behind me, kicking me in the middle of the back.

The force of her hit has me stumbling further into the room. The door slams shut by the time I whirl around to escape, but Jinx leans against it, blocking my way out.

"That was stupid."

"Maybe, but I had to try and stop you. I can't just let you kill people for fun."

She tsks. "Oh, love, I thought you'd figured it out by now. They're not exactly dead."

Narrowing and sliding my eyes to where Jackson's prone body lies, I curl my top lip. "He looks dead to me."

"I mean, if you consider the vessel in which his soul lived

the only way he can be alive, then I guess you're right. He's dead."

The only thing worse than a demon spirit is a condescending demon spirit.

"You're not consuming his soul... you're using it?"

Pulling her hands from behind her, she claps and struts toward me with an exaggerated sway to her hips. "You. Are. So. Smart."

"You're a bitch," I say, lifting my brow.

She pouts. "You wound me, Raven. I thought we were friends."

"I'd definitely remember befriending a psychotic demon. Sorry, we're not friends." I lift my chin and stare at her. Her milky white eyes swirl and glint with malice.

Ugh, I think I hate her.

You think? I ask Joan.

Jinx stops two feet away from me. "You're sure about that?"

My face screws up in frustration. She thinks she has the upper hand, but I can't think of how or what she might be hiding. There is no mistaking the eager twist of her lips as she prepares to drop a bomb. Stomach churning with unease, I purse my lips, trying not to let her see how she affects me.

"Raven?" a familiar voice asks right before fingers tap my shoulder.

Craning my neck, my eyes widen as I take in a mess of brown curls, brown eyes, and Morg's signature grin. I blink, unsure if what I'm seeing is real or if it's a vision. Reaching for her, I fully turn and grab her arms, gasping when she's completely solid. She's not a spirit. She's not a ghost. Morg is alive.

I knew it. If Jinx had truly killed her, she would have found a way to communicate with me from the other world, especially since I told her I was a medium not so many days ago.

Then she's gone in a puff of air. My hands are still raised like they're cupping her arms.

"Raven?" she asks from behind me.

I spin, only seeing Jinx, who is wearing a Cheshire smile as she twirls a lock of black hair. Stomach dropping with the sudden understanding, I take a few steps back, tripping on Jackson's body and landing on the ground with a hard thud.

"Are you okay?" Jinx asks using Morg's voice. Her facial features shift, and suddenly she's wearing Morg's face. "Raven, what's wrong?"

Scrambling back when she advances, I press into the wall and scream. Jinx cackles and hops over Jackson, landing in a crouch in front of me. She still looks like Morg, straight down to the teeth. Something flickers on the edges of my vision, and I move my attention to the shape materializing. It morphs and curves until Morg stands behind Jinx, who now wears her true face, and they both chuckle.

"Raven, what's wrong?" they ask in eerie unison.

A fist pounds on the door when I scream again. Kicking at Jinx with all my might, I try to force her back. The demon disappears, leaving me in the room with Morg, who isn't at all who I thought she was. Morg is a part of Jinx. She was never real.

Wood splinters as Everett breaks the door, bursting into the room in a flurry of bared teeth and flaring nostrils. He sweeps the room, cataloging everything from Jackson's body, to Morg, and finally me on the floor.

"Morg?" he asks with a deep frown. "I thought you were dead."

She winks at me, then spins to face Everett. "It'll take a lot more than that to kill me."

"Everett." I lick my lips, standing and keeping my eyes on my former friend. "She's Jinx."

"Seriously?" He steps around Jackson and stands next to me. "How do you know?"

"Raven, it's not true. She was controlling me, I swear." The way her voice cracks with her plea is damn good, but I'm not going to be fooled again.

"Stay the hell away from us." I point my finger at her. "Or I'll make you wish you were dead."

Following through on the threat might be hard, but I'm determined to find a way to harness Death's power to send the demon back to where she belongs. My heart aches with the loss of Morg all over again, this time for the friend I thought I knew.

She drops her grin and hurt flashes over her face. "We could have been good friends." Then the demon vanishes.

Why does my chest pang with regret? Like I've done something to upset her and I want to make it right? Morg isn't who I think she is; she's Jinx. Jinx is bad. There is no way I'm going to regret upsetting her, but seeing Morg sad, even if it was all a show, makes me feel guilty.

Footsteps pound down the hall, and I release a hard breath, sharing a look with a grim-faced Everett. Things are getting complicated.

CHAPTER 8

CARTER

It takes a lot to surprise me. Learning that Morg was Jinx all along doesn't surprise me. For some reason, I never really cared for the woman. She was reckless and obnoxiously loud. Not in a good way. Almost like she wanted the world to know how much she had to say, and she didn't care who was around, what sort of mood they were in, and whether they wanted to listen.

"I'm so sorry." Raven's soft fingers wrap around my forearm, her eyes filling with sadness.

She thinks it's her fault. Maybe not directly, but she feels like she has some blame in Jackson's death. I swallow the lump in my throat, looking away from where he lies, though I don't think I'll ever erase the image of his slacken face from my mind. He hadn't been here long, but he was quickly becoming a friend. His pranks were annoying, but all in all, Jackson was a great guy. Now he's gone. So is Morris.

"It's not your fault," I say, pulling her into a hug. "This would have happened if you weren't here. Shifters go missing all the time at Bad Moon Academy."

Raven shakes her head. "She was trying to get a rise out of me."

"Jinx is going to hurt shifters regardless of who her latest toy is. I'm more to blame than you are; we didn't even try to gather the other shifters. I left them to fend for themselves."

They died because I didn't protect them. The woman in my arms rests her head against me and my chest shakes with fear of knowing I may not be able to save her.

We must protect our luna, my wolf growls the words.

We will do all we can.

If she dies, our life will have no meaning, he says.

I'd like to say he's being dramatic, but my thoughts over the last few weeks have been centered around one person. Despite knowing my soul will be ripped to shreds if I lose her, I squeeze her tighter.

May the moon protect her.

You should be the one keeping her safe.

My wolf is annoyed with me, and I fully understand why. We're inadequate. Unworthy. I've never had to fight a demon spirit. Draco's frustrated words have never felt more true. My books can't fix this problem.

Raven deserves someone who can help her fight the demon. Not someone who can't do a damn thing to save her.

~

RAVEN

Carter is holding me so tight it's hard to breathe, but I don't ask for space. His chest shudders and my heart breaks. Jackson was his friend. Shifters are disappearing left and right, and he's not able to stop it. I doubt he's ever felt more helpless. For once, being able to connect with the other world doesn't feel like a curse. I'm the only one aside from Brayden who might be able to actually do something. I suspect if he could, Brayden would have taken Jinx out already. Resting my head on Carter's chest, I eye the shifter.

My phantom.

He stands with Draco, Everett, and Adler. They're making plans to deal with Jackson's body and gather the other shifters in the academy. I don't know how we'll protect them all, but there is strength in numbers. Layla and Bea linger in the hallway, having come up with everyone else. Bea hasn't seen Jackson because Layla has kept her far enough back she can't see in, but she's heard every conversation happening in the room.

"All right. Draco and I will handle this," Everett says, his alpha peeking through as he takes charge and starts solidifying the plan. "Adler and Brayden go together to get the others. We'll meet back in the main library."

Adler nods. Brayden slides his gaze my way, almost as though he's waiting for me to approve the plan. Everett notices his straying attention, and his eyes flash to mine.

"I trust you to do what's best," I say, speaking to all of them. "The shifters in this academy need us. You know what we have to do."

Tension bleeds from Everett's shoulders. Adler and Brayden dip their heads and leave to start their task.

"Why don't you and Carter take the girls to the library?" Everett suggests.

There's no snarling from my wolf at being told what to do. This is teamwork pure and simple, and it feels so right. I trust them. The sudden realization makes my heart flutter, terrified it'll only be crushed once more. There are only so many times one can be broken before pieces won't fit back together.

"Come on," I say to Carter. "Let's go figure out how to set everyone up."

He slowly relaxes his arms and steps away. The scarlet

creeping up his neck is hard to miss, but I pretend like I don't notice and grab his hand, linking my fingers with his and heading out of the room.

~

BRAYDEN

I tried to tell Raven about Morg earlier, but she was so angry at me I had to deal with that first. I regret dropping the subject as soon as she snapped at me; I should have told her. Not wanting to earn more of her ire, I foolishly let the subject slide and apologized to her instead. Had I told her like I intended, maybe she'd be less shaken.

It's a little late now, my wolf snarls at me.

Yes, well, one crisis at a time, hmm?

The demon isn't done with her games.

I know just as well as he does that things are far from over. Wasting time on what I should have said or done differently won't help Raven now. I'll do anything to make her happy, including going to find all the other shifters for her in this moon-forsaken place.

This academy has an ungodly amount of dust. The thin carpet lining the hall is coated in it, and every step I take kicks up a puff of dirt, making my nose twitch. Adler walks next to me, eyes sweeping over the walls, taking in the sheets covering the old frames. I'm not sure why they chose to protect certain portraits over others, but I'm not in charge of Pack Olympic's history committee. Some paintings are probably worth money if they're old enough and of someone important in shifter society.

Before we cross to the other wing, I stop walking and side-eye the fae. "So, what exactly are you doing here?"

His face lines with annoyance, but he clears his throat and steps toward me. For someone meant to be a nurturer, he's rather intimidating. Perhaps intimidator would've been more appropriate of a title. I turn to face him, realizing for the first time he's a little taller and bulkier than I am. Yes. Intimidator fits.

"I'm here for Raven." He shoves his hair away from his face.

"Well, of course you are. What I mean is, what do you expect to happen here?"

He stops a few inches from me, our eyes nearly level, and lowers his eyebrows.

"I'm not expecting anything, Brayden. What are you expecting? Seems to me like you're the one who should be questioned. You were stalking her, after all. Maybe it's you who wants something from Raven." His eyes drop down my body. "Or have you already gotten what you came for?"

His question hits a little too close to home, and I flit my gaze between his dark irises. Sure, Draco and I knew she could talk to ghosts. In his year of watching her, he learned as much when he found her on the front porch glaring at empty air and talking to her mother like she was there, but we weren't sure she could raise the dead.

The plan had been for Draco to ask her once they got closer, but when she reached for Jinx with a handful of Death's power, I knew she could do it.

"That's not why I'm here," I finally say. "The body is a perk for sure, but I'd be here with or without it."

"Good." Adler takes a few steps back but keeps his intense gaze set on me. "We still have a job to do?"

Scrunching my face, I nod. "Yup. Let's go find the rest of the shifters." I start off down the hall, staying in front of him so he can't see my face.

How the hell did he turn that around on me? I was supposed to be questioning him, but Adler ended up flipping the switch. Freaking fae. Maybe I underestimated him. He *is* worthy of Raven's affection after all.

~

RAVEN

Three hours later, there are twenty-one cots set up in the library. There aren't as many shifters as I thought there were, but it seems there is no end to Jinx's parlor tricks. Half of the students I'd seen must have been ghosts or forms she was manipulating. Like Morg. My eyebrows pinch together at the thought of my friend. There must have been some sign I missed. Something I should have picked up on to know Morg wasn't real.

You saw Jinx. She looks as real as you. If she can do that with her form, she can do it to others.

The men and I commandeer a secluded nook tucked away behind several shelves. Layla and Bea are set up with a few women I recognize from some of my classes, one of them being Penelope, the poor woman Ms. Fig called out. The birdface professor is nowhere to be found, so I'm assuming she's one of Jinx's illusions. Erron, Howard—the other zeta—and the remaining male shifters take another section of the library. While we're all separated, we're close enough I feel secure.

It'll be hard for Jinx to sneak in and cause trouble without us all knowing, especially since Draco has assigned a rotating guard shift. I've never seen Draco so focused as when he got the shifters gathered and barked orders at them. Some may not have appreciated being told what to do, but according to Joan, zetas are best for tactical planning. I expected some sort of tension to remain between Draco and Howard since my psycho tied him up, but Howard is just as efficient as

Draco when it comes to getting everything in order and making plans to protect us.

Since the food that appears in the cafeteria must be magically produced and clearly provides no real sustenance, Brayden and Draco dragged a few of the shifters with them to go hunt something to eat for a late lunch. They've been gone close to forty minutes. Howard is standing near the library doors, eyes flashing around the room in practiced militant attention.

"Raven, sit down." Layla hovers near where I'm pacing, a frown tugging at her lips. "They'll be back any minute. Everett and Adler are listening." She jerks her thumb toward where they sit.

There's still a chance Jinx could attack them, and we'd be too far away to help. I should have gone with them, but then everyone else would have been left alone, and I'd probably feel just as guilty as I do now.

"They're coming back." Adler stands from the worn wooden chair and comes to where I'm pacing. "They're okay, and they found food."

My nose twitches, and I sneeze, hating the layers of dust in this room. "We're going to the cafeteria," I say loudly, letting the shifters in the library know.

Howard sets to work getting everyone moving so we can go as a unit. The new plan is basically no woman or man left behind. We move in groups and we eat and sleep in the same places. My need for privacy is going to be pushed to its limits, but I'm more worried about what happens if we stay separated. The men said twelve shifters have gone missing over the last two years. That means more than half the people in this library are at risk.

∽

BRAYDEN

Placing the rabbits I killed on the table, I eye the shifters who came with, trying to pick out which one I want to have help me. Draco's an awful cook, so he's already out. Twins aren't identical in skillset, and I like to think I'm better at everything.

Pointing to a delta who holds his own score of rabbits, I tip my head to the side. "You'll do. And you"—I swing my gaze to the shifter who found the apple tree—"set those on the counter."

"Don't forget to say please." Draco's wearing a shit eating grin, and I shake my head.

It's good to be back in the flesh. I've missed having him near. The strange thing about twins is when you're away from the other for too long, it almost feels like you're incomplete. My other worldly visits weren't the same.

"Take your bad food luck out of here. Our luna is in the cafeteria." I head to the rack with old pans, snatch two, and head to the sink to rinse them. "Delta, start skinning those."

There isn't much to work with, but I spot olive oil, salt, pepper, and a few other spices on a shelf above the sink. Pushing into the pantry, I grab some potatoes. There's a bit of fruit, rice, pasta, and crackers, so I save those for another meal. Who knows how long it will take before we get more supplies? As long as I can add some flavor to the meal, have protein, and a little bit of starch, we should be able to keep everyone happy. It's been so long since I last cooked, but I'm determined to make a lunch worthy of a luna with the limited supplies.

"What's your name?" I ask the delta.

"Trey." He flicks his eyes to me before quickly dropping them.

I'm a beta, so he's being respectful. Part of me hates the timidness since I've been stuck in another realm for so long with only the dead to play with. Well, the dead and *him*. I wonder if he'll come for me, or if he'll even notice I'm gone. Who am I kidding? Death is well aware of how many minions he has. Raven snatched me from his hold, and I don't think Death will take kindly to her stealing his soldiers.

"Ever cooked a rabbit before?"

"No." He goes to wash his hands which are covered in blood.

It sounds gross, but this is survival. The food Jinx has been pretending to feed people isn't going to cut it. These shifters are being starved and don't even realize it. We're all going to need real food.

"Okay, I'll handle that. Why don't you cut up the apples while I prep this." I go to the stovetop and switch the burners on to test them. When the flames turn on without a problem, I release a sigh. I half expected them to be broken. "After you do that, you can help get this place cleaned up so we're not cooking in filth, sound good?"

Trey pauses, like my question surprises him, then nods and sets to work.

"Good, let's get cracking."

CHAPTER 9

RAVEN

About an hour and a half passes while we're in the cafeteria waiting for lunch. Some of the shifters are grumbling and fidgeting, obviously growing annoyed with the wait. Drumming my fingers on top of the table, I sigh and press my lips together.

"I'm so hungry," Bea says, laying her head down on the table.

"I'm sure it'll be ready soon."

As soon as the words leave my mouth, a low vibration flows from the floor to my feet, vibrating up my legs. The rumbling grows stronger and the buffet line rattles, the sterling silver pans and utensils banging around with the force of the vibration.

"What's that?" Penelope asks from a few tables over.

"Good question," I murmur, trying to lift my feet, but they're stuck.

Would it be too much to ask for one freaking break?

Uh, are you asking me? Joan asks.

Oh, no. Sorry, I'm just thinking in my head because I don't want to scream and scare people.

Is this another one of those tricks from the demon?

Must be, I say, chewing on my bottom lip.

Carter grunts. "I can't move my legs."

"Me either." Adler leans back, but his feet don't move from where the ground is holding them hostage.

"Jinx's magic, I'm assuming." Draco scowls.

"Look! The buffet!" Lincoln, the guy from my class with Ms. Fig, shouts.

Every shifter in the cafeteria swings their gaze to the food which has magically appeared. The rumbling subsides, and as soon as it stops, I can move my feet again.

"Thank the moon!" Lincoln rushes to the buffet line, bypassing the plates and going straight for a roll.

"Don't, Lincoln! It might not be safe."

He sneers at me. "We've been eating it for weeks now. I think you're just trying to control us." Taking an exaggerated bite, he chews and shakes his head. "See," he says around a mouthful, "it's fine."

A few shifters exchange looks, but no one else gets up. I watch Lincoln swallow the last of the roll, washing it down with some of the tea which appeared at the end of the buffet line. He laughs and mutters about how we're all paranoid idiots, all the while continuing to eat straight from the line of food.

"I have a bad feeling about this," I say to the small group at my table.

"Let him eat it. He's so determined to be right, let him see how hungry he'll be in a few hours. Then maybe he'll realize he needs real food and not her magic crap." Everett leans his elbows on the table, rolling his eyes. "He's the idiot."

My lips twitch because I agree, but I don't get the chance to respond. Lincoln starts to cough, having eaten too fast.

Slamming his hand on the metal counter, he pounds on his chest with the other, trying to dislodge whatever's stuck.

"Great, now I have to save him or look like an asshole," Draco says. He uses his supe speed, flashing away from the table and over to Lincoln. He smacks the shifter's back a few times, but it doesn't help.

Lincoln's face is tomato red now. I rise from my seat, wondering if I should go to help, but stop when Draco picks him up from behind and does the Heimlich maneuver. That'll fix the problem.

Only it doesn't.

Squeezing his hands into Lincoln's stomach, Draco tries again and again to dislodge the food, but it's not working.

"I should go—"

His body seizes, and his eyes roll back. I run over to help Draco hold him steady while he thrashes through the fit. People are yelling, but I can't understand any of it. Lincoln's foaming mouth, scarlet skin, and convulsing is all I see. All I hear is a strange grunting hum coming from him, like he's trying to scream something at me but he can't get the words out.

"What do we do?" Draco asks me, eyes wide as he dodges Lincoln's head which slams back before shooting forward. Lincoln folds over, going suddenly limp.

"No!" I try to lift him, but his body won't move.

Draco eases him to the ground, putting him on his side so he can feel for a pulse on his neck. Running my hands over his arms, I check each of his wrists, grimacing when there's no beat to be found. Rigor mortis shouldn't set in for at least a few hours, but his body has stiffened already.

A dark chuckle fills the room, and shouts erupt as shifters scramble away from the flood of ghosts; they spread through the cafeteria like an infection. Adler grabs Bea and he, Carter, and Everett move toward one of the groups of shifters by the windows, out of the path of the specters who are heading straight toward Draco and me.

I drop my hand from Lincoln's skin, falling back on my butt when the ghosts reach for him, their cold bodies passing through mine. Some of them glance at me, eyes lighting with a spark of something. They recognize the link to the land of the living. My medium powers call to them. Soft whispers fill my head, each one trying to tell me its story. More glance in my direction, called to me by the same power. As one, they stop moving toward Lincoln and start moving toward me. One reaches for me, a spindly, transparent finger jutting toward me like a knife.

"Raven?" Draco's voice is distorted, like he's speaking through a pane of glass.

Swinging my gaze in his direction, I gasp when I realize I can't see him. Ghosts are surrounding me on all sides, each trying to tap into my power. My chest tightens when the finger jams into my skin, brushing against my heart with an icy caress.

"No," I whisper, breath misting from the chill.

They won't take me like they did Alice. I don't care if I am the only connection they have with the land of the living, they're not going to take me down. Snapping my eyes shut, I breathe in and reach toward the dark power within the center of my being, drawing up a handful of the vile black mass and sending it to my hands, letting it pool there as I open my eyes. Staring at the ghost whose hand is inside of me, I bare my teeth, lifting my hands. I release a shout, shooting the power from my hands and to the spirits surrounding me. Filling them full of black swirling magic.

Ear shattering screams fill the space around me. The specters flicker in and out like there's a crappy reception on an old box television.

"Send me home!"

"Save me. I'm beggin' you to help me."
"You can't let her keep us here!"

The voices grow louder and louder. Begging for freedom. Begging for a way out. Begging. Begging. *Begging* until all I hear is their pleas. Until all I can feel is their pain. My vision dims, and all I can see is my hand and the black magic coursing out of it and into the ghost in front of me. My fingers cramp, freezing as they slightly curl in. The ichor-filled power pulses through me and booms out of my palm in a wave of darkness, taking the spirits one by one. Onyx colored smoke swirls around the empty space, as if savoring the last drops of their souls, before floating back to my arm and disappearing all together.

Draco snatches me up from the floor and holds me in his arms, a fierce growl rumbling in his chest. He spins around, searching for more of them, but they're gone. Even Lincoln's body is missing. I blink, thinking I'm imagining it, but when I glance at the floor where Draco laid him down, he's not there.

Adler, Carter, and Everett rush over, faces lined with worry.

"Did I make him disappear?" I point, and they all look at the ground.

"Everett and I moved him while you were busy with the ghosts." Carter touches my shoulder, like he needs reassurance I'm real.

"It was only a few seconds though." Pinching my eyebrows together, I meet his gaze.

"It was about four minutes for us. Draco ordered it after we couldn't break through the wall of ghosts." Everett sighs. "The worst four minutes of my life."

Adler hums in agreement, lips pulling into a severe frown.

"How were we able to see the ghosts?" Layla asks from

behind Carter. He steps aside to let her near. "I thought you were the only one who could see them."

"I don't know. I guess if they're tied to Jinx, she has enough power to make them appear."

She frowns, obviously not happy with that answer.

"I wish I knew for sure what was going on." Lifting a shoulder, I pat Draco's chest so he'll put me down. He hesitates, squeezing me closer to his body before finally setting me down. He doesn't let me go though, instead, he wraps his arm around my waist and holds me against his side. I shoot him a look but decide not to say anything because his eyes are glowing yellow.

"What is going on out here? I'm in the middle of cooking, and I can't concentrate with all the scream—" Brayden cuts off, eyes stopping on his brother before his gaze clashes with mine. The door to the kitchen swings back and forth, squeaking with each pass. "What the fuck just happened?"

The guys and I all exchange looks. Draco's raised brow reads *yeah, what the fuck just happened?* So I run my hands over my face and shake my head.

"You better sit down."

∾

AFTER GIVING BRAYDEN THE QUICKEST RUNDOWN OF WHAT happened, I sent him back to the kitchen, promising we'd be okay and that the best thing he could do is continue to cook. Everyone is hungry. The shifters in the cafeteria are solemn. Lincoln's abrupt death due to Jinx's food and the incident with the ghosts has drained any sort of cheer out of them. Even my group is quiet while dinner is cooking.

Chewing on my lip, I glance at the door to the kitchen. Brayden is back there with Trey.

"You know, Little Red, if you want to go check on them,

you can." Draco taps his finger on the table we're sitting at. "Or are you scared of my brother like you are me?"

"I'm not afraid of you." I look at him. "Your brother... is a different story."

Draco hums. "You'll have to tell me the tale of your interactions another day. Go see how he's doing. Moons know if I do it, he'll flip out."

"That's encouraging." Setting my shoulders, I glance at Bea who is sitting with Layla. Layla's doing her best to hide how scared she is, but the lines creasing her forehead are pronounced. "Here I go," I say to no one in particular, but Draco pats my shoulder before I walk off.

"So brave."

I lift my hand and flip him off. A delectable scent wafts from the kitchen, and the closer I get the more my mouth waters, and the more it feels so *wrong* to be hungry after everything that happened. Hesitating for a second, I place my hand on the swinging door and take a deep breath. What Draco said bothered me. Will his twin really be upset if I interrupt? He was mad when he burst out of the kitchen to see what was happening. Squaring my shoulders, I roll my eyes at myself. It's Brayden. My phantom friend. Why am I so freaked out by him?

Maybe because you brought him back to life and he's fully functioning? Didn't you say raising the dead after too long creates zombie-like reanimations? Joan asks.

I've only seen it once, and that's what Mom taught me. Meddling with the long deceased is a dangerous game. Brayden is... not normal.

She snorts. *Obviously. He's a bit off kilter.*

"You're making me nervous, Little Red. Get in here." Brayden's voice carries through the door.

Pushing into the kitchen, which is now as close to sparkling clean as an old kitchen can get, I pause and look around. Trey is scrubbing a mop back and forth near the pantry, furiously cleaning up the last grimy tiles.

"Wow."

Brayden peers into the oven, checking on the food. "I basted it about ten minutes ago. Five or so more and it'll be ready. The potatoes are already done." He points to a bowl with a towel lying over it.

Joining him, I stare at the pan filled with meat and diced apple pieces. The heat from the oven warms my skin, but Brayden's fingers are freezing when they wrap around my arm and pull me into his side. He moves his arm around my waist.

"Are you hungry, Little Red?"

I narrow my eyes and glare at him. "I'm not sure when you died, but manhandling a woman is not hot."

Liar, Joan whispers.

Shush, you'll only encourage him.

I do not see the problem.

Of course she doesn't. Brayden spins me and backs me into the counter so fast my heart skips. Bracing my hands on the butcherblock, I crane my neck and purse my lips.

He inhales deeply, a pleased rumble filling his chest.

"Leave us," he growls at his helper.

Trey drops the mop and rushes out of the kitchen, head ducked like he's afraid to catch Brayden's eye.

"Well, that was rude." I press my hand onto his chest when he leans toward me, fighting for space. "Brayden, what are you doing?"

He runs his fingers up my sides, tracing my curves and moving them to the back of my neck. "You're scared of me?"

"Not of you."

A line forms between his eyebrows. "Explain what that means? Because your heart is pounding."

Yeah, and some of that has nothing to do with being afraid.

"How are you. . ." I trail off and gesture up and down his body with my free hand. "So together?"

With a smirk, he laughs. "That's the strangest compliment I've ever received."

I groan and push on his chest, but he doesn't budge. "That's not what I mean. You were dead. . . and now, you're here, fully functioning. Even with my necromantic powers, you being this aware is not normal."

"Normal is rather boring, don't you think?"

"Stop doing that," I say with an exasperated sigh. "I'm not joking, Brayden. I don't understand, and I want you to explain it to me." I want answers, especially since I apparently stole him from Death. Considering what I did with the spirits earlier, using his power to make them disappear, I'm definitely making my way to the top of his shit list.

His blue eyes darken, and he glances away. "I'd have to understand to do that, and if I'm honest, I'm not sure I do."

Searching his face, I blow out a breath. "Start with explaining what you were."

"Growing up, I used to have nightmares of a creature wearing a black robe and carrying a scythe. My parents and brother wrote it off, telling me I shouldn't watch scary movies before bed. The thing is. . . no matter where I slept, what I did before bed, or how much I tried to manifest positive images before I fell asleep, he always returned. Even after Draco and I were attacked at a party in the woods and brought to Bad Moon Academy, the darkness followed me. When Jinx tried to take me, it didn't work. She killed me, but she couldn't consume my soul or my wolf because another had already laid their claim."

"Death," I whisper, moving my hand from his chest and placing it on mine.

He nods. "You stole from a Horseman. I don't think he'll take kindly to that."

Trying to process what he said, my eyes widen and my mouth pops open, stuck on a word which won't quite come out.

A Horseman? Joan asks.

She's learned a little bit about the world from me, but the apocalypse isn't something that's come up in our regular conversations and thoughts. I pull up some of my memories of the Four Horsemen, trying to explain what he means.

She whistles. *You done fucked up.*

I didn't mean to!

Brayden's thumb brushes over my cheek, and I lean into the touch.

"I thought there were four? They symbolize the apocalypse."

"They do, but Death is not stagnant while he waits for the great battle. He's always been the reaper of souls; he's only biding his time until his brother's rise to the call of the Underworld."

The lights flicker, distracting me from the conversation. I glance around, searching for Jinx who is probably the cause, but she doesn't appear.

Stepping away and sighing, he turns the oven off. "I know what happened earlier was traumatic, but we have much bigger problems than Jinx. She's just a demon spirit."

Just a demon spirit, he says. Then again, if what he told me about Death is true, I've probably pissed off an even stronger demon. A Horseman. More than simply Death then. Jinx is nothing compared to him. Which means we'll have to find a way to get rid of her sooner rather than later.

"Food's ready."

I grab a few spatulas, waiting for him to grab the pan out

of the oven with his hot pads. When our gazes meet, his face ripples with warring emotions: happiness and sadness.

"We'll figure it out," I say.

"I hope so, Little Red. Otherwise, I'm not sure we'll make it out of this alive."

CHAPTER 10

RAVEN

Brayden and I work together to make sure everyone is served before we get our own plates. We join the guys once we're done, sitting next to each other like old pals. Carter eyes the two of us and chews some of the roasted rabbit and apples. Adler waits until we're seated to start eating, but Everett is almost done with his helping.

"This is surprisingly good," Everett says around a mouthful of potatoes.

Grinning at him, I take my first bite, making a curious noise when the flavors burst across my tongue. The meat is similar to chicken in taste and texture, and the apples add a bit of sweetness to the non-traditional meal.

"Wow." I take a drink of water.

Brayden nudges me with his elbow and a smug smile spreads across his face. "Never doubt a chef."

"Bray's always been a good cook." Draco pops a piece of apple into his mouth. "You should try his chocolate pie." The twins share a reminiscing look.

"I like pie," Adler says. He's sitting next to Carter, looking a bit out of place among the shifters.

"Well, then, number five, I'll make you some when we get out of this mess." Brayden moves the longer pieces of his black hair off his forehead with a little head flick.

"Number five?" Adler asks, glancing at me in confusion.

"Brayden," I warn, but he ignores me.

"Oh... you know, you're the fifth part of our harem." He stabs a piece of meat and points his fork at Adler. "Normally it's another wolf, but given the circumstances and your chosen form, I don't think our luna minds including you. Right, Raven?"

My cheeks burn under Adler's amber gaze, so I glance away and bite my cheek. Joan *had* claimed Adler, it's true, but he doesn't know anything about what being with a luna means. I don't even know if he wants to be with me, and now Brayden's forced the issue.

Carter clears his throat, drawing my attention. He's rubbing the bridge of his nose, and his forehead wrinkles in annoyance. "What Brayden so ineloquently said is: you're one of us."

"Raven."

Steeling myself for the inevitable rejection, because what sane man would want to be a part of a harem, I meet his gaze. I mean, these guys are one thing, but Adler? He's different. He's not a pack animal; while he can shift, changelings are nothing like shifters.

His eyes soften at the edges, and he stretches his arm across the table, placing his hand in front of my plate as though he's waiting for me to take it. Curious as to what this means, I place my palm against his and hold my breath.

Burning amber eyes bore into mine. He runs his free hand over his scruff before resting it on top of mine. "I humbly accept this strange but fascinating offer."

Oh, thank the moons. Joan releases a hard pant. *He had me worried for a minute. Now we can plan the claiming ritual.*

Claiming ritual?

Oh yeah, a bit of blood and loads of peen.

A bit of what now?

Joan snorts. *You'll be fine.*

Adler squeezes my hand, and I forget all about Joan. "I hardly remember what it's like to have a family. Lou is the closest I ever came to having a mother." He drops his gaze and shakes his head. "It'll be nice to belong."

Joan moans. *All the dicks are ours! Moons, can you imagine how it'll feel. Each one distinctly different and ravishing you? I'm a little jealous I don't get to bone the wolves, but I can live vicariously through you.*

"Oh, gross."

"I'm sorry." Adler begins to pull away, and I panic, worried I've offended him. I yank his hand toward me.

"No, sorry. Joan is being disgusting."

She chuffs. *Excuse me? Wolves mating is no different than you mostly hairless apes fucking.*

I didn't mean it like that... okay, I did, but you're right. I'm sorry.

Grumbling some more, she says *it's fine* then shuts me out.

"I think she's mad at me." Pursing my lips, I try to coax her back out, but she's giving me the cold shoulder. Adler's fingers flex against me, and I gasp, dropping his hand because I've nearly pulled his entire body over the table. "Sorry."

"Family," Draco says, drawing out the word. "You may come to regret joining us." He cuts his eyes to his brother.

Brayden tips his head to the side and flips him off. "Unlike you, Adler isn't easy to scare. Isn't that right, Adler?"

"You don't scare me."

With a wink, Brayden takes another bite. "There's still time."

"Moons, I forgot how annoying you were." Draco runs his hands through his hair.

He laughs and looks at the guys. "So, I'm in?"

They all look at me, and I widen my eyes, not entirely sure how to answer. Draco hums and drums his fingers on the table.

"I think she likes him."

"Obviously," Everett says and scoffs. "He's in."

Carter claps him on the back. "Welcome to the club."

"Ugh, it's not a club." I spin my fork in the few pieces of apple left on my plate.

It shouldn't be so easy to joke right now, but with all the sadness and death, the last thing I want or need is to be wrapped in sorrow. I'll take my joking where I can get it.

"Hmm. I disagree. It's like a fan club but better because we all get to have sex with you." Draco grins when I choke on my own spit. "Careful, Little Red. Wouldn't want you to die before you fulfill your promise to me."

"What did Joan say that was gross?" Everett asks, saving me from Draco's line of questioning but embarrassing me in an entirely different way.

"She, uh, said she was jealous she didn't get to bang your wolves."

Four matching growls rumble around the table.

"Tell her not to worry, we'll bring you enough pleasure she won't even remember wanting to have sex." Everett winks at me, running his hand over his jaw, his thoughts obviously down in a gutter.

"So our wolves won't mate?" I ask Carter, the reasonable one of the group.

His eyes are hooded, making me rethink the last thought,

and he takes a second to answer. "No, they won't. We only have sex in our human forms."

Oh thank god.

"There's the matter of the ritual," Brayden says, shoving his empty plate away. "We should do it before the full moon, it'll make us all stronger."

Draco nods. "I like this plan."

"I agree," Everett says.

Carter glances at his friends, then slides his gaze to Adler. "It's not our choice."

Dropping the mental wall between us, Joan gasps. *Oh, woman, if you say no, I will find a way to murder you.*

If you kill me, don't you die too, Joan?

Semantics. She replaces the wall, still mad about my comment, and leaves me to my own devices. She didn't even explain what the ritual entails.

"Tomorrow night."

They all share a look, the shifters grinning like devils.

Why do I have a feeling I'm not ready for whatever happens during this ritual?

∼

ADLER

I TRY NOT TO STARE AT HER WHILE WE FINISH EATING, BUT I can't seem to help myself. After two years of denying my attraction to her, my control is slipping. Nearly losing my mind when she disappeared a few weeks ago was all it took to make me forget about being noble and protecting her. I didn't want to corrupt her, to be the reason she was exposed to the super natural side of the world. She's neck deep in this life now though. There's no better way to protect her now than to stay close.

Make her mine.

Being a changeling is a shameful, lonely existence. She knows I was shunned. Knows I'm cursed, and she doesn't give a *damn*. Those vibrant jade irises lift to meet mine, and the unbridled desire I see there steals my breath.

Screw nobility.

I'm tired of holding myself back. Nothing is standing in my way now. Not even the four men sitting with us can deter me. I'm taking Raven in whatever way I can.

∽

CARTER

Being placed on guard shift second, I roll out of my cot around three in the morning on Monday. Raven groans when I shake her awake but stretches and rubs her eyes because she's on duty too. I try not to stare at the way her boobs jut into the air when she arches her back, but I'm a man. By the time she sits up, I've moved my gaze to her face. She still looks tired. Like a trooper, she stands and reaches for my hand.

"I'd ask you to carry me, but I'm firmly against being carried like a damsel. I'm considering it though; that's how sleepy I am."

Squeezing her fingers, I pull her along to where Draco and another shifter wait. She grumbles something about the lack of coffee and a smile pulls at my lips.

"Any trouble?" I ask Draco.

He shakes his head, sweeping his eyes over Raven. "Maybe she should go back to sleep. I can cover her shift."

This gets her attention. She pulls her hand from mine and

straightens her back. "No way. I don't need you to cover for me."

Tipping his head to the side, Draco hums. "All right, Little Red. I won't fight you over it, but there's no sleeping while you're on guard."

She scowls, and he smirks, having gotten the reaction he hoped for.

"Go to bed, Draco. We have a job to do."

The other shifter has already left, so Draco sighs and rubs the back of his neck. "Be careful."

"I'll make sure she's safe." He lifts his gaze to meet mine, nodding and heading off to his cot.

Raven runs her fingers through her long, red hair and surveys the room. Everyone is sleeping peacefully. I lean against the oversized librarian's desk, placing my arm on the wooden top. She makes her way over to me, taking the spot a few inches away from me. Her cherry scent wraps around me and makes me want to bury my head between her legs while we're up, or maybe that's knowing the ritual is happening tonight.

Turning her head toward me and inhaling, she steps closer, leaning into my side. "Why can I tell you're turned on?"

My hand finds her lower back, and I hold her securely against me. "The ritual solidifies the bond, but it's already started to form since you accepted Adler as our fifth."

"Oh," she says softly, eyes dropping to my lips. "What happens at the ritual?"

Casting my gaze around the room, checking for anything amiss like I'm supposed to, I debate on whether I should show or tell her what will happen. Telling is a lot less fun, but it's probably the most responsible decision. She'd never forgive me or herself if something happened to the shifters while I demonstrated a fraction of what she'll feel later tonight.

She turns, pressing her chest against mine and craning her neck. Those luscious tits press into me, so pillowy soft and full. My cock was halfway hard before she moved, and now it's fully erect, straining for her through my jeans. If she feels it, she doesn't react. She simply stares into my eyes and waits for my answer.

"We bind the pack with blood, then the bond is consecrated, as a unit."

Those green eyes light with interest, and her scent intensifies. I bet if I slid my finger into her panties, I'd find her soaking wet. My cock aches, and it takes every bit of will power I have not to rip her clothes off and fuck her against the desk.

Take her.

No, I tell my wolf. *We will have her, soon enough. I cannot break the trust of our unit.*

She's ripe.

I ignore him and run my hand over her hair, smoothing it down. "Does that turn you on?" I whisper the question, delighting in the way she sucks in a breath.

Her heart is pounding. "Yes," she confesses, glancing down.

"Good." I place my finger under her chin, making her meet my gaze. "You will get everything you've ever wanted."

∽

RAVEN

Everything I've ever wanted. Truth be told, I hadn't considered anything like this before, but being surrounded by them, having their lips trailing all over my body, and being filled in every way is something I haven't been able to avoid thinking about. Heat sweeps through my core and I press my legs together, trying to relieve some of the pressure.

You mother freaking hussy. He only told you about the ritual and you're ready to go? Joan blows a raspberry.

You're one to talk, Joan. You were ready for me to claim them before we even knew their favorite colors.

We still don't know that! She's shouting now, so I put up the mental wall between us.

"What's your favorite color?" I ask.

His eyes crinkle at the edges. "It used to be blue."

"Used to be?"

With a nod, he picks up a strand of my hair. "I think I like red now."

Swallowing, I look away, hiding my surprise. His favorite color changed because of me? Should I feel proud about that? Because I do. It feels wrong to want this ritual to happen, especially with the possibility of Jinx coming around at any given moment, but I want all of them. I'm halfway to grabbing Carter's hard cock and fulfilling one fifth of my desires when Everett places his hands on either side of where Carter stands, pressing his front into my back and sandwiching me between them.

Carter groans, moving his hips against me ever so slightly. "Everett, it's not time."

A dark chuckle brushes over the skin on my shoulder seconds before he kisses me there.

"Our luna is in need." Everett places his hand on my lower stomach, wedging between my body and Carter's and pressing his erection into my ass.

"We have to wait," Carter says softly, moving his hands to my hips and rolling them forward.

"For sex, maybe. But this is different." Everett's tone is just as quiet, both working hard not to wake anyone else up.

I whimper in need when my clit presses against Carter's

jeans. The sleep shorts are a soft cotton and don't provide much of a barrier. He releases a low growl, moving his hands from my hip to my ass and squeezing me roughly.

Everett's hand on my stomach floats lower, slipping beneath the shorts and my underwear. His finger is hot against my slit, plunging deep into my soaking wet heat. He toys with my clit, dropping kisses over my shoulder.

"Good girl. So wet for us."

Carter's lips capture mine, swallowing my response and dragging a throaty moan from me. Everett grinds into me while he moves his finger over my clit. I dig my fingers into Carter's hair, taking control of the kiss and teasing his tongue with mine, earning a chuckle from Everett.

"That's it, baby. Take control." Then he shoves two fingers inside of me, moving his other hand to cup my breast and squeezing it. "We can't fuck you yet," he whispers, moving his fingers in and out of me. "But when we do, I'll take all of this" —he tweaks my nipple, making me gasp into Carter's mouth —"and more."

Carter takes one of his hands from my ass and presses against my clit with his thumb. Everett moves his arm slightly to accommodate his friend, still sliding his fingers in and out of me. Breaking away from my kiss with Carter, I press my mouth into his shoulder and swallow every whimper and moan. The thrill of being caught has my heart pounding and only serves to make me even wetter. They work together, making my body tremble with an impending orgasm, and as if knowing how very close I am, Carter pinches my clit and Everett adds a third finger, stretching me in the best way and breaking me all at the same time.

My core clenches as warmth floods through my body. I bite my cheek to keep from crying out. Together they keep me standing, holding me up when my legs weaken. Everett moves his hand from my pussy, leaving me aching, and

Carter slips his hand up to rest on my waist. Turning my head to the side, I sigh in contentment. Wet fingers trace over my lower lip then slip inside my mouth, brushing over my tongue. I close my mouth, sucking his skin clean.

"Very good," Everett whispers next to my ear. "This is just a taste, Raven. Tonight is going to change your life."

And damn if I don't get wet all over again.

CHAPTER 11

RAVEN

By the time everyone wakes up, I'm already tired again but there's no time for rest. In order to keep the deal with Jinx, I have to be in class by ten. Howard and Draco make sure everyone has a buddy while they go about the day as though nothing is wrong. There's no real food for breakfast, so we decide to skip the meal and wait until Brayden and Draco get another kill. I'll take a growling stomach over the possibility of Jinx's poisoned food.

"I want to come to class with you," Bea half-whines, stomping her feet.

Problem is, she's already taken my class. She's taken all the classes the academy has to offer except what's on her current schedule.

"If you could come with me, I'd let you, but you know Jinx won't allow it. You have to go with Howard; he'll keep you safe."

After seeing the way he worked to make sure everyone was taken care of and swallowed his pride to take Draco's orders, I have no doubt about his commitment to keeping everyone alive. I don't like the idea of her going off to class without me, but this isn't about us. It's about everyone.

Blowing out a hard breath that ruffles some of her mousy brown hair, she groans. "Why do we have to pretend anyway? It's stupid."

"Blame the demon spirit. We'll see each other at lunch?" I nudge her with my elbow.

"Whatever." She huffs and walks to where Howard is waiting to take her to class.

I fight off a smile. She's absolutely right, but it wasn't my idea. Getting a glimpse of her attitude makes me feel a twinge of guilt for Aunt Lou. Bea isn't even a fraction as rebellious as I was. Next time I see my aunt, I owe her a big hug. She's been nothing but good to me, and all I've done is throw it in her face by breaking rules, staying out late and getting trashed, and needing to go to rehab to get my shit together.

"She has spunk." Carter appears at my side, his assessing gaze locked on Bea's back. "Kind of like you."

"Thanks?" I ask with a chuckle. "Ready?" Glancing around the library one last time, I check for anyone who decided to take their chances and stay behind.

Everyone has left except for Layla, who is sitting on her cot, head in her hands. Now that they're gone, she's stopped pretending like she's okay. Her face is heavy with sorrow and my heart pangs in sympathy. I remember my first death. After experiencing several, I've found it gets easier to ignore the grief threatening to drown me. It never gets easier to lose someone, but it does get easier to hide the true extent of the impact death has on you.

"Give me a minute," I tell Carter.

His eyes track to Layla, and he presses his lips together, nodding and going to wait by the door.

She doesn't look up when I approach, merely takes in a

sharp breath. "Whatever you're going to say, I don't want to hear it."

"Okay." I sit next to her. "It's time for class."

A derisive laugh escapes her. "Yes, let's all play pretend so the bitch can kill us all on Friday. Sounds like a great plan."

"We have five days to come up with a way to stop her." I frown. "I'm going to try to figure out how to send her back to her realm. I've never done much necromantic work, but there are plenty of texts about magic. Surely one of them has information we can use."

Before she even says it, I know she's about to be rude. There's a glint of something dark in her gaze, like she wants to hurt me just so I can join her in misery.

"Give it a rest, Raven. You keep acting like you're the chosen one. News flash, this isn't a movie. You can't save anyone. Not Morris. Not Jackson or Lincoln. The only person you're good at getting out of trouble is yourself."

"I know you're hurting, but I'm your friend. Not the enemy." With that, I stand and head toward Carter. "Come to class or don't, but I can promise you, you don't want to face Jinx alone," I say, glancing over my shoulder.

Her face crumples, and her chin trembles. I almost think my reaction made it worse. She wanted me to get mad, to lash out at her. The only reason I understand what she's doing and why is because I used to do the same thing. Especially right after Dad died.

"Everything all right?" Carter's hands are in his pockets, and he rocks back on his heels when I stop in front of him. "That seemed tense."

I lift a shoulder. "Pain is ugly."

"You're a lot kinder than I would be." He moves his gaze over my head, taking in a sobbing Layla. "She's wrong. You can save people, especially with the five of us here to help."

"I hope you're right."

His face softens, and he clears his throat. "Let's go, we don't want to be late."

The clock on the wall reads nine-fifty-three. We have seven minutes before History of Shifters is scheduled to start. I resist the urge to check on Layla again. She'll either pull herself together or fall apart. Either way, she doesn't want me there to witness it.

There are times when people want help finding their way and aren't afraid to lean on another for support. Other times all you can do is leave people drowning in their pain and hope they find a way to swim out on their own. Knowing she doesn't want help doesn't make the choice to leave her any less difficult.

"You have to make the choice, Raven, I can't make it for you." Aunt Lou is standing at the kitchen counter, resting one hand on the granite. Her face is red from crying. She spent all night worrying about where I'd been.

"Then what's this?" I hold up the pamphlet for a rehabilitation center that specializes in youth addiction. "You're not asking me to go. You're forcing me."

Aunt Lou blows out a hard breath, glancing at the ceiling and fighting off tears. By the time she looks at me again, her eyes are dry and her face hardens. She moves to the cabinet where she keeps her stash of alcohol. It used to be big, but I took more than my fair share, and she's purposefully not buying more. Like she thinks by letting it run out, it'll cure me.

Too bad she can't see I'm diseased. There's nothing that can cure what ails me.

She slams a bottle of cheap whiskey in front of me, leaning against the counter next to where I stand.

"You want to call the shots? Fine. Drink."

"What?" I ask with a gasp. "Now you're okay with it?"

Fire flashes in her eyes, and she cracks the lid open, holding the nearly full bottle out to me.

"You're so hell bent on an early death. Drink. You're still drunk from whatever you did last night."

The strong bite of booze fills the air, making my mouth water, and I lick my lips, eyes wandering down to the bottle. Reaching for it, I gently extract it from her hands and lift it to my lips, waiting for her to scream at me. I take a swig, not even flinching at the harsh taste.

"Do me a favor, tell Mirabelle I said hi." And with that final punch to the gut, Aunt Lou leaves me in the kitchen, ignoring the tears filling my eyes.

I stare at the bottle, hand shaking as I hold it. My stomach is sour with all the liquor I've consumed in the last twelve hours. I catch my reflection in the stainless-steel refrigerator, and a sob rips from my chest.

I'm just like Mom. Selfish and broken, dragging the rest of the world down with me. There's no reason for me to be here. Aunt Lou hates me. Mom and Dad are gone. I don't have any friends. What's the fucking point?

No. Fuck that. I'm not like my mom. Swinging my arm back and splashing whiskey all over myself, I hurl the bottle at the fridge, laughing when it breaks. Brown liquid mars my reflection, making me look even more pathetic. Stepping closer, glass crunching under my Converse, I swipe my hand across the stainless steel. I stand, staring into the impossibly shiny appliance. Aunt Lou obsessively cleans it and now I've ruined it with streaks of whiskey.

I keep messing up. A big piece of glass pierces through the bottom of my shoe, stabbing into my heel. Pressing my lips together, I stay still for a second, letting the pain ground me, then carefully walk out of the mess, slipping my shoe off and pressing a paper towel to the blood. Everything crashes into me like a train into a car on the tracks.

Sobbing again, I drop my forehead to my arm, letting it all out. They're gone. I won't ever see them laugh again. I won't see Dad shake his head at Mom for being ridiculous and dancing around the kitchen. Or the way her eyes crinkle when he tells a dumb joke. There will be no more camping trips. No more Friday night movies. Nothing. That's all there is. Nothing.

Strong arms wrap around me, pulling me into a soft body. Aunt Lou smells like lilacs and earl grey tea. Dropping the towel from my still bleeding foot, I turn and cling to her, not caring that my snot and tears are seeping into her shirt.

"I'm alone," I whisper. I'm not even sure she hears me because she doesn't respond right away.

"Oh, Raven," she says a second later, rubbing her hand over my messy hair. "You're not alone, baby. We have each other. It's you and me, but you have to want it, Raven. I can't watch you go down the same road as your mother. It'll kill me."

Biting my lip, I pinch my eyes shut and breathe her in. Her heart beats steadily, so full of life. She's here. I've been fighting her ever since I got here, but I think it's time to listen. I really don't want to go to rehab, like some sort of helpless being, but I don't know how to stop.

"There's no shame in needing help," she says, as if reading my mind. "But like I said earlier, you have to want this. You need to make sure you're ready to cut the bullshit and pull your head out of your own ass."

I chuckle at her gruff words and nod. "Okay." Squeezing her tighter, my throat closes, trying to keep me from accepting her help, but I fight the sensation, swallowing my stubborn pride and the sickness in me to answer her. "I need help, Aunt Lou." My voice cracks, fresh tears spilling out of me.

"I know you do, baby. I know you do." She keeps me wrapped in her arms, not letting go until my cheeks have dried and my breathing has evened.

That day was my breaking point. Aunt Lou's tough love may seem harsh to some, but it's what I needed. Layla will figure out what she needs too; it's only a matter of time.

Carter is halfway through his lesson about the first war between supes and humans when Layla shuffles in. Her head is down, and she slides into her usual seat, not meeting either of our gazes. He doesn't pause or miss a beat; he keeps on with the lesson as though she's been there all along. I'm thankful he doesn't make a big deal about her arrival, because shame is weighing her shoulders down, and I suspect she's beating herself up for what she said to me.

While I'd like to say I didn't take it personally, I'm not that person. What she said stung, but she was lashing out. I've already forgiven her. I continue writing notes, using it as a distraction from the current reality. Nothing like thousands of deaths and civil unrest to keep you from thinking about how fucked up your life is.

"For being slower and the weapons available in the early twentieth century, humans still found ways to slay hundreds of shifters in any given battle. Cannons were loaded with silver, which served to take care of the shifters. Fields were filled with explosives, so when the vampires tried to sneak up on a legion, they were blasted apart, giving the humans enough time to burn the head and body in separate places."

"What about the witches?" Layla asks, suddenly perking up.

"The witches are an interesting set of supes, because they've worked hard to stay out of the wars. When shifters and vampires were busy attacking humans across the world and vice versa, the witches were busy fortifying their covens, building their numbers, and growing stronger."

"Didn't the witches attack shifters and vampires though?" I ask, remembering tiny details from the brief overview our school gave. The main points were to let you know, regardless of how human they looked, supes were dangerous.

"They did." He ruffles his hair and yawns. "A few covens of dark witches went on an attack, going after other witches, shifters, vampires, and hunters alike."

My ears twitch at the word hunter.

Not with the hunters again, seriously, Joan whines in my head.

Shut your trap. They're so interesting.

"The hunters are gone now... right?"

Carter grins. "You've been reading?"

Lifting a shoulder, I stare at my nails. "Sometimes I study."

"You're right. Hunters are extinct, though not because of the dark witches. A vampire named Nix can be credited with that."

"She killed them all? Why?" Layla asks, glancing between the two of us, all of her earlier awkwardness now gone in light of learning more about this world.

"Hunters were the strongest of supes, once fully trained, of course, and they're driven by a need to kill bad things. So given vampires or even shifters being, well, wild, they would come in and take care of the supes who posed a danger to humans and the other supes. Anyway, long story short, some hunters pissed off Nix, this very old vampire, and she and a few other vampires went and wiped them out."

"If they were stronger than them, how did they do that?" I wrinkle my brow. "That doesn't make sense."

Carter shrugs. "You'd be amazed at how strong vengeance can be. Nix worked with Blood Mafia, a big grouping of vicious vampires, and launched a series of surprise attacks. Once she took care of the mature hunters—or the ones who awakened and had the full use of their powers—it was easy for her to take out the rest."

"So she's really dangerous." Layla runs her fingers through her hair.

"She is, but she's been in hiding for at least twenty years, so we don't really have to worry about her. Blood Mafia keeps to themselves now in San Francisco. The elders have come to terms with them."

"Shifters and vampires living in harmony?" I snort. "What would Jacob and Edward say?"

Carter gives me a funny smile, like he's trying to understand but doesn't quite get there.

"Eh, I'm more concerned about how Selene would feel." Layla shoots me a grin.

"True, she's a badass. I want to be her when I grow up."

"I don't know what you're talking about with Edward and Jacob, but I do love *Underworld*, and I've come to find after being changed that most of those same stigmas are true between vampires and shifters. It's almost like our nature won't allow for more than one supernatural race." Carter rubs the bridge of his nose and yawns again. "Okay, why don't we call that good for the day? We have two minutes before class is out."

Flipping my notebook closed, I shove it into my backpack and head to Layla's desk, stopping to wait while she gets her stuff put in her bag.

"Pretty wild, huh?"

She searches my face, looking for any sign of anger left over from her comment to me earlier. When she doesn't find any, the tension bunching her shoulders together eases and she chuckles.

"That a few vampires took out an entire race of supes? I think you mean terrifying."

"I think we're safe from vampires, at least while the wards are up. We can worry about them once we take out... the trash." I wrinkle my nose, hating that I almost said I want to kill Jinx out loud. Something tells me she wouldn't be too happy about that, though a part of her has to anticipate it.

Layla lifts an eyebrow at my quick recovery. "It's starting to stink." Pressing her lips into a thin line, she glances at Carter who is waiting by his desk for us.

"Ready for lunch?" he asks.

Our stomachs growl in answer and he shakes his head. "I sure hope they brought more food than yesterday."

I laugh and start to head out of the classroom. Layla grabs my arm once we're in the hallway, turning me toward her.

"Hey, can I talk to you?"

"Everything all right?" Carter asks, eyeing my friend. He's not her biggest fan right now.

"Yeah, can you give us a minute?" I smile to let him know I'm okay, and he takes a few steps away. It's the most privacy we're going to get without separating.

Blowing out a hard breath, she screws her face up, like what she's about to say is hard for her. "I owe you an apology. I didn't mean what I said earlier about you only being able to save yourself. I'm just so scared. And mad. This isn't how my life was supposed to go."

I glance at the floor and shrug. "Trust me, I had no plans to become a shifter either." Swinging my eyes up to meet hers, I say, "You're forgiven. I'm on your side, Layla."

"I know." She squeezes my arm then releases it. "I'm really sorry for being a jerk."

"It's okay, Layla." I pull her into a hug. "Everyone handles pain differently. You're not defined by that moment. We're friends, right?"

Lifting her hands, she wraps them around me and nods.

"Then that's that. Now come on." I release her and turn toward Carter who is staring at me with the strangest look on his face. "Time to find some food."

∼

CARTER

Raven is too forgiving. I don't know how she does it. I'm still mad at Draco for what he did four weeks ago, but she hasn't brought it up, almost like she's processed her anger and moved on already. I still can't though. The look in his eyes when she came over to our table... was too wild. I knew then that he'd gone against our pact to never turn someone.

"What are we even doing in this town, Draco?" I glance around, eyeing the bar that's in need of new siding and a lightbulb for the sign.

Lou's.

He's seriously taking me to this place?

"Even after years of being stuck inside the academy, you can't shake off your city slicker snobbery?" Draco tosses a dark look over his shoulder. "Give it a chance. You might like it."

With a scoff, I run my hand over my hair, making sure it's not too messy after shifting back from wolf form. When he convinced me to come on another run and bring our clothes, I didn't expect to be brought to the middle of nowhere for a beer. It is nice to be outside of the wards though. I shrug off my uncertainties and follow him inside, determined to make the best of what's left of this month's freedom.

The lingering scent of cigarettes from years ago clings to the walls of this place like my ex-girlfriend, with a death grip. Not even the fresh coating of paint can get rid of it. Still, the place is clean and the booths aren't torn up like I expected. Draco leads us to a table in the back, slides into his seat, and turns to watch the room.

A big guy behind the bar narrows his eyes and tips his head up as if to say *you're welcome here, but don't fuck around.* The dinner crowd is settling in, mostly older guys with beer bellies and scruffy beards.

"Hey there," a woman in a black apron says, plopping two laminated menus in front of us. "Whatcha drinking tonight?"

"Whatever local IPA you have on tap."

Raising her eyebrow at his short response, she clucks her tongue and nods. "All right. I'll be right back."

My eyes stray back to the dining room while we wait. Guys are laughing and joking across multiple tables with the type of familiarity that comes from years of living in the same town and growing up together. The kitchen door swings open and a bright flash of red hair catches my attention.

She's young, probably fresh out of high school, and beautiful. After finishing putting on her apron, she scans the room, eyes passing over our table like she doesn't even notice us. There's something about the way she wears her smile that doesn't seem genuine. Like she's putting on the face everyone is expecting her to wear.

"See something you like?" Draco asks, voice taking on a hard edge.

Glancing at him, I take in the slight yellow glow in his blue eyes and the way his fingers curl into fists. He shoots his eyes in her direction, the tension lining his face easing when he looks at her, but the lines return as soon as he turns back to me.

"What did you do?" I ask, leaning forward. "We made a pact, Draco."

"Two IPAs." The waitress sets our beers down on the table, interrupting the conversation. "Are you eating?"

"Yeah," I say and order enough food to feed four people. My stomach is rumbling and cramping, a reminder of why we made the agreement in the first place. Once we figured out what was going on at Bad Moon Academy, Brayden, Draco, Everett, and I agreed we'd never be the reason someone was taken to the moons forsaken place.

As soon as she's gone, I pinch the bridge of my nose and eye him. "Tell me you're not thinking about biting her."

"I'm not thinking about biting her." A cruel smirk twists his lips.

Sitting back, I try to convince myself he didn't do it. He'd come back last night a bit wild-eyed and bloodied. I'd written it off as a *good night of hunting. Is it possible he bit her? Changed her even though he knows better?*

He keeps glancing at her, like an addict looking for his next hit. I press my lips together, my annoyance growing with every passing second. I get ready to say something, but stop when he sits a little straighter and looks me dead in the eye.

"The weather is nice out here, don't you think?"

Scrunching my eyebrows together, I try to figure out what he's getting at. "What?"

Tipping his head to the side, he laughs softly. "Yeah, today's been pretty intense."

"Draco, what the hell are you talking about?"

He picks up his beer and sips, eyes sparkling with mirth. Then it hits me. A delectably sweet scent, like ripe strawberries sprinkled in sugar, or peach cobbler, wraps around me in a warm hug. I take a deep breath, swallow my frustration, and smile at the woman as she places the food in front of us. The rare steak smells delicious, and my mouth waters when I see a small pool of blood under the slab of meat.

"Should I get your friend's water?"

Moons, her voice is like a siren's call. Some women have a slightly higher pitch to their voice. While not grating, it can be a little annoying. Her voice is like a robust wine. Rich and a little bitter. Dark and tantalizing with a slight huskiness coating every syllable. Her electric green eyes sweep over us as she sets the last plate down. Glancing over her shoulder, she searches the room. I flit my gaze over her body. She's wearing black pants and a shirt but there's enough curving to hint at what lies underneath the fabric.

I'm so distracted by her that I don't notice Draco reaching toward her until she glares at him.

"Don't touch me." *Her words hold so much command, I wouldn't be surprised if she already shifted. I can't smell her wolf, so I know she hasn't.*

Draco pulls away from her, and I glare at him.

"He didn't mean anything by it, did you?" I kick him under the table.

"I'm sorry," he growls, face flashing with violence.

He doesn't intimidate me though. I'm just pissed. I keep my grin on my face until she leaves then scowl at him.

"You bit her?"

Popping a fry in his mouth, he shrugs and looks at her as she goes around the bar. "Yup."

"Well, congratulations, you just sentenced her to death."

He turns toward me in an attempt to avoid looking at her, but his eyes keep slipping back to her as I lecture him about what he's done. I don't even think he hears a thing I say.

I still get irritated when I think about that night. Raven's face lights up when she sees Draco with the guys. There are no vestiges of annoyance and there's no trace of resentment. She's forgiven him already like she did with Layla. She continues to surprise me, and I'm not sure any of us deserve her, but I'm determined to do whatever it takes to keep her safe and make her ours. If that means swallowing my pride and forgetting my annoyance with Draco, so be it.

∽

DRACO

Finally Brayden and I have time to be alone. I corner him in the library when we come back to grab fresh clothes after hunting. The edge of my brother's mouth lifts, and he draws his lower lip between his teeth. He knows I'm irritated with him, and he's enjoying it.

"What were you thinking?" I ask, running my hand through my hair and sitting on my cot. "You forced your way back. What if she'd been mad? What if she rejected the bond because of it?"

Spreading his hands in front of him, he gives a small shrug. "She didn't, so I don't see the problem."

"The problem is that, once again, you didn't think about the consequences." I let him connect the dots, watching as his eyes soften, and he swallows when he gets my meaning. Moons, I'm pathetic for feeling so hurt about him stepping in to try and save Alice.

"I didn't know what would happen." He doesn't try to tell me that knowing he'd be killed would have changed his mind. "I'm sorry for leaving you."

My face pinches, and I look away. "It's fine."

"Then why are you mad?"

"I'm not mad," I snap then cringe. "Fuck. Fine, I'm pissed. You fucking left me."

"It's not like I had a choice, Draco. Those things were attacking Alice. What did you expect me to do? Standby and do nothing as she was killed?"

"No, dammit."

He scoffs. "So what then? I'm sorry. I came back to you as soon as I figured out how to use my reaper form."

Grinding my teeth together, I nod. I know this. We've talked about what happened when he first showed up in ethereal form, but now he's here. Fuck. I'm such a fucking pussy. My hands shift and I slam the claws into the cot, grunting when they get caught in the springs. With a snarl, I try to rip them out, but one is lodged in tight enough that I snap it. I hiss and press the now free palm against the bed, trying to work the claw out.

"Draco, stop." He approaches me like I'm the scary one. "You're going to make it worse. Let me help."

I shake my head, continuing to try and get it out on my own. The tip of my claw breaks as it pulls free. With a gasp, I shift it back to a hand and shove the finger into my mouth, rolling my tongue over it to help it heal the broken nail.

"Shit. Seriously, Draco, what the fuck?" He grabs my shoulders and shakes me. "Don't be psycho. That's my job."

Dropping my hand to my side, I release a dark laugh and roll my eyes. "It was an accident."

He shakes me again, a little harder, then butts his forehead against mine. "Good, because I plan to hold onto the title psycho a bit longer if you don't mind. I like making Carter squirm too much."

I nod and clap my hand on the back of his neck. We stay like that for a minute before I shove him away.

"You're lucky I like you," I tell him, standing from the bed and adjusting my shirt. "Otherwise I'd have to kill you."

He cackles. "There he is. I like this version of Draco better than mopey Draco."

Flipping him off, I start toward the door. "Love you too, asshole."

With a snicker, he shouts, "Love you, bro!"

CHAPTER 12

RAVEN

Lunch is uneventful. Everyone made it back to the cafeteria unharmed and there have been no Jinx sightings. Adler, Brayden, and Draco have been gathering fresh meat and using the limited supplies in the pantry to figure out what to make for the next few days. It's nice to see them all working together, knowing that we can be a team is important to me, especially if we're sealing the deal tonight.

I'd like to breathe easy, but I know as soon as I start to relax, she'll pop up to cause trouble. Jinx won't let us off without a little bit of psychological torture. She enjoys it too much. Everett drones on about controlling the wolf inside, but I'm so tired from my early morning guard shift I end up propping my head up with my hand and nodding off. I'm in the middle of chasing bunnies, a dream courtesy of Joan, when he whispers in my ear.

"Wakey, wakey."

"Five more minutes," I mumble, slowly opening my eyes to find it's just me, him, and Bea. The little shifter giggles when I wipe my palm over my chin, only to find a small trail of drool. "Ugh, you should have told me, Bea!"

"You were snoring so peacefully," she says, laughing even harder when I make a noise in mock frustration.

"You let me snore? Traitor," I whisper the last word, and she tilts her head to the side.

"Come on, Raven, you know I'm on your side." Bea slips out of her desk and walks over. "What are we doing tonight?"

"I know you are." I reach out and pat her arm then flick my gaze to Everett who turns his head and whistles, not helping me one bit. With narrowed eyes on him, I say, "Uh, the guys and I have something to take care of."

"Oh my god, you're going to have sex, aren't you?"

Her squeaked question has both Everett and me turning to give her an appraising look. She's fourteen, so I guess it's not too unusual for her to know what sex is, but still, she's so young and I'm not really comfortable talking to her about my gang bang.

"Um, it's the luna ritual," is all I can muster.

She nods. "I've read all about it. Five men for one luna." She continues to rattle off random facts about lunas and their harems, making me feel a little uneducated. I haven't even studied anything about my shifter status.

You don't need a book. You have me.

True, but I feel like I should have at least tried to figure out as much as I could before agreeing to this.

Joan sighs. *I've given you all you really need to know. The men complete us, and in turn, our power will grow as a unit. A luna with a harem is a formidable force. Great sex, built-in cooks, and unlimited snuggles... any other questions?*

As if it's that simple. Joan doesn't understand why the idea is so bizarre to me. I've grown up learning that marriage is between two people. Sure, I've heard of polyamorous relationships but this is a little different. They're all mine, no sharing, no other women. Just wholly and completely *mine*. Them being excited about it and not bickering about things has made it a lot easier, but the whole idea is still weird to me.

But blood? What sort of ritual includes blood?

It won't hurt, Joan says. *It's only a short part of the ritual and all the peens will seriously make up for that bit.*

Oh god. There are five of them, Joan. This is a horrible idea. How will it even work? There are only so many places they can go!

Suck it up, buttercup. You're about to be deep in harem love, and you're going to be so annoyed with yourself for waiting this long to get all that deliciously thick—

Joan!

What? You were thinking about it.

Ugh. Wolves. I put a thin wall between her and me in my mind, politely asking for space but giving her the ability to push through if she really wanted to. Knowing how nervous I am, she doesn't come in and continue her lecture about how much I'll love my harem. It seems we're learning more about when to back off so the other doesn't get overwhelmed, and it's nice knowing she understands when I need a moment.

Or maybe she's trying to be good so I actually go through with the ritual tonight. One thing I know for sure is that I need a long, hot shower to feel even close to ready for what is in store for me.

EVERETT

The guys head to the locker rooms to shower, leaving the women behind. I'm a little uneasy about separating, but Raven is strong and the other women, while not lunas, are also capable of taking care of themselves for an hour. There are only six showers, so we rotate showering, getting dressed, and watching out for any sign of Jinx.

Adler leans against the wall next to where I stand, tipping his head back to rest against the brick. I try to think of something to say that doesn't sound douchey or like a lie.

"Can you believe it's only Monday?" I run my hand over my face. "Fucking Mondays, am I right?"

He laughs and looks at me. "Even in the supe world, Mondays are the worst."

Blowing out a hard breath, I nod and kickstand my foot against the brick. "Though you have to admit, there is a pretty good end to this day."

"Mmm." He runs his hand over his scruff, eyes flitting around the room before returning to me. "What am I walking into?"

Smirking, I say, "Well, for starters, there's going to be a lot of dick."

Carter scoffs as he walks by with a towel secured around his waist. "I think he's more concerned about what the ceremony means and how it works."

"First of all, the ceremony does have a lot of dick, so, he needs to know about that."

With a sigh, Carter tosses a scowl in my direction. "You're being crude."

"Oh, pardon me, would you rather I call it a penis?"

Adler snorts and presses his lips together to hide a smile.

"Shut up and tell the man what he needs to know." Draco backhands my stomach when he goes by, grinning like a fool.

"Speaking of dick," I say, raising an eyebrow at Adler who simply smiles harder. "All right, all right. So the ceremony is a big deal. Long story short, Raven is a luna, and now that she's accepted that we're her harem, it's time to seal the deal."

"You make it sound like a bunch of frat boys looking to score." Carter pulls on his shirt and fluffs his blond hair with his hand. "What Everett is so eloquently trying to say, is that the bond between a luna and her harem—or pack if you will—isn't officially formed until we complete the blood rite and consummate it."

"Oh, the blood rite. My favorite." Brayden makes a slurping noise as he steps out of the shower, foregoing the towel and strutting to the bench butt naked.

"Bro, put on some fucking clothes." I give him a hard look, and he stands, closing the distance between us in two giant steps. Kicking off the wall, I cross my arms and narrow my eyes on him.

"You'll be seeing a lot more of this later tonight, Everett. Maybe you want to touch it." Brayden reaches for my hand, and I growl, shoving his chest and putting space between us.

"Knock it off." Carter pinches the bridge of his nose. "If you guys fight, I swear I'll junk punch the both of you so hard you won't be able to enjoy the evening."

"Rude," Brayden says with a scoff. "I was only teasing our little alpha. He seems way too worried about my junk." He grabs himself and winks at me. "Maybe he wants a taste?"

"Fuck you, dude." I'm not into dudes even in the slightest, and he knows it. He's being an asshole.

"Enough." Adler's tone leaves no room for argument, and my wolf snarls at me inside my head, begging to be let out to put the fae in his place. Turning his heavy gaze on me, he steps closer. "Understood?"

A foreign power, rich with promises of violence, crawls over my skin.

He's strong.

Stronger than us? I ask. Not that I want to challenge Adler. I'm more than happy to stop messing around, especially if it makes Brayden put some clothes on. The question is more out of curiosity.

My wolf pauses for a few seconds then whines. *I can't tell.*

Hm. Interesting.

I search Adler's face then dip my head in understanding. "You got it, boss."

Brayden cackles, but quickly shuts up when Adler starts for him.

"Easy does it, big boy. I'll play nice."

Adler releases a growl which has me wondering if he can shift into a wolf of his own, and sweeps his gaze around our small group.

"If what Carter says is true, tonight we swallow our pride and any grievance we may have with each other. The luna needs us to be united."

"You're goddamn right," Draco says, yanking on a pair of ridiculous pants.

"Let's get ready," Adler says to me, jerking his thumb toward the showers.

I don't answer him, but I do turn and strip out of my clothes before jumping into one of the private shower stalls. The hot water beats against me, and I scrub myself harder than necessary, frowning as I stare at the wall. If he's stronger than me, what does that mean for the pack dynamics?

Does it matter? My wolf asks.

You're the one who wanted to rip his head off for trying to tell us what to do.

The fae is a good fit for our pack. The luna chose wisely, and we shouldn't question her.

I turn and let the water wash away the soap from my hair and back. *I wasn't questioning her. More wondering what it means for us as alphas?*

Things will change a bit, but when we join with the luna, our power will grow. The unit will be strong together.

Finishing my shower, I can't help but wonder why he's suddenly so calm. Adler's show of force must have been stronger than I thought. Since my wolf knows the most about what the bond means, I groan and run my hands over my face.

Seems like Adler was right. Time to put aside my pride.

∾

RAVEN

After a simple dinner of rice and rabbit, Layla, Bea, a few other women, and I go for showers, rotating shifts between bathing, hair drying, and keeping watch. Bea goes last. I help blow dry her hair, feeling a little motherly and silly, but she smiles the whole time, so it's worth it. Between the six of us, we get done in about an hour and fifteen minutes.

My stomach begins to knot as we make our way back to the library, beating the men who also went to clean up. Since they're gone, we sit together at one of the large tables, talking about our past lives but not going too deep into them so as not to make anyone cry.

"I was a veterinarian. When I saw the wolf so close, I assumed it must've been injured, but boy was I wrong." Jasmine releases a soft laugh, making light of it.

"Well," Layla says, saving her from an awkward conclusion, "I was on a hike with a date. The wolf ran out in our path. Get this, the guy turns and bails, leaving me with the wild animal. Talk about one hell of a way to end a date. Needless to say, it didn't work out."

We all laugh at that and the door to the library opens; pine scented soap fills the room, coiling around my heightened senses. I take a deep breath. There's something oddly appealing about a freshly washed man. Like the water somehow strips away everything but their raw masculinity.

As they filter in, our table grows quiet and Penelope and Layla shoot me curious looks. We talked briefly about the ritual, and I'm more than embarrassed to learn essentially everyone is waiting for me to get railed. Crass, but honest. Everyone knows I'm about to have my mind blown. I'm not a virgin, but damn, this whole situation makes me feel like a blushing bride on her wedding night, which isn't entirely far off of what tonight is. It's basically the shifter version of a wedding.

My men gravitate to each other, as if they're pulled by an invisible force, and as one, they turn their gazes to me. The hair on my arms rises, gooseflesh rippling over my skin. With a sharp breath, I shove away from the table, driven by the same urge, and wave bye to my friends, ignoring the small smirks they all share.

At least they didn't make me feel like a slut for this. They didn't even care. That's how you empower a woman. Let her live her life free of judgment. If I want to take five men, who the hell is going to tell me no?

There you go, now you got it, Joan whispers. *They grow up so fast.*

I swear to the moon if you embarrass me for this, I'll never forgive you.

She chuffs. *Relax, Raven. I'm going to sit back and enjoy my spoils. Once the ritual is complete, their wolves will meld with mine. Trust me, while I'm excited to feel the pleasure they'll bring you, I'm more excited about being connected to my wolves.*

Right. I keep forgetting this is about more than me. It's about Joan. It's about the guys and their wolves. It's about the beginning of our little pack.

"There she is," Brayden drawls, eyes straying down my body. "Damn, boys, what did we do to deserve this?"

His words draw a flush up my neck and the other's chuckle, giving me their own searing looks. All of this attention is going to make me nervous, so I wave off his comment.

"So, where is this happening?" I raise an eyebrow and

place my hands on my hips. "I refuse to become a real luna in the ballroom."

Carter shakes his head. "I think you'll be surprised." He extends his hand, and I stare at it for a beat before slipping my hand inside of his. Adler snatches my other one, placing a kiss on the back of my hand. My breath hitches.

"Come along, Little Red." Draco swaggers out of the library with his hands in the pockets of his leather pants. Brayden and Everett hold the door for us, and we all leave the library together.

"Get some!" a guy I don't know calls, and Everett snorts.

This is a horrible idea.

CHAPTER 13

DRACO

The pitter-patter of Little Red's heart makes my wolf hungry. All he sees is prey, though he recognizes this prey isn't meant to be torn apart. We'll eat her up sure enough, just not in the savage way we do with other prey. My hand rests on the door to my bedroom, and I hesitate for a mere second.

What if she doesn't like it?

No, I shake off the creeping self-doubt, knowing the guys and I have this locked down. Raven likes all of us, even fucking Brayden. I don't know how, but my asshole of a brother weaseled his way into her good graces. I love my brother, though I can't deny there's something scary about him. Maybe it's the whole dying and coming back stuff. I know that isn't true; it's the simple answer. Brayden's always been more extreme than I am, and I know I'm out there.

Wrenching my door open, I shove all of my thoughts about Brayden to the back of my mind and focus on what's important tonight. Raven. I press my back into the door, gazing down at our little red-haired vixen. Her impossible emerald eyes widen as she takes in the five twin size beds we shoved together. Using the sheets Brayden and I stitched together—our mother taught us how, don't judge—we made a large, fitted sheet. We sewed together the flat sheets too, in case Raven wanted some warmth. Given all the bodies that will be in the bed, there's no need for a comforter.

Perhaps not the most romantic of places, but I found some of the old candles in the ballroom and placed them around the edges of the room, using those for lighting. There's a small bowl and knife we'll use for the first part of the ritual lying on my desk.

Raven lets go of Carter and Adler's hands, brushing past me to stand at the edge of the bed. Her heart kicks against her chest even harder. Since she's facing away from me, I can't see her face to know what she's thinking.

The guys come in, and I close the door, carefully making my way over to her. I walk my fingers up both of her arms, gripping her biceps and pulling her into my body. She comes easily, relaxing in my hold and releasing a soft sigh.

"Little Red. Luna. Raven." So many names for her, and each feels equally right. "Time for the binding."

She turns her head, looking up at me with curiosity. "The blood?"

The worry in her question draws a laugh from me, and I nod. "It'll only hurt a bit."

Everett brings the knife and bowl over, holding the blade out for me. I release Raven and take it and run my finger over the sharp edge. This will do perfectly. Nice clean cuts is what we want. They'll heal better that way.

"It's time to begin," Carter says.

The men make a half circle around Everett, each waiting their turn, and Raven stands awkwardly next to me, hands curled into fists at her side to try and hide the slight tremor running through them, but I see it.

Fear can be fun sometimes, especially when there is trust between partners. To accept us as hers speaks volumes of how she feels, but she can't fight back her natural reaction. Part of her will always be the scared human in the woods. With time, she'll learn to embrace her wilder side and stifle those reactions.

Get on with it. My luna grows impatient.

Settle down, I say to my wolf, but focus all the same.

Everett nods when he sees I'm ready. "Zeta, what do you offer our luna?" he asks, repeating the words Carter taught us earlier.

"I bring my blood and allegiance. My heart and my soul." Raven gasps as I slide the blade over my palm, cutting it open and squeezing my hand over the bowl. Six drops fall into the dish.

Adler hands me a towel, and I wrap it over the wound, sliding my gaze to Raven and winking.

Carter steps forward, and we trade places.

"Delta, what do you offer our luna?"

"I bring my blood and allegiance. My heart and my soul." He repeats the same line I had and cuts himself. Six drops of blood splash over mine, and Brayden takes his place.

"Beta, what do you offer our luna?"

Brayden eyes Raven and bares his teeth in what he must think is a grin. "I bring my blood and allegiance. My heart, my soul, and Death."

Always a showoff. I scoff and glare at him.

She narrows her gaze, but she doesn't say anything to him. He tips his head to the side and cuts his palm with a fast slice, going deeper than we had, but still only allowing six drops to fall into the bowl. Carter offers him a towel but he shakes his head, letting his blood drip over the floor. It's impossible to miss the way he stares at the crimson liquid, like he's only just realized he's alive again. He's lucky I don't mind the mess.

The fae steps forward, grabbing the bowl from Everett and taking his place. Everett snatches the knife from Brayden.

"Psycho," he whispers, smirking at my brother.

"Control freak," Brayden says back before joining Carter and me.

"Alpha, what do you offer our luna?" Adler asks like a natural born shifter. This has to be strange to him, but he hasn't said as much or reacted to anything we've told him. He makes a good addition to our pack.

"I bring my blood and allegiance. My heart and my soul." Everett is quick and efficient. He wraps his hand and takes the bowl back from Adler so he can have his turn.

"Nurturer, what do you offer our luna?" Everett asks.

Adler holds the knife point up, letting the blood slide toward the hilt as he studies the dagger.

Raven's eyebrows pinch together at his silence, and I'm two seconds away from ripping his head off when he clears his throat.

"I bring my blood and allegiance. My heart and my soul." His blood mixes with ours, and he tosses the knife up, catching the tip of the blade between two fingers.

"Luna?" he asks.

Carefully extracting the knife from his hold, Raven clutches it at her side, her knuckles turning white with how hard she's gripping it.

"Luna. We offer ourselves to you. Do you accept us as your own?"

Her eyes cloud, the look she gets when her wolf is speaking to her, and she slowly lifts the knife.

Placing it against her pale skin, she nods. "Yes. Six wolves, one pack. One bond to hold us together. You are mine, and I am yours." The blade bites into her skin, and her blood wells to the surface, dropping into the bowl.

I take the knife from her, and she glances at me, eyes suddenly lighting like she was in a daze and woke up. Her gaze drops to her hand, then jumps to the bowl. She dips her finger into the blood and coats it.

Stepping forward, I close my eyes while she draws a line from the middle of my forehead down to my chin. I catch her finger with my teeth, just barely, and she makes a noise in the back of her throat.

"Six wolves, one pack," she says before going to Carter to repeat the same thing. When she reaches Adler, he sets the bowl on the bedside table. She marks him and repeats the words.

"Now you come to the middle," Carter says, but she's already moving, guided by her wolf.

Once she's between us, she lifts her hand and puts the same line of blood on her face.

"Six wolves, one pack," we all say together.

A wolf bursts from Raven like a ghost, leaping toward me.

I grunt when her power slams into me, twining around my wolf before bursting out of me and into Carter. The luna weaves her way through each of us, taking bits of us with her as she goes. She jumps back to Raven, hitting her square in the chest and disappearing from sight. As soon as the wolf is gone, my wolf howls in my head.

Not because he's sad, but because we can feel her. I can sense every part of the pack through the link. My wound heals, no need for shifting with the bond. One of the many perks. The main perk releases a burst of laughter, red hair tumbling over her shoulder.

"That was amazing!" Raven's chest heaves, and her smile is nearly my undoing.

How can something so beautiful ever want to be with someone like me?

I grab her, spin, and pin her back against my front. My heart thumps in my chest, terrifying and exciting me all at the same time. She's so deliciously innocent. Running my nose up the column of her throat, I inhale, groaning when I catch a whiff of her arousal. Beneath the trembling heart and hesitation, she's more than ready for the next half of the ritual. The consummation of our pack. "Let's get you out of these clothes," I whisper into her ear, smirking when she shivers in response.

∾

RAVEN

Draco's voice rumbles over my skin in a dark caress, making my pussy clench in need. His strong hands move from my arms to the hem of my shirt, easing it up. Lifting my arms to help him, I cross my hands over my chest before dropping them. I'm not going to cower. This is our night, and I won't hide from them.

"Very good, Little Red." He presses his palm against the base of my stomach, nudges my neck over with his nose, and places a kiss on the sensitive skin.

My eyes flutter closed and a moan passes my lips, letting them all know I'm ready.

Another set of hands pulls on my pants, and I stare into Adler's stormy amber irises. His rougher, yet equally as gentle fingers undo the button then the zipper. Separating the two sides, he slips his palms inside, brushing over my thighs before slowly dragging the material down. Draco holds me steady as I step out of them and Adler tosses them aside, backing away so Brayden can take his place.

He traces my cheekbone with his thumb before tipping

my chin up so he can take a kiss. His lips are so soft, a stark contrast to how he presses in, suffocating me with his mouth in the most delicious of ways. A faint trace of copper bursts across my tongue. The blood from the binding tastes perfect in this moment. A reminder of what we are now. When my bra springs free, I smile against his mouth, only slightly annoyed I didn't feel him messing with the strap.

Backing away from the kiss, he narrows his eyes on me. "I can't wait to wreck you."

Squeezing my thighs together, I try not to let him know how wet he just made me, but nothing escapes his notice and his chest rumbles in approval.

"It's not my turn yet, Little Red." He slides the bra down my arms, freeing my tits to his hungry gaze.

"Who said anything about turns?" I ask, shoving my chest toward him and chuckling when he licks his lips.

Draco nips my neck, making me yelp in surprise. "We said something about turns. Be a good girl and listen."

"Make me," I whisper, biting my lip to fight off a big grin.

"Naughty little thing," he says, moving his hand from my stomach to cup a breast, pinching my nipple hard between his thumb and forefinger.

My back arches in response, and I whimper, not exactly hating the pain, but not quite sure I enjoy it either. Brayden steps closer, grabbing my other boob and gently caressing that nipple, offsetting the pain Draco delivered.

"Are you going to listen?" Brayden's breath brushes across my lips, his mouth centimeters from mine, teasing and tempting.

I'm so wet right now, and my core aches with the need to be filled. While I'd like to explore the twin sandwich a little more, I'm eager to get to the main part, so I nod.

"Good girl," Draco says, releasing my nipple from his

fingers and trailing his hand down my stomach, resting it above my panties.

Brayden leans closer, and I move to meet him for another kiss, but he pulls away a second before our lips touch and steps aside. "Patience."

I'm about to tell him where he can shove his patience when Carter approaches, wasting no time hooking his fingers into the edge of my thong. My gaze collides with his, seeing a hungry, carnal desire deep in the depths of his green eyes I haven't seen before. Without ceremony, he yanks my underwear off, lifting the soft material to his face and burying his nose in them, taking a deep drag of my arousal. Part of me wants to look away from his intense stare, but I don't. I hold it and watch his pupils dilate and eyes flash yellow with his wolf as he inhales me. It should be wrong, but it's not. It's fucking delicious how turned on he is right now. With a small smile, he stuffs them into his pocket and turns away from me, side-stepping my reaching arm.

Huffing, I drop my hand and let out a soft growl. "Don't I get to touch you?" I ask them all, shooting an annoyed look around the room.

Adler is on the edge of the group, watching this all unfold with a curious glint in his gaze. This is as new to him as it is to me.

"Yes." Everett slides in front of me, completely naked and *very* erect. He flicks his gaze over my shoulder to meet Draco's. The zeta reluctantly releases me. "Come here," Everett says, opening his arms. The other's clothes drop to the floor and my stomach tightens.

Every shred of doubt evaporates, replaced by a soul deep need to take them all, mark them with my teeth. Make them mine.

Taking two steps, I throw myself at him. He catches me mid jump, letting me wrap my legs around his middle and gripping my ass to keep me in place. My lips catch his in a needy kiss, tongue slipping into his mouth and tangling with his, earning a deep, rumbling growl from him. Spinning with me in his arms, he tosses me onto the mattress. No sooner does my back hit the bed when he climbs over me, pressing his hips between my legs and lowering down so our bodies are perfectly lined up.

Pulse pounding against my skin, I suck in a breath when he teases the head of his cock over my slit, running his silken length back and forth.

"Luna," he says in a gruff voice. "I'm yours."

I moan when he positions his dick and thrusts into me, stretching me in one, hard stroke. Wrapping my legs around his waist and linking my feet above his ass, I pull his mouth to mine and take what I can from him while he rocks into me. Lifting my hips to meet his and grinding against him, I match his pace.

"Harder," I say, breaking away from our kiss with a pant.

He groans, grinding against me with his cock deep enough to make me tremble.

"Any other day, I'd fuck you so hard the bed would break, but today is about more than me." His words make my forehead wrinkle in confusion, then he pulls out of me, slapping my pussy and kissing me. "Sharing is caring, Luna."

Cold air sweeps over me as he rolls to lie on his side, fingers tracing over my tits, tweaking and tugging on my nipples. I turn my head to demand he finish what he started, but stop short when a hot mouth seals over my clit, sucking hard.

"Oh fuck." I glance down and see Brayden between my legs. Digging my fingers into his black hair, I shamelessly roll my hips, forcing more of myself against his mouth as Everett smacks my breast. A ridiculous string of noises passes my lips, begging for more, and Everett smacks the other one.

With a dark chuckle, Brayden lets go of my clit, moving his tongue over my slit before parting my folds with his hands. My grip on his hair tightens, and I direct his position with my hands, not at all worried he doesn't like how I'm nearly suffocating him. He sticks his tongue inside of me, swirling it around before moving back to my clit for another mouthful, humming and licking my most sensitive parts.

"Brayden," I gasp his name, pulling on his hair to ask for more.

His eyelids flutter open, and he stares at me, lips clamped around me as he teases me to the brink of an orgasm. I lift my hips, but he slams his hands onto my thighs, ripping his lips from me and shaking his head. "Not yet," he says, denying me an orgasm but making my heart flutter in excitement.

He rises to all fours, running his hands over my core before sliding into me with a grunt.

"Luna, I'm yours." He slides into me, once, twice, three times before pulling out and moving to lie on the mattress on my other side, wrapping his fingers around my neck as his lips meet mine in a demanding kiss. Delicate fingers run over my thighs as another one of the men climbs between my legs. Sliding my gaze to the side, I watch Carter hold the base of his dick as he studies Everett's hands on my breasts and Brayden's lips claiming mine. I tug him closer with my feet, grinning into Brayden's mouth when his nostrils flare, and he gives a hard stroke up his length before slowly pushing into me.

Carter's thick as all hell, and I'm thankful he's taking it slower than Everett had because it hurts a little. Not enough to make me want to stop, but enough that I don't want him pounding into me like a piston until I'm used to him.

Everett's strong hands knead my breasts while Brayden's fingers tighten slightly on my neck. I have a moment of panic, brought on by the incident with Jinx trying to choke me, but his mouth demands my full attention and it passes.

"Luna, I'm yours." Carter grunts when he's fully sheathed, then rolling his hips maddeningly slow, he works me.

There are so many caresses, so many touches, I can't distinguish which one makes my heart skip, or my breath hitch, or makes me moan. Heat sweeps over me, enveloping me in a fiery hot embrace. My moans are stifled by Brayden's rough lips, breasts claimed by Everett, and center filled with Carter's deliciously thick length.

My walls clamp around him, trying to keep him locked inside of me, but he withdraws, stepping back so Draco can take his place. The cruel twist of his lips lets me know he won't let me come either.

"Little Red," he says, foregoing the official title, but the nickname feels so *right*. "I'm yours."

Rougher than Everett, he slams into me, making my back arch and mouth drop open. His cock is full and pulsing, instantly making me whimper for more. Brayden moves his lips over my chin, down to my neck where he clamps on, suckling and marking me while his brother batters me with punishing strokes. Everett's mouth closes around one of my nipples, and he bites when Draco thrusts in, swirling his tongue over the pebbled skin as Draco withdraws. He repeats this until Draco growls, ripping his dick out of me and stumbling back, cursing to no one in particular.

The others pull away, and I get ready to scream, because there's no way they'll work me this hard to leave me high and dry. But the protest dies on my lips as Adler takes Brayden's spot on the bed, lying on his back beneath the pillows and tugging me to him. I don't need to be told twice, so I roll over, climb over his hips, and take his velvety length in my hand, fingers barely touching around his girth.

"Luna, I'm yours." His eyes darken as I rise up on my

knees, putting the head of his cock right at my center and sliding onto it, running my hands up to cup my breasts and gasping when my clit presses against his skin.

"Damn right you are," I gasp out, leaning forward to press my breasts against him.

"You're so perfect," he says, lips kissing both of my cheeks before coming in for a kiss. I slip my tongue over the seam of his mouth, pressing for more. A hard palm cracks against my ass and stinging pain races through my body, but seconds later a hand soothes the pain away.

"You like that?" Everett asks.

Looking over my shoulder, I see him centered behind me, wet cock ready to press inside of my ass, but he hesitates, flicking his gaze to mine. I nod, letting him know I want it, and his eyes flash yellow.

"Hang on, Luna."

I stop moving, fully taking Adler's dick, and swing my gaze back to my rock. The one who kept me sane without even realizing it. His eyes search my face as he gathers my hair, gripping it in one hand and bringing my mouth back to his.

We kiss, devouring each other as Everett spits on my ass, using his saliva as lube to push a finger inside, slowly, carefully preparing me for his cock.

"Breathe in," he says, and I listen. "Now relax."

I force my body to melt against Adler, focusing fully on his lips as Everett pushes inside of my ass. A bite of pain crashes over me, and I break from the kiss with Adler, dropping my forehead to his.

"Easy, Raven. You can take it." He's so sure I can handle it, but I'm ready to tap out. "Breathe in," he says, echoing Everett's instructions, so I do, counting to three before expelling it, all the while never looking away from his steady eyes.

"Moons, babe, you're so. Fucking. Tight." Everett groans the words out, finally fully seated. He gives me a minute to adjust before he moves, slowly rocking his hips to get me used to the overly full feeling.

Adler tugs on my hair, rolling his hips up in time with Everett.

"Oh," I say, unable to fully express the sensations washing over me. Too much, not enough, faster, slower, more, less. I can't decide what I want.

"Raven," Carter says.

I lift my eyes from Adler to Carter who is kneeling in front of me, his thick cock reaching for me. Licking my lips, I move for him without needing to be asked, and his dick twitches seconds before I swirl my tongue over the head, lapping up the little bit of cum waiting for me.

"Can you swallow me?" Carter, of all fucking people, asks with a serious face, eyes lighting with hope.

I hesitate, unsure of exactly what that means because I've only given head once, and I'm pretty sure I did it wrong. Understanding flashes across his face, and his eyes soften.

"It's okay, I'll teach you."

Adler and Everett both roll their hips at the same time, and my mouth pops open, a soft cry floating out of me.

With what seems like unending patience, Carter lets me recover before scooting forward slightly, positioning himself for my mouth. I wrap my lips around him, holding on to his back to keep from collapsing in a heap of overly sexed bliss. He shushes me when Adler and Everett slam into me again, placing his hand on the back of my neck and pushing his thick cock inside of my mouth.

My eyes prick with moisture when he goes too far, and he murmurs soft words, telling me I'm such a good girl.

"Now swallow," he says in as close to a demand as he can get.

Fighting the urge to gag, I swallow, feeling my throat constrict around him.

"Just like that, Raven. Fuck, you listen so good. Do it again."

I do, making him moan as Adler and Everett continue to fuck me, unrelentingly filling me with their dicks and pushing me toward a ledge. The bed dips as Draco and Brayden come to either side of me, stroking their cocks with their own hands.

No! My mind screams. *Mine.*

Adler somehow senses my distress and moves his hands to my shoulders, helping to hold me up for Carter so I can move my hands to grip their lengths, taking over their languid strokes and squeezing them as I work them faster.

"Swallow," Carter says.

I listen, swallowing again and making him growl. He pulls back, giving me room to breathe, then begins to pump himself in and out of my mouth, not going as deep but fucking my face all the same. Keeping my lips firmly sealed over his length, I moan as tingles float up my spine.

Adler takes my nipple between his lips, swirling his tongue over it, and thrusting up at the same time Everett moves inside of me. My fingers tremble around Brayden and Draco, and as one, the six of us gasp.

An invisible force pours out of me, coiling around each man before slamming back into my chest, just like after I marked them with blood. The power of the pack bond fully settling sends a ripple of pleasure down my spine, filling me with an undeniable certainty that this was meant to be.

I hum, making Carter gasp. Adler and Everett move in tandem, gliding in and out of me faster and faster until my walls clamp around Adler—the only warning I get before I'm thrown from the cliff.

In a freefall, plummeting through each man's pleasure as

if it were my own, I come so hard I squirt, coating Adler in my essence as each of them pour their seed into or on me. Carter's semen is hot and salty, shooting down my throat, and I swallow again without being told. Everett and Adler come at the same time, dicks throbbing inside of me as they reach their release. My hands give a final tug on Draco and Brayden, and hot cum sprays over my back, coating parts of my hair in the process, but I don't give a damn.

Joan presses against me, forcing a partial shift. I'm helpless to stop her because a surge of luna power shoves my attempts to wrangle control back. Fur ripples over my hand, and my fingernails turn to claws, sharp and deadly. With five quick slashes, she gouges each man, slicing deep into their shoulders with a savage growl.

The shifters throw their heads back and howl. Adler glances around before tipping his head back and releasing his own version, lighter and less animalistic, but joining in on the pack song anyway. Joan retreats within me as quickly as she pushed out, curling up in the corner of my mind with a satisfied smirk.

Now they are ours, she says.

With their voices twining around me, reverberating over my skin, and calling to my soul, I throw my head back, hair falling down my back, and let loose my own howl.

This is wild, untamed claiming. And it's fucking perfect.

CHAPTER 14

ADLER

I didn't expect something like this to work on me since I'm a fae. During the ritual, I prepared myself for the inevitable fallout when it failed because of me. I'm not like these guys, but it doesn't seem to matter because Raven's wolf laid claim on me. I run my fingers over my shoulder where four pink scars lie, all that's left of her claws slashing across me.

With her head resting on my shoulder, arm slung across my body, she hums a song I don't recognize, but Draco harmonizes with her, not seeming to care that the rest of us are in the bed as well. It doesn't feel strange though, it almost feels too natural. Something like this shouldn't be so right. Thank Mother Faerie it is. The shifters have accepted me as one of their own, and now we are permanently marked by Raven.

The Luna's Pack.

I'm not a wolf, but something primal stirs within me, and the bond between us snaps tight when I focus on it.

Carter lifts onto his elbow, brushing his blond hair from his face. "The link is working."

"What does it mean?" Raven asks, stopping the tune she's humming to glance over her shoulder at him.

"It means"—Brayden stands from the bed—"that we can feel each other. If someone is hurt, we'll all know it."

"Mind speak?" Raven swings her gaze to him, eyes dropping down his body as he lifts his arms up and stretches out.

"No mind speak," Carter says.

A soft stirring of jealousy fills my stomach, but I squash it. There is no room for jealousy with family. The thought punches me in the gut, and my thoughts turn inward, forgetting all about listening to what they're discussing. The last family I had hated me. I was five when they sent me away, three days after my first change.

"Mama, Mama!" I call, running toward her with a grin. She'll be so surprised to see me wearing Therion's face. Even more so when she realizes my fae magic has manifested. So young too. "Mama!"

"Therion," she scolds, turning from the stove. "What's all this yelling about, hm?"

I giggle, then swap my face for Therion's. "Surprise, Mama! I'm magic!"

Her scream is so loud I slap my hands over my ears and back away. With a pale face, she shakes her head, whispering to Mother Faerie to save her from this curse. A broken child.

Is she. . . is she talking about me?

"Mama?" I ask in a small voice. "I won't do magic again, Mama. I'm sorry." Magic is good in Faerie; I don't understand what I did wrong. "I won't pretend to be Therion," I say on a whimper when she screams for Father. My heart is galloping inside my chest like the horses of the wild hunt: wild and erratic.

Mama has never been so angry.

"Shut up, child. Cursed being. Great Mother, what did I do to

deserve your ire?" Mama raises her hands toward the ceiling as though she's pleading with Mother Faerie herself.

Lifting my gaze, I search for our creator, but there's nothing there. "Mama? What's wrong?"

With a hiss, she smacks me across the face. "I said shut up!"

"Adler?" A soft voice rips me from the memory and gentle hands shake me. "Are you okay?"

Before I open my eyes, I tuck those memories and the pain which accompanies them into the far recesses of my mind where they can't reach me. Where they'll stay until I choose to revisit them and tear apart my heart all over again.

When I finally meet her gaze, her green eyes have darkened, and she searches my face with a scowl.

"Your pain is coming through the link." She runs her fingers over her mark on my skin, lips pressing together in thought.

"It's not those," I say, scrubbing a hand over my face.

"Then what is it? Whatever it is, it's making me sick to my stomach." Flicking her eyes back to mine, she runs her palm over the scruff on my chin. "I almost couldn't breathe through it."

"She's right. You nearly made us all cry in agony. What was that?" Everett asks from where he lies next to Draco.

The shadows on the ceiling flicker with the candles, and Brayden moves toward the bed, growing larger with each step he takes until the mattress dips and he settles on Carter's other side, tossing an arm behind his head.

"Are we sharing our trauma?" His voice is light but there's a dark curiosity lacing each word, almost daring me to speak the truth.

"No," Raven says quickly. "You don't have to tell us if you don't want to." She holds my cheek and stares into my eyes. "When you're ready, I'll listen."

Hating how long I've had to hide who I am from her, I

grimace and decide to give her some of my past. "I was thinking about my family."

Understanding flashes over her face, and she drops her gaze, thumb running over my whiskers. "Carter taught me a little bit about changelings. They sent you away?"

I nod in confirmation, worried that if I answer with words, the whole story will spill out of me. Anger flares in her irises, and she brings her other hand to my face, holding me in place as she says, "They have no idea how special you are." Then the woman who's changed my entire life course leans forward and presses her lips to mine in a tender affirmation of her words. "No idea," she whispers, mouth moving against mine before she kisses me again.

My soul cracks with her words, and I close my eyes again, hoping to Mother Faerie this isn't a dream.

~

RAVEN

Perfection is a fool's wish. Scars are what makes a person beautiful. Physical, psychological, it doesn't matter. There's nothing more worthy of love than a broken soul with stitches holding it together. A smile filled with so much depth you can reach inside and find nothing but darkness lurking within it. Or a person who, no matter how hard they laugh, can't quite conceal the hurt in their eyes. Being damaged doesn't mean you aren't worthy; it just means the people who choose to love you, despite all your chips and cracks, see who you are beneath the marks the world has left on you. *That* is real.

Adler's pain echoes through the link, still filling my stomach with churning unease. Whatever memories haunt him are dark. He didn't have to explain what happened. His family threw him away like trash, trading him for a human because the fae believed he was cursed.

I wish they could see the man I see now, because they'd know there's nothing cursed about him. He's broken and imperfect but there's nothing wrong with him. He's more than a changeling. Dropping my forehead to his chest, I inhale him, breathing in his familiar sandalwood scent. There's a small pulse of hope flitting through the link, almost like he's trying to keep the emotion from us. Sending a wave of calm and reassuring thoughts, I wrap my arms around his torso and hug him, resting my cheek against his chest.

"This is what makes a pack special," Carter says quietly. "There's nothing that compares to a Luna's pack. We are one. We share pain. We share joy. No one needs to carry the weight of regret or shame because we'll do it together. Together we are strong. Together we are one."

"One," Everett says.

Draco exhales, like he's been holding his breath for a few minutes, and says, "One."

"One, for better or worse." Brayden chuckles, probably thinking how it's going to get a hell of a lot worse before it gets any better.

"One," I say, squeezing Adler again.

His chest expands with a deep breath, and he breathes the word too, completing the pack. Holding us together.

He is the nurturer, but he needs it as much as he's going to give it to us, Joan says.

I know.

The pain he let out without realizing it told me all I needed to know. Adler is afraid of family. If I'm honest, part of me is scared to hand my heart to five people. Each of which hold the ability to break a piece of me. The only person I've let in since Mom and Dad is Aunt Lou. I've given them my trust.

Here's hoping they don't destroy it.

CHAPTER 15

RAVEN

Going back to the library where everyone else is together is the last thing I want to do, but because I have a conscience, I can't stay with the guys in this comfy, oversized bed and its mismatched sheets. So, I climb out from under Adler and Carter's arms, scoot to the edge of the bed and search for my underwear, only to remember someone stole them.

"You can't have them back," Carter says, crawling up behind me and wrapping his arms around me.

I sink into the hug for a second, soaking up all this free affection while I can. The marking and ritual has made them all more willing to give their touch, and I'm worried once we leave the little cocoon of love, they'll begin to hold back.

Things have changed now, Joan says softly. *It will be hard for them to resist the urge to be near you or to kiss you. You don't need to worry.*

Trusting her not to lie to me, I sigh, looking up at Carter. He drops a kiss on my forehead then grins like a little boy who stole a piece of candy.

"Fine, you can have them." I roll my eyes and pat his arm

before tugging it away so I can stand and get dressed. "I don't want to go, but we should get back to the others."

"The good news is we aren't on guard duty tonight," Draco says, rising from the bed and pulling on his pants. "Howard will take care of it tonight."

"Thank god. I'm exhausted." As if to prove my point, a yawn rises up, and I'm helpless to fight it off.

Brayden, Adler, and Everett are the last ones to get out of the bed, and it's all I can do not to stare at each of them, devouring every inch of naked flesh like I may never see it again. Carter nudges me with his elbow before pulling on his shirt.

"You're drooling, Luna."

I scowl at his use of the name. "It's Raven. I don't want to be called Luna."

"Why?" Adler rubs his scruff, standing nude and in no hurry to get dressed as he studies me.

"Because. . ." I trail off, trying to come up with a good reason. "I don't want to be called Luna," I finally say.

Squinting at me, he nods and lifts his shoulder. "All right." Then he bends over and picks up his shirt, choosing to put that on before his pants.

Turning to face away from him, I stare at the flickering candles on the desk. Luna. I'm officially an alpha. Does it matter that I don't feel like one? Sure, Joan has made me strong, but who is going to listen to me? What happens when they realize I have a hard enough time keeping my own life together and I can't care for a pack like they expect me to? My eyes catch on Draco's. He skirts around the group, sliding next to where I stand by one of the clusters of candles.

"You have that look in your eyes, Little Red." Lifting a finger, he drags it through the flame, slow enough to make my heart spike in alarm but not enough it actually burns him.

"What look?" I finger comb some of the knots out of my hair and side-eye him. "I don't have a look."

His lips press together, and he pinches his thumb and forefinger to the wick, snuffing out the flame. "You do. What are you worried about?"

"Aside from the demon spirit who wants to eat us all?" I give up trying to get rid of the knots and drop my hands to my side. He's staring at me, not letting my sarcasm distract him from getting his answer. This is part of the dangers of letting someone in. They learn to read you, and now he has access to my strongest emotions with the pack link.

"I'm not sure what I'm supposed to do now. I know we have to take care of Jinx, but after that? What does being luna mean? Do I have to be responsible for shifters?"

He hums and moves his fingers to another candle, extinguishing that one with a pinch as well. "You're worried you can't handle it."

Obviously.

I nod instead of snarking out loud.

"There is no you." He swings his gaze to mine, brow furrowing. "*We* are a unit. You may be the official leader as far as power goes, but we share the burden of responsibility now." Jerking his thumb in the direction of the others, he shakes his head. "Do you always let people in then retreat into your shell like you're all alone?"

"No," I say just as Adler says, "Yes."

I scowl at him over my shoulder, and he lifts his hands in surrender.

"When you arrived at Lou's, you let me in a little, then shut me out time and time again."

Opening my mouth to protest, I try to think of the times I shared pieces of me with him, or with any of the team, only to realize I hadn't. I worked with them for so long, but I never told them much of anything. Shooting the breeze with the crew is a whole lot different than letting them in. Anyone can pretend to care when it's superficial.

"It's okay," he says, stepping toward me and Draco. "Lou didn't tell everyone else, but I know why you didn't want to. You weren't the only one hiding from the world."

Swallowing my pride, I glance away and nod. "Together then."

"Together," they all respond, each voice rich with its own tone, circling around me and squeezing my heart.

As a pack, we'll defeat Jinx and escape this place.

∽

We get back to the library as everyone is settling down for the night. Most of the people are lying in their cots and reading, staring at the wall, or talking to whoever is closest to them. Since it's nearly eleven, I go to check on Bea, relieved to see her fast asleep in her cot. Layla and a few of the ladies from earlier smirk at me when I appear.

"So, how was it?" Layla asks, fanning her face. "Thinking about it is enough to make me want a harem. Were they big? Different sizes?" She leans closer. "Did they have piercings?"

"Oh my god, stop. I'm not talking about this with you."

One of the other women sighs. "At least someone is getting laid. Look at her skin, it's glowing."

"Pretty sure that's the light," Penelope says.

"Whatever," the other one rolls her eyes, "she's totally glowing."

I have to bite my lip to keep from laughing at them. "It was... good. Different than I expected in general, but I had a good time." With a shrug, I sit on the edge of Layla's bed.

"A good time. Pfft. Please, we need dirt. How many times did you come?" Layla pokes me, all the tension between us is gone, and I'm glad she's enjoying trying to pry details from me.

Shooting my gaze to where Bea lies, I shake my head. "So what did you guys do while we were gone?" I deflect.

"Nothing much." Extending her legs, Layla lies down and places her hands on her stomach. "I used to wish for down time, you know? And now that I have it, all I want to do is be busy. It's ridiculous."

"Well, down time and being forced to stay inside because of a demon spirit aren't exactly the same thing." I scoot forward so she can pull the blanket out from under my butt and toss it over her legs. "Soon enough we'll be able to do whatever we want."

I glance around the group, taking in the pursed lips and doubt lining their faces. They fully expect this to be the new normal. That or they expect to die. Closing my mouth, I chew on my cheek and wait for someone to say something or change the subject, but they don't. One by one, the women all decide it's time for bed, so I slink off to my little cot and climb in. The men have already fallen asleep, so I lie back and close my eyes, praying to whoever will listen that we all make it out okay.

CHAPTER 16

⌘

EVERETT

After another menial breakfast on Tuesday morning, I take Raven and her friends out for a run in our wolf form. Adler joins us, taking to the sky as soon as we get outside. The women all gasp when he shifts into a giant golden eagle. I'd be lying if my ego didn't take a hit, but to be fair, Adler's other form is pretty majestic. Given how much other animals fear my wolf, the only ones I get to see up close are rabbits and deer.

Since they're all busy staring at him, I strip down and shift, releasing a long howl at the sky to get their attention. Their wolves hear my call, and it only takes them a few seconds to strip out of their clothes and join me in wolf form.

That's more like it, my wolf huffs.

He's a prideful bastard, but he *is* an alpha, so I don't give him a hard time. Instead I hand over control to him, letting him lead our little group deep into the woods. Raven's red wolf keeps pace with mine, hardly panting even though we're running full out. The other women and Bea stay farther behind, but they're all betas or deltas. They don't want to try and outrun an alpha or luna because it would only result in a fight for dominance. This isn't the time or place to test those limits, and they all seem to defer to Raven anyway, accepting her as their leader without Raven having to force it on them.

The best alphas are the ones people follow without being told. Those are the leaders that inspire and bring out the best in the group. My wolf is proud of our mate, and so am I. I'd say we chose well, but that'd be a lie. Raven is the one who picked us, and I'm honored to be part of her pack.

A rabbit dashes between bushes, making my heart leap. With a twitching nose, I change directions and yip at the others. A few sets of scampering paws reach my ears, so I yip again and the wolves split apart, knowing what to do off natural instinct. Raven sticks with me, and together we corner the rabbit, chasing it until one of us has to make the killing strike.

Resting my steady gaze on her, I lower my head to the ground, letting her know she's in charge. Her nostrils flare and a growl rumbles out of her chest as she leans back on her haunches, preparing to pounce. I watch as the red wolf shows mercy, making a quick end for the terrified creature.

After we eat, we meet up with the others who have also had their fill and head over to the waterfall to wash off and get a drink. Hunting in wolf form is always strange, but since there aren't a lot of food options, it's the best we can do for now.

"Oh god, I haven't been swimming in so long." One of the women wades out into the water, and I avert my gaze, focusing on Raven instead. She nudges me with her nose, gently biting my neck and yipping playfully as the others splash into the water. Everyone has shifted, Bea included. Raven growls at me before leaping into the water, paddling out in wolf form before diving under and shifting. When her mane of red hair flips out of the water and she smiles at me, green eyes lighting in challenge, I follow after her and shift once I'm deep enough.

The others swim around, but I don't even glance in their direction. My eyes and attention are laser focused on one person and one person alone. Raven.

∼

RAVEN

Everett glares at me when he surfaces, fully shifted into his human form. "No one said we were going skinny dipping."

Flicking water at his face, I swim farther into the pool. "Like you've never done it before."

"That was different." He swims after me, catching me around the waist and pulling me close. This time he treads water to keep us up, and I smile at the memory of us dunking under the water the first time he tried to pull this move.

"How?" I ask, reaching up to wipe water off of his eyebrows.

"We were alone for starters." One of his hands runs over my thighs, and I suck in a breath, glancing at the others.

They're all busy splashing and playing, but I'm not comfortable getting frisky with Bea so nearby. Thankfully, he laughs and moves his hand back to my waist.

"And," he says with a teasing smile, "I didn't have to worry about keeping my hands to myself."

Placing my hand on my heart, I pout my lip. "Aw, poor thing. How will you survive?"

Bea screams, and I snap my head in her direction, heart jumping to my throat. She and Layla are splashing each other, big grins painted across their faces. Tension bleeds from my shoulders, and Everett pulls me closer, pressing my body against his.

"They're okay," he whispers, drawing my eyes back to his. "And I'll think of a way to get you back for this."

"Get me back? I didn't do anything!" I wrinkle my nose at him.

Grabbing my hand, he places it on his very hard cock. "Yes, you did."

"That's not my fault. You need to control yourself." I shrug and move my hand to his shoulder. "Besides, didn't you get enough last night?"

"Nope," he says, popping the P.

Adler screams above us, and we all stop to glance up and watch him circle the canopy before he lands on a branch with a loud chitter.

"Come on down," Bea screeches at him. "Don't be scared!"

He flies off the branch, swooping low enough he could grab her with his talons if he wanted to and she squeals, ducking below the water as he makes what sounds like a bird laugh before landing on a branch again. Gasping for air when she surfaces, she glares at him.

"I won't forget that!"

Adler chitters and swings his gaze to mine. I can almost see the mirth dancing in them from here. Shaking my head at him and grinning, I swim away from Everett and join the women and Bea, splashing and playing for a half-hour until it's time to head back.

∾

Later that night, when we're all settled in bed, I can't seem to fall asleep. Dread is niggling in the back of my mind, telling me I've already gotten too comfortable. There's no way Jinx will let us off so easy. Something bad is bound to happen; it's only a matter of time. At some point, I close my eyes, the weight of exhaustion forcing them shut. Though a little while later, a soft pitter-patter catches my attention, and I wrench them open. Creepy Alice's face hovers near the edge of my bed. I slap my palm against my mouth to keep from screaming.

Her stringy hair hangs like a curtain around her, blocking the dim light from a lamp on the librarian's desk. With a pale, scar-ridden hand, she reaches for me, a sweep of cool air washing over me. Damp, wrinkled fingers clasp around my wrist, a freezing cold vice. She blinks as a roach scuttles out of her mouth, and then I feel it. A tug on my medium powers. Almost like someone's stuck a straw against my spine and is trying to siphon my essence.

"Alice?" I ask in a barely audible whisper.

Placing a slimy finger against her dry mouth, she shushes me as she pulls me from this world and into a memory.

There's a heavy fog blanketing the ground, so dense the headlights are no use. It must be midday because it's not dark, but that's almost worse, like the sun somehow amplifies how white the mist is. Creepy Alice sits in the backseat of a van with me, while the Alice—who is very much alive in the memory—lies on the floor of the van between the bucket seats. She's asleep or knocked out. Two burly men sit in the front, dead silent during the drive. They don't even look at each other.

I swing my gaze to Creepy Alice, who is watching me through her curtain of dirty hair.

"What is this?" I ask, knowing it's safe to talk since it's only a memory.

With a firm shake of her head, Creepy Alice faces forward. Snatching a cockroach who tries to make a run for it, she pops it into her mouth.

Do you think she realizes how gross that is? *Joan asks.*

Ugh. I don't know, but it's part of her other world form.

A screech sounds when the guy driving lays on the brakes, and the vehicle lurches to a stop in front of the wrought iron gates. The familiar howling wolf at the top tells me exactly where we are: Bad Moon Academy. My eyes stray to Alive Alice who still hasn't stirred. The passenger gets out and opens the gate, the screaming metal slicing through the air. A few seconds later his dark form appears in front of the car, and he gets in, slamming the van's door shut.

The driver eases inside. I expect him to stop, but he doesn't. A loud bang fills the air. Pack magic closing the gate. Or Jinx's magic —as I've learned. An icy hand wraps around my arm and everything blurs. When Creepy Alice lets go of me, we're standing in the foyer. I glance toward the door, expecting the men to carry her inside, but she appears in front of me, pointing in the other direction. I turn, catching a glimpse of her in a maid's outfit. Not the sexy kind people wear for Halloween, a legitimate maid's outfit. Conservative and meant to blend into the shadows, to be unseen by those who occupy the academy.

She walks right past me, so close I could almost reach out and touch her, except she's not really here. This is only a memory. The Alice who is alive in this particular flashback goes around the staircase and heads down the short hall lined with bookshelves. We follow her, and Creepy Alice doesn't stop me so I assume this is what she wants me to do. Alive Alice begins dusting the bookshelf, humming softly to herself.

"I don't know how many times I have to say it, Jinx. Find a goddamn way like you promised me." A loud voice booms through the foyer, making Alive Alice stop humming and go stock still.

High heels click across the marble floor, following after heavy footfalls.

"Of course, Alpha. Like I said, getting ready for the first full moon takes time. There aren't enough souls yet for the sacrifice—"

Alive Alice gasps, pinching her eyes shut and covering her mouth with her hand, but it's too late.

"What was that?" the alpha asks. The footsteps pound closer until a large body stands at the end of the hall, casting a looming shadow over the hardwood floor. "There's your soul."

"No. She's not ready. I have plans for this one, Alpha. I need another."

He growls and Jinx's tinkling laughter floats down the hallways.

"Don't be like that. She will be ours soon enough, but, as I said, I already have plans for her." Jinx peeks over the alpha's shoulder, winking at Alive Alice as though she wishes to reassure her.

Alive Alice only shrinks farther into the bookshelf, cringing away from their scrutiny. I can hear her heart pounding and I'm not even in the real moment. Everything blurs, shifting again as Creepy Alice pulls us through time, only giving me flashes of memories. An altar in a part of the woods I've never been to. Twelve people standing behind it wearing chains. Jinx's face twisting in an evil smile as she raises her hands to the full moon and the shifters all scream at the same time. Alive Alice cleaning the blood that splashed on the altar while Jinx sings a song about death and power.

Another blur and we're in the foyer again. Alive Alice watches from a nook near the stairs as four new shifters are brought in. Two identical faces with longer black hair, one with blond hair, and another with short brown hair. They're carried in by four stocky shifters and placed on the marble floor. The guys leave in a hurry, not staying to find out what becomes of my men. Alive Alice shifts forward, glancing around like she expects a ghost to pop out and scare her, then races to them.

She checks their pulses. Tension bleeding from her shoulders. A cackling laugh rings through the academy and Alive Alice scurries away. Color bleeds together as Creepy Alice drags me from that memory to another in the foyer, of her standing at the stairs and being assaulted by ghosts. The spirits press in on her just as they *had the first time she showed me a part of the memory, only this time, someone shouts "Kill her!".*

Jinx stands at the top of the stairs, a mad grin pushing her cheeks back. "Now."

Brayden and Draco burst into the foyer from the side hallway, running for Alice as she screams and scratches at her face.

"Brayden! What do we do?" Draco stops a foot away from where the ghosts circle.

His brother grimaces, glaring at the circling vultures then at Jinx. "I've had enough of this." Then he steps into the swirling mass of spirits and stands in front of Alive Alice. A blast of murky gray light pierces his chest, and he shouts in pain. Another burst of light slams into Alice, and she falls back, landing against the edge of the staircase, a sickening crack filling the air.

"Brayden!" Draco shouts, trying to shove through the shadows, but he's pushed back by an invisible force. He slams his fists into the spirits, like he can break through them, but it doesn't work. His twin is still crying out in agony as his soul is sucked from his body.

"No!" Jinx screams, stumbling down the stairs. "Stop it!"

Her shouts do nothing to stop her creatures, if she can even control them, and soon Brayden collapses to the ground.

"What have you done!" Jinx scolds them, sweeping her hand in a violent gesture and making them disappear. Her fingers curl into a fist, and her chest heaves as she stares at Brayden's lifeless body. "He was off limits."

"What the hell?" Draco rushes her, but Jinx knocks him into the wall with a flick of her hand.

Alive Alice coughs, and Jinx spins, dropping to her knees and pressing her hands against her chest.

"You're alive," Jinx whispers. "Good." She leans toward Alive Alice, hovering her lips above her mouth and puckers her lips, sucking air and drawing a pure white stream of essence out of Alive Alice. As soon as the stream vanishes into Jinx's mouth, Alice's body goes limp.

I'm thrown back into reality like someone tossing a bag of ice on the ground to break it apart. Air rushes from my lungs and my back arches off the mattress. Alice—the ghost of her—is still kneeling in front of me. Her head is tipped to the side, and her fingers hover near the edge of the bed. Grasping them, I tug her toward me, ignoring the creepy feeling which accompanies her semi-solid state, and hug her. Thankfully, there are currently no crawlers skittering around her body, and Alice's form buzzes against my touch, like she'll blink out if I squeeze her too tight.

Releasing her, I sit up and stare into her eyes. Something shifts in her gaze, like she's made up her mind, and she flickers out of sight.

"Raven?" a soft voice whispers.

I glance at Bea lingering near the edge of her cot. She's clasping her fingers together, and she shifts her weight between her feet, but it's the haunted look in her eyes which has my heart squeezing in sympathy.

"Come on," I say, lying down and scooting so she can take what little space remains.

As soon as I pat the mattress, she rushes over, making Howard shoot to his feet where he's standing guard. She settles in under the thin sheet and blanket, and Howard dips his head at me, letting me know all is well. I wave at him then rest my head on the pillow. The cot is so narrow we're almost pressed up against each other, but with Bea it doesn't feel weird. It's as natural as if she were my own sister. Not for the first time, I wish I'd had a real sibling. Being the only child is lonely. With her steady breathing, I finally find sleep.

"Raven." Bea shakes me awake the next morning. "Something is wrong."

Usually, I'm slow to shake off sleep, but the way her voice dips with fright has me sitting with a ram-rod straight spine in two seconds. I blink rapidly and swivel my head, searching the room. Shifters are floating above the ground, suspended in their sleep. Carter, Draco, and Everett are still in their beds, unaffected by whatever magic Jinx is using thanks to their bracelets. Brayden and Adler are floating above their cots, still sleeping.

"Bea, why aren't you floating?" I eye her up and down. She's fine, except for her blown pupils and the reek of fear curling around me.

"I don't know," she says. "I woke up when it started happening and grabbed you, then it stopped."

The demon spirit can't make you float?

I wish I knew why or how this demon stuff works, I tell Joan.

"Oh goodie, you're awake!" Jinx struts into the room wearing six-inch platform heels, a slinky black dress, which is so at odds with her other outfit from the last time I saw her, and her long hair is loose and curled. "And your little friend here, curious how close you've gotten, don't you think?" She slices her gaze toward Bea, who flinches and presses her face into the pillow like she can hide from the spirit if she tries hard enough.

There's a second where I think perhaps Bea is like Morg and the other students Jinx placed about, a strategically crafted part of her, meant to get close and learn my weaknesses, but I shake the doubt off. Bea isn't a spirit. I know Morg fooled me, but I know in the core of my being Bea is real. She's not Jinx's minion.

"What do you want?" I ask the demon, glaring at her.

"Can't I come to visit without needing something?" She pouts her ruby-red painted lips.

When I scoff, she throws her hands into the air.

"Fine, you got me all figured out, don't you?"

"Hardly," I drawl. "I thought we had until the full moon." Gesturing to the floating shifters, I shake my head. "This isn't part of the deal we made."

Jinx grins and walks closer; the clacking of her heels jolts the guys awake. "Hello, loves." She blows them a kiss. "Miss me?"

A deep growl sounds and Draco shifts, landing in his wolf form, black coat almost as dark as the shadows in the library. The curtains are drawn and someone turned off the lamp on the librarian's desk, so I can't tell what time the clock reads or judge the time of day from the changing sky.

"Draco," I say. "Not yet."

With a tinkling laugh which grates across my skin, Jinx tsks and sets her hand on her cocked hip. "You poor dears. You think there's still hope?" She giggles and rolls her eyes. "They never learn," she says to herself.

"What do you want?" Carter appears next to my bed, followed closely by Everett and Draco in his wolf form.

Squinting at me, then sliding her gaze to each man, her smile slowly begins to fall. "Not the warmest reception I've received, but no matter." She waves her hand around, her ample cleavage jiggling with the motion. To their credit, none of the guys seem to notice or care about how she looks. All they see is an enemy.

"The point," I say, snapping my fingers twice.

"Careful, Raven. I may have agreed to our deal, but the only person holding me to it is myself. All of this," she jerks her thumb behind her to where the rest of the shifters float, "can go away in a matter of minutes if I want it to."

I scowl at her but keep my mouth shut, knowing she'll follow through with that threat if I push her too far.

"There you go," she coos. "Now, the alpha is on his way. If my senses are right, he'll be here by lunchtime tomorrow. You all need to be good little pets and do as you're told. If you step out of line, I'll kill them all." She flicks her gaze over her shoulders. "Wake up!"

Jolting from their sleep, eyes widening when they realize

they're floating, and gasping when they see Jinx, everyone starts to beg to be let down. Well, everyone but Howard, Brayden, and Adler. They're staring at Jinx with fire flaring in their eyes, a promise of revenge.

"Hear that, loves?" She shouts the question, silencing the shifter's pleas. "Not one step out of line or you die, understood?" Her gaze drops to Bea, and she winks at her.

"We understand," I say, stepping in front of where Bea is on the cot.

"Good." With a snap, the shifters fall from their suspended state, dropping to the floor with hard thuds as Jinx disappears.

CHAPTER 17

ADLER

I watch as the shifters begin to head to class, the numbers in the library dwindling until it's me, Brayden, Draco, and Erron. The headmaster is hunched over on his cot, trying to make himself invisible. The twins stand together, glaring at him like he's going to be our next meal.

"Should we go do some research?"

Their gazes swing to me in unison, and I'm the new focus of their intense scrutiny. Brayden's lips quirk and Draco scowls.

"You sound like Carter now," Draco says.

Shrugging, I stand from the tiny cot we're passing off as a bed and stretch my arms overhead.

"Are all fae as big as you or is it just changelings?" Brayden's eyes flash over me. "You're huge."

The question is simply curious, but still, I grind my jaw together. I've made it a point to either be in my other form or stay with others, knowing inevitably this moment would happen. Now that we're a pack, I can't hold back with good conscience. While revisiting my home world to explain the ways of Faerie to them will dredge up unwanted memories, I'll do my best to answer their questions without going too deep into my personal history. There are some things I refuse to share.

"Most fae are big. Erron." I make a *come here* motion with my finger. "We're going to study."

He peers at me then flicks his gaze to the twins, eyes dropping when Draco releases a soft growl.

"Draco," I say. "Leave him."

"He's a bastard. Do you know what he did?" he asks, turning his scowl on me.

"Raven told me but that doesn't mean you get a free pass to mentally torment him. He's terrified." I glance at the quivering headmaster. "He's already broken. You'll have to find a new toy."

Brayden snickers and Draco punches him in the arm, muttering "shut up" before turning and storming out of the library.

"You know, Adler." Brayden draws out my name like he's figuring out the best way to say it and sound half-cocked. "You're supposed to be the nurturer. Not the pisser-offer."

I close the small gap between us in four steps and stare down at him. "You're sorely mistaken if you expect me to coddle you. Nurturing is about more than cooing and hugging." He'll soon find out how *nurturing* I want to be if he wants to push me on the Erron matter.

Tsking, Brayden reaches up and tweaks my nose. I snatch his wrist and squeeze it.

"Oh, Daddy, I'm sorry." Brayden throws his head back and cackles.

Fucking psycho.

"Erron is off limits for you to torment, understand?"

He swings his dark blue eyes to meet mine, and his forehead wrinkles. "You're serious?"

I nod.

With a sigh, he throws his hands into the air. "Fine. He's yours to deal with. Draco and I are going hunting."

Since I know we need food, I don't try to argue that they should join us in the staff library. Besides, the headmaster will be of no use if they're present. He'll just retreat into his trembling shell and try not to breathe.

Once Brayden leaves, I turn to the omega. "Come on."

I'm no wolf, but Erron scrambles off his cot and scurries over, quick to follow the command. We walk the short distance to the library, Erron practically stepping on my heels. When we reach the door, I stop and turn to face him.

"Don't think because I protected you all your wrong doings are forgiven. Your road to redemption won't be easy, if you even make it."

He shrinks away from me, nodding and dropping his stare to the floor. "There isn't a day that passes without regret."

Scoffing, I turn to open the door. "Your regret won't raise the dead."

Sniffing, he shuffles in after me and slinks to the table and couches where the current stack of books lies. I don't shame him for crying, nor do I acknowledge the fat tears rolling down his cheeks. Picking up the smallest book of the stack, *High Demons of the Underworld,* I hold it out to him.

"No slacking."

Erron grabs the book and begins to read. I stand and watch him for a second. His hands are shaking, but he reads like he's supposed to. Turning my attention to the books, I grab one about witches and settle into the plush leather chair.

Time to see if I can find out something more about Raven and her powers. She sees the dead and brought Brayden back. With great power comes great consequence. One cannot simply raise the dead and not have side effects.

∼

BRAYDEN

After finding a few wandering chickens on the property, Draco and I drag them back to the academy before he sets off to find Raven. I don't like him going alone, but he doesn't seem concerned, so I'm not going to make a big deal about it. Since I served some of the fruit that was left in the pantry for breakfast, I'm low on supplies, but I can make it work for lunch.

Pretty soon we'll be down to eating whatever it is we manage to kill or find in the forest. During my run, I noticed a few mulberry trees, a small patch of strawberries, and what looked like the tops of carrots. It won't be much, but anything is better than attempting to eat whatever food Jinx conjures.

I'm in the middle of plucking a chicken when a slight vibration works its way through the kitchen. Glancing at the clock, I shake my head when I see it's eleven. Jinx is consistent, I'll give her that. Every day at five, eleven, and four the vibration happens; then about ten minutes later the buffet is full of fresh food and the coffee pot or juice containers are full. She's expending massive amounts of power to make the food appear, and taste, real. Draco, Carter, and Everett told me twenty-four shifters have been taken since I died. Twelve each year I've been gone.

Ripping out a feather, I stop and sniff. Is that. . . pesto chicken? With a scoff, I toss the feather into the growing pile and roll my eyes.

"You'll have to do better than that if you want them to eat

your food," I sing-song. "Even my measly dishes are more appealing to them right now."

"Who are you talking to?" a soft voice asks.

I spin, swinging the chicken at the intruder. Bea, Raven's little friend, screams and ducks, covering her head with her hands. Letting the chicken fly, I drop to my knees. The bird thuds into the wall and plops to the floor in a gross squelch.

"Are you okay? I didn't mean to scare you." I reach for her, then stop short, unsure if I should touch her because she is trembling, pressing her forehead to the tile. "Bea?" I ask, softening my voice. "It's okay."

Ever so slowly, she lifts her head, squinting at me and glancing around. Her eyes land on the chicken I let fly, and she bursts into giggles. Sitting all the way up, she slaps her hands over her mouth, still laughing.

"So you're okay?"

She nods, laughing so hard tears begin to fill her eyes. "I. I wanted to help," she says around giggles.

"Well, you scared me. What sort of thirteen-year-old sneaks around like that?" I raise my right eyebrow, pretending to be upset.

"I'm fourteen." She stops laughing and fixes her shirt as if that'll make her seem more grown up.

"Oh, fourteen. My apologies to the lady." I place my hand at my stomach and give her a small bow, earning a snort.

"You're weird," she observes, though her eyes are more curious than rude. There isn't a single ounce of malice written on her face.

Staring into her brown eyes, which are too knowing for how young she is, I nod. "That I am." Slapping my hands to my knees, I shove off the ground and go pick up the chicken. I'll finish plucking it then wash it. By the time I slap the bird back on the counter, she's standing and tapping her little fingers against the wood.

I start plucking, side-eyeing her as I do. "So, what can you cook?"

Lifting a shoulder, she blows out a breath. "I know how to make macaroni, grilled cheese, pizza. . ." She trails off. "Nothing useful, I guess."

"Well, here's your first lesson in cooking." I yank out the last feather and slap my hand against the skin of the chicken. "Wash this in the sink."

Her eyes round like saucers, but she gives me a curt nod and picks it up, holding it away from her body so it doesn't touch her shirt.

"Good. Water should do it, not hot though, don't want to cook it while you wash."

"Oh my god, you can cook it with hot water?"

"Cook what with hot water?" Raven pushes through the door, smiling at Bea before glancing at me. "Hey."

"Chicken can cook in hot water!" Bea says this like it's some new discovery for the whole world.

"Huh, who knew?" Raven wrinkles her nose at me, grinning at Bea's horror. "Need any help?"

Jerking my thumb toward the other two chickens, I turn and show her what we need to do. She doesn't miss a beat, nor does she bat an eye at the somewhat gruesome task. We've been so spoiled with the food supply in the human world. Not very many people cook like this anymore, but Raven isn't bothered by it.

∽

RAVEN

Bea and I help Brayden make a simple chicken dish with onion powder and garlic salt. We turned the last three potatoes into mashed potatoes. It's enough for everyone to have a small scoop, hardly adequate to fill someone up, but it'll do.

The most important thing is protein and carbs. We have more than enough chicken for everyone to have a good-sized portion and some of us ate in our wolf forms, so I'm not worried about people being hungry today. A quick glance around the kitchen tells me we have about a day before things get dire.

Brayden pats his pants like he's forgotten his keys and phone, something I think is more of a strange habit while he's thinking, and purses his lips, eyeing the modest spread.

"Okay," he finally says, grabbing the platter of chicken and nodding at me and Bea. "Here we go. Bea, grab the spoons."

I grab the bowl of potatoes, following him out of the swing door and setting it on one of the tables close to the buffet line. Jinx's food is annoyingly aromatic, and I glance over my shoulder to make sure she's not holding a fan toward us so we're forced to breathe in the basil and parsley.

"This looks good," Layla says, holding out her plate so Brayden can give her a serving.

Since we're rationing, we have to serve the food. The temptation to grab one more slice of chicken or spoonful of potatoes is too tempting, especially for hungry shifters.

They better not eat all the potatoes, Joan snarls the words inside my head when the spoon scrapes against the bottom of the bowl.

Relax, that was the last person in line. There's enough for Bea, Brayden, and us.

With a huff, she grumbles more about being hungry, but I ignore her. She's hangry, and I don't blame her. We've literally been starved and used as food this past month. What we've been eating hasn't been enough to really help, but since whatever illusion Jinx has spelled the academy with makes me appear healthy, I've sort of been ignoring the fact.

Bea grabs her plate, and we serve her, then Brayden and I take the last and go join our pack at one of the bigger tables.

Draco slides the seat next to him out of its spot, and I take it, waiting until Brayden sits across from me before beginning to eat. Even though everyone else has already scarfed most of their meal down, I can't forget my manners that say you wait for the chef to sit and eat before you start.

Who knew when Mom taught me the simple lesson that I'd be using it inside of an academy where I'm likely to die?

Lifting my fork, I start to take my first bite. A second after the creamy potatoes hit my tongue, a blast rocks the building. Every shifter in the room sits a little straighter, tips their chins a little lower, when a wave of power washes over the room. It hits me like a fist to the stomach, but instead of making me want to glance down in submission, my hackles rise and a growl creeps out of my throat.

An alpha.

Joan, if there were ever a time to make a power play, now is not it.

I won't cower before the likes of him!

Growling at her inside of my head, I shove her back into the corner. *You have to, Joan. You heard Jinx. She'll kill everyone.*

My wolf snaps her teeth at me inside my head, and I prepare to slam a wall in front of her to completely block her out, but she goes preternaturally still and quiet. It doesn't take a genius to figure out why.

The alpha has arrived.

CHAPTER 18

RAVEN

A strong presence brushes over my skin, and I can't help but turn around to get a glimpse of the infamous alpha who offers up changed shifters for power. Standing at just over six-feet, he's smaller than I expected, but based on the punch of power when he walked in, his looks are one-hundred-percent deceiving. His short blonde hair is spiked with an ungodly amount of gel, and if it weren't for the nasty sneer and glint of *possessiveness* in his cold brown eyes, he'd probably be decent looking.

A handful of men spread out behind him, scowling at the lot of us in the cafeteria like we're nothing but scum. The alpha's eyes sweep over the cafeteria before resting on the buffet behind us. I tense, waiting for the moment when he realizes we're all eating something different than what Jinx tried to serve us, but he simply glances to the side, studying Howard.

I glance at the buffet, noticing it's empty save for a pan of chicken. Why did she make her food disappear? Is she worried what he'll think? Of course, if he thinks she's lost control somehow, he won't be happy.

"Howard, it's been too long! How are you liking your position at the academy?" The alpha's voice is a deep baritone, but it's not smooth like Brayden's or Draco's—it's full of gravel and sharp objects. Threatening and not one bit soothing.

One of the guys sets a few bags of food on a table near him, scowling at us all before falling back in line with his buddies.

"It's good, Alpha. The students are learning a lot." Howard doesn't seem excited to see him; if anything, he looks terrified. There's a story there, but I'll have to figure out what it is another day.

"Is that so?" The alpha makes a noise of surprise and glances around, eyes pausing on me. Knowing it's the smart thing to do, I force my gaze to my lap.

Joan growls in my head, but I'm the only one who can hear it.

Don't, I warn Joan when I feel her creep forward.

Leave it to me to fuck things up.

He's a threat, she says like it's a simple give and take.

An idle one at the moment, but if you provoke him, he'll become a very real danger to you and everyone in this room. What about Bea?

I sense more than hear his approach, the weight of his attention growing even heavier with each step he takes toward me. When he stops near the table, I can see the edges of his shoes.

"Hello," he says, a gruff rumbling of the word. "I'm Peter."

"Nice to meet you." I don't look up, too afraid of how Joan will react if I do. She's not happy with my submission, but right now, ensuring no one is hurt because of me is more important than keeping her satisfied.

"Look at me."

The command slams into my chest, and even though I don't feel a pull to comply with his demand, I lift my gaze because of it.

His lips are drawn back in a cocky sneer, and his eyes flash yellow, his wolf looking hungry enough to strike at any given moment. Peter doesn't merely want my submission, he wants to devour it.

"What's your name?"

Pulling my shoulders back, I set my chin high and meet his stare. "Raven."

The alpha takes another step toward me and picks up a strand of my hair, spinning it around his finger. "Such a pretty thing, aren't you?"

I don't dignify him with an answer, and while I know I can't react, I imagine unleashing Joan so she can show him exactly how ugly we can be when provoked.

"Strong too." He sniffs. "A powerful beta." Tugging on my hair, he sighs. "Such a shame you're a half-breed."

"She can still be useful for something," one of his lackeys says, winking at me.

The shifters who came with him snicker, and he glances over his shoulder and joins them.

If he touches you anywhere else, I'm killing him.

Thank you, but let's try to keep control of ourselves. They're trying to intimidate us. My words do nothing to help calm Joan down, so I give up trying to reason with her and place a simple mental wall between her and me.

"Come for a walk with me Raven." He struts away with all the swagger of a man who thinks he's god's gift to women.

Again, this is a demand and not a request.

Keeping control of my emotions and making sure I don't react on the surface, I nod and rise from my chair, gently pushing it in and shooting a quick look at the men. They're all tense and on the edge of doing something very stupid. Brayden's fingers have already shifted to claws and Draco's eyes are glowing yellow, but he glances down to keep the alpha from seeing. Everett, Adler, and Carter have a handle on their emotions, and continue to look at their laps and stay as still as statues.

"Come along, pet."

Adler flicks his eyes to me, eyes burning with rage, and I give a slight shake to keep him from saying something. Right now, he's under the radar. The bond is keeping him safe from the alpha's attention for now, but if he does something to draw attention to himself, the alpha might realize the shifter energy swirling around him has nothing to do with Adler and everything to do with our bond.

"Coming," I say, adjusting my shirt and squeezing Bea's arm. "I'll be right back."

The alpha and his four men watch me walk over, not even trying to hide their leering. My skin crawls, and I fight the urge to snarl at them in warning. This walk he wants me to take is going to test every ounce of control I have over my wolf. I'm not sure I'll be able to keep her in check, and if I'm honest, part of me wants to let her out.

∾

ADLER

Watching her walk away with that creature has got to be the hardest thing I've ever done. He's filth. Dirt which needs to be swept away, but Raven is trying to keep the peace to make sure Jinx doesn't follow through with her threat. There are enough of us to take the alpha and his men on, but there aren't enough of us to stop the demon spirit from killing our people.

The fork I'm clenching groans and bends, folding in half

thanks to my anger. The farther they walk down the hall leading to the foyer, the more my chest heaves. Heart slamming inside of my chest, I set the trashed piece of silverware aside and ball my hands into fists. I've never been the type of guy to want to punch something to relieve stress, but I'm suddenly overcome with the urge to slam my knuckles into the alpha's face over and over until he's no longer able to so much as look at another woman, let alone Raven.

A loud laugh floats down the hall, and I scowl at it.

"She'll be okay," Carter whispers to me, putting the bent fork on his plate. "Joan, her wolf, won't let him do anything to hurt her."

Draco and Brayden are grimacing at one another, both look like they're about to lose control. Seeing them as worked up as I am makes me feel like I'm not alone. Everett glances around the table, a small vein on his forehead bulging as he battles against his own alpha nature. Carter is the only one who appears to be fully in control, that is until I see the long crack running the length of his plate. He squeezed it so hard he broke the hard plastic.

"She better be," I whisper back. "Otherwise, we're going to be responsible for a lot of deaths."

We all share a look, each of us silently agreeing to make the alpha and his men pay if they do anything to hurt Raven, even if it costs us the lives of the other shifters. It's fucked up, and probably a little selfish of us, but if these men feel the way I do, we'd sacrifice a thousand shifters to save her.

CHAPTER 19

RAVEN

A dark wave washes down the bond, funneled through our pack link and fueled by five variations of rage, each tainted with the promise of violence. I think of the beach and the calming waves of the ocean, sending how at peace I feel when I sit in the sand through the link and hoping it'll help.

"Do you know why you're here?" Peter asks, pity flashing over his face.

Pinching my eyebrows together, I slide my gaze his way. "To learn about shifter society so I can go live with the pack."

His eyes are a soft brown, not full of the complex colors Everett and Adler's irises contain.

"Hmm. How are you finding your studies? Learning a lot?" He edges closer to me as we walk into the foyer, invading my space. "I'm sure you've been having a hard time keeping up."

If my guess is right, he's only trying to intimidate me. If I'm wrong... Well, I'll think about that when the time comes.

"It's interesting," I say honestly. "There are so many things they don't teach us in public school."

Clicking his tongue, he shakes his head. "Humans and their fear of knowledge. I've never understood why they're so against teaching more about shifter society. Your kind has a lot they can learn from us."

I don't really feel like debating the merit of public school agendas, so I shrug and glance toward the stairs. Jinx is standing at the second-floor landing, grinning like a maniac. Today she has her black hair in pigtail braids, and she's wearing a simple white shirt and skinny jeans. If it weren't for the milky white eyes, she'd look normal. Human almost.

"There she is," the alpha's voice booms through the room. "Raven, have you met Jinx?"

He's looking at her so he doesn't see the flash of panic and the widening of my eyes. Do I say yes? Does he expect me to know her?

"Uh—" I begin but Jinx cuts in.

"We haven't had the pleasure, Peter, you know that. I don't meet the shifters until the full moon, after they've passed their classes."

Peter cocks his head to the side, stopping at the base of the staircase. "How are you, Jinx?"

With all the grace of a countess, she sweeps down the stairs as though she's floating and holds out her hand for the alpha to take and kiss.

Ugh. It's disgusting. They both act so above us. Even when he talks to me it's like he doesn't expect me to have enough brain power to piece together an intelligent response. Condescension is so ugly.

Jinx giggles, and I want to vomit at the sound. She's vile.

"Now, Peter, behave yourself." She smacks his chest, and he throws his head back, barking out an obnoxious laugh.

I squint at a picture on the wall to keep from glaring at them. He may have his back turned, but his men can see my every reaction. Better them to think I'm studying art than thinking about murdering the alpha.

He stops laughing and moves away from the stairs, walking back toward me. The essence of his power rolls over me, and every footstep makes Joan's hackles rise. I know something is seriously wrong with this guy because she's never had this sort of reaction, not even with Everett who is an alpha as well.

"Is everything prepared for the ritual?" he asks, running a finger down my arm.

Gooseflesh rises in response, but not because I'm excited. Repulsed is more accurate. He inhales, a low growl working its way up his chest.

"Fear has such a lovely taste." He grabs my wrist and yanks me against his body.

My heart thumps in response, and I nearly lose control of Joan, but I suck in a hard breath and grind my teeth when my chest slams into his.

"Peter, she's mine," Jinx says in a soft warning, stepping toward us.

He snarls at her in response. "They're all mine! You keep what I allow you to keep, do you understand me?"

Another sickening punch of power crashes into me, and my stomach turns. Bile rises in my throat, but I swallow it down, taking another deep breath to keep control of my emotions. He still thinks I'm a beta. More importantly, I'm not breaking the agreement I made with Jinx.

Running his nose up the column of my neck, he groans and squeezes me. "So sweet." Then he shoves me away from his body so hard I stumble, trip, and land on my ass against the marble floor. "Too bad you're a half-breed."

I bite back my response and stare at my shoes. If I fight, it'll only provoke him more. This is not the time to be a smartass.

"She can't even harness her beta energy. Look at her, she looks more like an omega." One of the guys spits on the marble. "Pathetic."

"Pathetic indeed." Peter scoffs. "I expect a full reaping this time, Jinx. Every shifter. No excuses."

"Understood, Alpha." Jinx curtsies. "Every single one."

"Good." His eyes track to the hallway. "Carl, go get Howard. Let's see if he still wants to fight his alpha."

One of the guys takes off to the cafeteria with purposeful steps, driven by the power the alpha forced into the command. I frown, forgetting about keeping my unfazed mask in place, and Peter squats in front of me, gaze skating over my body.

"Such a waste," he says with a shake of his head.

"Why? Because I'm changed?" I ask, keeping my voice soft so as not to challenge him directly. More like I'm still learning the rules and silly little me forgot I'm not supposed to question him.

"Ha. The bitch wants your dick, Peter."

Like hell I do. Joan will rip his head off before he gets a chance to touch me in that way. My stare is focused on my shoelaces, and Peter waves his hands in front of my shoes, forcing my attention to him.

"Because you're not really a shifter. You were raised human. Sure, you can turn into a wolf, but you'll never be a shifter. You're not natural. You're an abomination." He smirks when my face lines with annoyance. "And I don't fuck monsters."

I'm saved from having to answer the mess of hate he's spewing because the guy he sent returns, dragging an unwilling Howard after him. Chancing a glance at Jinx, I check to see if Howard's struggle will be a point against us, but her lips curl, and she claps.

"Let me have him, Peter."

His eyes narrow then he looks at her over his shoulder, standing and stepping away from me.

"You're being greedy, Jinx. I'm giving you everyone in this building, except for Howard, for the reaping. Don't be ungrateful."

The demon spirit pouts but nods. "You're right."

Peter scoffs. "Of course I am." Then he turns to face Howard. "Now, let's go see those fighting skills, Howard."

THE ALPHA HAS HIS MINIONS GATHER THE REST OF THE students in the basement gym so we can watch the fight between him and Howard. We stand in a semi-circle around the soft mats. I'm the closest to the fight, by order of the alpha, and Bea and Layla stand next to me. The men kept their distance so as not to reveal the pack bond we've formed. Frustration sizzles through the link, popping like hot bacon grease and burning me every so often. They're not happy.

"On the mats, Howard." Peter rips off his cotton shirt, tossing it aside. His pants are loose enough he can get in a good kick if he wants.

The zeta resists the order for a second, eyes swinging to meet mine, like he somehow expects me to stop this. I'm not in control here, at least not with Jinx's threat. Screwing my face up in apology, I try to let him see why I'm not helping. His body deflates when he realizes I won't be stepping in and using my luna power to counter the alpha's command.

"Now, Howard." The alpha's bouncing back and forth on his toes, throwing jabs in quick succession. He's so focused on showing off he doesn't notice why the zeta hesitated.

Clearing his throat, Howard steps onto the mat, tugging

his shirt over his head and throwing it aside. "I don't want to fight you."

Peter laughs. "Well, it's a little late for a change of heart, isn't it? You challenged me in front of the pack."

"I did, and you beat me into submission. I don't want to fight you again." Howard stops a few feet away from the alpha.

Size wise, they're almost equal, but Peter has an edge of wildness about him that Howard doesn't. Alpha power explodes through the room, and he growls at Howard.

"Fight me."

There is no choice for Howard. The punch of the command rips a snarl from his lips, and he charges the alpha. Peter swings his fist in a fast uppercut, hitting Howard square in the jaw and launching him into the air. While his body is airborne, the alpha spins and kicks, shoving his foot into Howard's stomach.

The shifter flies back into one of the mirrored walls, his body cracking the pane before slamming into the mat with a hard thud. A few of the women cover their mouths with their hands or glance away, but the rest of us, Bea included, watch as Peter kicks the shit out of Howard, pummeling him over and over. Forcing him onto his back every time he tries to recover. Kicking his ribs hard enough that sickening cracks fill the air. By the time the fight—if you can even call it that—is over, Howard is black and blue, bleeding, and scarcely breathing. He coughs, blood splattering over the mat where he lies.

Lifting one hand, he bangs it against the mat in forfeit. I wait for Peter to acknowledge his tap out, but he doesn't. The alpha curls his fist up, pointing his elbow over Howard's stomach and drops to his ass, digging the point of his arm into Howard's torso. Howard howls, so high and pitiful my heart skips for him, then he begins coughing again, crimson liquid seeping out of his mouth.

"Time for the finisher." Peter's hand partially shifts into a claw.

He's going to kill Howard.

"No!" I shout, stepping out of the line. "He submitted to you. Please, don't kill him."

Jinx whistles low, stepping away from her spot on the wall and strutting toward us.

"My, my, alpha. We have a fighter here. Perhaps she wants to challenge you? Or maybe we can pick one of her little friends to die? She has to learn a lesson somehow, right?" Her milky eyes bore into me, reminding me of every life on the line.

Dropping my gaze, I bite my lip and shake my head. "No, I'm sorry. I shouldn't have said anything."

Peter chuckles. "You're right. You shouldn't have. Watch me kill him."

My stomach cramps and revulsion rolls over me as his power tickles over my skin, trying to force me into submission. Lifting my gaze so he doesn't think there's anything wrong, I watch him swipe his claws across Howard's throat. Heat sweeps up my neck, and my eyes grow damp, knowing part of this is my fault. I could have stopped him. My luna power could have overcome his. I know in the core of my being this alpha isn't stronger than me, not even with Jinx's magic helping him. I should have stopped him, but I didn't.

Bea whimpers, and I have to dig my nails into my palms to keep from running to her and blocking the sight. Red pours out of the wound, spilling over the floor, and pooling around the zeta's lifeless body. Swiping at my damp cheeks, I keep my eyes on the wound as I was told, hoping the alpha buys the act of submission.

We will never submit to him, Joan growls. She prowls back

and forth, baring her teeth whenever she thinks he might be looking. Thank the moon he can't see her.

"Do you want to challenge me?" Peter asks, standing and walking over to me. He grips my chin and yanks it up. His eyes are filled with so much malice it makes my skin crawl. He's as bad as Jinx.

"No," I whisper, holding his gaze for a beat.

Softening his hold, he runs his thumb over my lips, making my body tense. His touch leaves behind an empty feeling, and I want to reach up and scrub my mouth until it's red and raw. Until I can no longer feel the vile promise lingering there.

His gaze hardens as he takes in my damp cheeks. "This is a human reaction. Shifters aren't this weak." Shoving me away from his body, he scoops up his shirt and pulls it on, glancing around the room of changed shifters. "You will never fit in. You cannot go home, and you will not join the pack. There's no sense in wasting your lives if we can harness the power of your wolves. You will serve a purpose in death. You should be thankful for that."

A squeak sounds behind me, and I glance over my shoulder, seeing Layla hugging Bea to her tight enough I worry about her being able to breathe. The shifter's eyes meet mine, panic widening them.

Peter pauses, studying the two of them with his lip curled in disgust. "Weak and fragile." Snapping his fingers, he points up the stairs, directing his men to go. "All of them, Jinx. I'm getting the class reports from Erron to send to the elders then I'll be back on Monday. I expect it to be done."

The demon spirit dips her head, but he's not paying attention to her as he stomps up the stairs.

CHAPTER 20

EVERETT

More than one of the women runs to the locker room, hands pressing against their mouths to keep from throwing up before they reach the toilet. Raven kneels next to where Layla is holding Bea.

"She was going to say something," Layla explains, shaking her head. She loosens her hold so Bea can turn around.

She sobs, sniffing loudly and throwing her arms over Raven's shoulders. "He didn't have to kill him."

Our woman cries as she holds the girl, but she doesn't make a sound. She's strong for the little shifter. Layla scrubs her hands over her face, shooting her gaze to the big pool of blood. Her face pales.

"Carter, help me clean up." I nudge him with my elbow and point to Howard.

"No, no. He's mine," Jinx says, stepping in front of me.

"He's dead." Carter pinches the bridge of his nose. "What are you going to do with a dead shifter?"

Turning to glance at Raven, Jinx drums her fingers together. "I have an idea."

Carter and I glance at each other, knowing exactly what the other is thinking. Draco, Brayden, and Adler all step forward to stand next to us. A deep growl builds in my chest, and I let it rumble up my throat, warning Jinx.

She cuts her gaze to us, grinning when she sees us all in a line. "Oh, how cute."

Brayden moves, grabbing her by the neck and lifting her off the ground. He only has a hold of her for a few seconds before she disappears, reappearing across the room with a nasty scowl.

Straightening her shirt with a huff, Jinx's eyes blaze even whiter. "You may be marked by Death, Brayden, but not even you can hurt me."

Our luna can. My wolf's gruff voice fills my head.

You're right, but she's not going to risk the lives of everyone around her to try and kill Jinx.

Raven stands, shoving Bea behind Layla and walking over to us, lips pressed into a firm line, her wolf's yellow gaze bleeding through.

"What are you doing?" she hisses at Brayden.

Brayden clenches his jaw and refuses to pull his attention from Jinx. "Someone needs to take care of her."

Flicking her hair over her shoulder, she glances at Jinx. "He didn't mean it. We played along while the alpha was here. You can't break our deal." The words tumble out of Raven's mouth so fast, her panic bleeding through.

The shifters in the room ease back, moving behind the treadmills like they can hide from whatever is about to happen. Those who went into the locker room come out, pausing to take in the scene, then scurry to join the group. The heady scent of copper fills the air. My wolf paces inside of my head, struggling to let me maintain control. We've learned to respect one another, but a mate link will drive a wolf mad if he thinks she's in danger.

Draco snatches his brother's arm and pulls him back, clapping his hand on the back of his neck and forcing his forehead against his.

"Don't fuck this up."

Brayden sneers at him, shoves away, and turns to leave, crashing into Adler in the process. The fae is a few good inches taller than Brayden, and he uses it to his advantage, leaning over him and simply staring at him. Adler doesn't speak, but he doesn't need words. His face is set, eyes narrowed and lips clamped shut, but a brush of strong, foreign power flutters through the pack link. Brayden grinds his jaw and glances down, submitting to the fae.

"A luna and her harem. How sweet." Jinx steps toward Raven, who spins on her heel to face the demon. "You're right. You played by the rules, but I need a favor."

Placing her hands on her hips, Raven shakes her head. "I'm not doing you any favors."

"Maybe I misspoke"—Jinx chuckles—"by favor, I meant you have to do it."

"That's not what that word, you know what, never mind. What do you want?"

Jinx swings her hips as she approaches Raven, trying to be cute, but frankly the demon-spirit is disgusting.

"You see, I need Howard." Pointing to the dead shifter, she pouts her lip at Raven. "Fix my broken toy."

The link crackles and pulses, dread sweeping through it.

Carter flashes to Raven's side with his supe speed. "You don't have to do it."

"Wrong." Jinx swings her hand up.

Bea squeaks, flying into the air upside down like there's a

rope tied to her ankle. Her hair and hands dangle over her head, and she cries for Raven to save her. The link pulls taut, threatening to snap.

Shrugging Carter off, she drops to her knees, blood seeping into her pants, and holds her trembling hands over Howard.

"I'll do it. Put her down, carefully."

Tsking, Jinx wags her finger. "Not until you do what I asked."

Raven nods, glancing at us with wide green eyes. The link is flooding with too many emotions, each so strong they overpower one another until all I can make out is a mass of darkness. A pit of despair yawning inside the link. Carter falls to his knees at her side.

He places a hand on her back. "I'm here."

I join them, kneeling on her other side and putting my palm above his.

Draco, Brayden, and Adler kneel on the other side of Howard, nodding at Raven when she looks at them with damp cheeks. With one shaky breath, she snaps her eyes shut, whispering to herself. Every word spoken fills the link with ichor, the tar like substance sludging up the connection with Raven. I meet Carter's gaze over her head, wrinkling my brow when my stomach clenches.

Make her stop, my wolf says, sounding afraid for what has to be the first time.

I don't know how, and even if I did, I can't. She won't stop until Bea is safe.

He whines when whispers fill my head, bleeding through the link. The voices of the dead. Images flash through my mind. Guns firing, bullets piercing chests. Endless rivers of blood. Hands clutching chests. Pained moans as bodies writhe in pain. Metal crumpling when two vehicles collide head on, crushing the people inside. Screams reverberate, bouncing around inside my head. My wolf snarls at it, snapping his teeth to try and make it stop. I shove at the images and sounds, but they won't leave. If anything, the more I fight them the louder and more vivid they become.

"Raven," Adler says, fisting his hands. "Stop."

She shakes her head, face wrinkling in annoyance, but she continues to mutter, drawing more of the vile power into the pack link.

"Death." Brayden growls, eyes flicking to mine. "She uses his power to bring people back."

He hasn't explained a lot about what happened when he died, but unease is written all over his face, telling me my wolf's worry is valid. Whatever she's doing is dangerous.

"Vivo," she says loudly, snapping her eyes open. They're greener than I've ever seen them, almost electric in color.

Jinx gasps, but we all ignore her to watch Raven bring Howard back to life.

Howard draws a raspy breath, sickly wet with the fluid in his lungs, and his fingers twitch. Slowly, his chest rises, filling with air, and his eyelids flutter open. The zeta's eyes are dull and milky, not entirely white like Jinx's. His wound is still open, but there's no blood left inside of his body, so all that's left is gaping slash marks and bright red tissue. He makes a few incoherent sounds, reaching for Raven. I grab his wrist to keep him from touching her and release a warning growl.

"It's okay," Raven says, placing her fingers on my arm. "I'm his connection to the world. He doesn't want to hurt me; he wants to understand."

Glancing at her, I take in her damp cheeks, red eyes, and trembling lips. She squeezes my arm, so I release Howard, glaring at him to make sure he doesn't try anything stupid. Grasping his hand, Raven scoots closer to him, dragging her legs through the blood as she goes. The warm liquid covers me when I move with her, the rich copper scent growing stronger with the displacement.

"Howard," she whispers. "It's Raven."

More incoherent sounds.

"His neck is torn apart. I don't think he can talk," Carter says. "See if you can force him to shift."

"Okay." She licks her lips, glancing at each of us. A seed of doubt breaks through the ichor filling the bond, growing and blooming into an ugly flower of self-deprecation.

"Hey," I say, pressing my palm more firmly into her back. "Nothing's changed. You will always be our luna."

∽

RAVEN

"You will always be our luna." Everett's words soothe some of my worries. They've never seen what I can do, at least not like this. Bringing Brayden back was different, because Death kept his mind and body intact, making it easy to bring him to the land of the living. Howard's body is destroyed. He's only been dead a little while, so his soul lingered on this plane. Finding it and shoving it back into his body was easy enough, but I'm not a healer. I can't fix what's broken.

If his supe power works like it did when he was alive, then shifting might help him. It's worth a shot at least.

"Howard, shift." My luna power threads into the words.

His shoulders tense and fur ripples over his skin. The forced change takes seconds, and when it's complete, a tall tawny brown wolf with white eyes stands before me. Blood darkens his coat near his throat. Tossing his head back, he unleashes a scratchy howl, which breaks and turns into a human-like moan.

What did you do to him? Joan asks in horror.

Jinx bursts into giggles behind me, clapping her hands. I scowl at her over my shoulder, watching as she lowers Bea to the floor. Layla grabs her little arms and pulls her to the group of shifters hiding in the back of the gym, as far away from Jinx as she can get.

"You did it!" She pats her thigh. "Come here, Howard. Come here, boy."

"He's not a dog," Draco says, gritting his teeth.

"Please." Jinx slaps her thigh harder. "You're all mutts. Come. Here. Howard."

She's not a luna; she can't command him. Howard growls, but it crackles and turns from canine to human like again. The resulting sound is strange and not at all threatening. It's like he's playing monsters instead of being one.

"He's still broken," she says, wrinkling her nose and squinting at me. "You did it wrong."

"I didn't do it wrong. This is what happens when you bring the dead back." I gesture to the wolf. "They were never meant to come back. He'll never be the same."

Lifting her hand, she curls her fingers, the same way she did when she killed Jackson. "Well, I guess you'll have to try again."

Then Howard moans again. The strange sound makes my heart squeeze, and I try to block him from her attack, but she shakes her head.

"It doesn't work like that."

The wolf collapses behind me; human-like screams pour from his mouth as Jinx rips his soul from his body. I turn, staring as he convulses, paws twitching like a dog having a bad dream. When the cries stop and the wolf stills, Jinx sighs.

"Try again or I kill Bea."

Rubbing my arm over my face, wiping away snot and tears, I bite the inside of my cheek and hold my hands up over Howard again, muttering the same words from before. Mom's face flashes in my mind, but I pinch my eyes shut, trying to block her out, but the more I try, the more the picture of her hands stuck in Dad's grave grows.

I guess we're not so different after all.

CHAPTER 21

Raven

Jinx makes me revive Howard five times before I fall apart. Chest shaking, sobs growing louder with each breath, I hold my hand over his body, trying to force myself to make it work again. But every time I try to call on Death's power, I hit a wall. All I see is Dad's slacken face and gray skin. All I can think about is the way Mom's gaze blazed with insanity. All I feel is his cold hand clutching my ankle through the dirt as he uses it to dig his way out of the grave on Mom's command.

"You see, baby? It worked!" Mom's eyes are bright, cheeks red from the chill in the air. "He's back." She digs her nails into the dirt and starts digging a hole like a dog searching for the special place he buried his bone.

Shivers skate down my spine when his grip grows stronger, pulling me toward the hole when he yanks on it. He's trying to force his way out of the dirt, but there's too much covering him. He won't make it unless we get it off of him. Imagining him choking on mouthfuls of dirt spurs me into action, I lean forward, peel his hand off of my ankle, and start digging alongside Mom.

"Good, baby, just like that. He's almost out." Mom uses both hands to pull a big pile of dirt off the grave and giggles. "Hold on, hunny! We're almost there!" she screams at Dad, as though he can understand her.

Maybe he can. For all I know, the man buried beneath all this earth will be exactly how he was before he died. Except deep down, I know that's a stupid wish. That cold grip was nothing like how my father felt. His embraces were warm and smelled like a campfire. His rough hands patting my shoulder as he passed were always sparked with love, not the cold, nothingness I felt seconds ago.

Whoever we're unburying is not my dad.

Shoving my hands into the dirt, I continue to dig despite all of this. My heart won't let me stop. He already died once, and I can't bear for it to happen again. Not when I can do something about it this time. I drag another heap out of the hole, and Mom catches my arm, gasping. I follow her gaze which is set on Dad's grave, mouth dropping open when I see him.

Dad is staring at her like she's the light at the end of a tunnel and he can't wait to reach it. Strange noises rattle out of his mouth, but none of them form actual words. Mom crawls into the grave, grasping both of his hands and pulling him out of the dirt. Maggots tumble from his body, spilling from holes they've burrowed into his skin. I fall onto my butt, scrambling back as she brings him out.

"What did you do?" I whisper, eyes rounding like saucers. "Mom, what did you do?"

Her head snaps to me and her lip curls. "I brought him back."

I open my mouth to say something, but she screams in frustration, shaking Dad like a ragdoll.

"He's fucking alive now, Raven! Don't be an ungrateful little bitch."

Shock blasts through me, sucker punching me in the gut and stealing my breath away. I've never seen her like this, never heard her talk like this. Who is this deranged woman and what did she do with Mom?

With a scoff, she swings her gaze to my dad. "Teenager Raven is difficult, as always."

As always? My face wrinkles, and I try to reason as to what she means. Sure I'm moody, but so is she. I listen, get good grades, and follow the rules. What the hell does she mean by difficult? I'm not a golden child, but some parents would kill to have a kid like me, especially one who keeps her nose out of trouble and in a book instead.

"Come on. Let's get him home." *She stands, placing her hands under his elbows and bringing him with her.*

Dad wavers on his feet, head swaying back and forth like it might fall off. "Grogrgiosasaba."

"Mom, we can't take him home. He's not right."

"Enough, Raven! Either help me get him in the car or you can walk home."

My chest hollows out. Hurt ripples through me when I realize she means it. She'd leave me here to take this abomination home.

Pressing my hands against the mat, shoving them deep in the blood, I shake my head, rocking back and forth.

"Giving up already?" Jinx asks with a tsk. "I thought you had more gumption than that."

"Leave her alone. Howard won't be whole again." Adler's protective voice caresses my skin.

Everett pulls me into his arms; the blood that covers me smears over his skin and clothes, but he doesn't care. He wraps me in a tight hug, as though he can squeeze away the memories and what I've done.

"Fine, it doesn't matter anyway," she says.

Howard's body convulses, and a spiral of white mist floats

out of his mouth, shooting toward Jinx. She made me bring him back so she could steal his soul?

"You're a bitch." I spit the words at her over Everett's shoulder.

"So I've been told." With a smirk, she winks and disappears, taking Howard's essence with her.

CHAPTER 22

RAVEN

The guys carry Howard's body to the river deep in the forest, laying him on the bank as the rest of us gather and build a raft made of fallen branches. Layla sniffles, wiping her arm across her runny nose, and sets another branch on the funeral pyre before heading off with Penelope to go get more. Leaving him in the academy felt wrong, so I asked if we could send him off with a warrior's farewell, how the Vikings used to. It was that or dig a hole, and I don't think any of us wanted to do that.

Something about burying a shifter six feet under is too real. Too final. The way we're planning it now, he'll be sent off, traveling down the river until his body burns and the wall surrounding the academy grounds stops the raft. He may not be able to float off on a huge journey, but it's more symbolic this way. Plus, Jinx won't be able to take him like she did with Jackson, Morris, and Lincoln.

"Here you go," Bea says, handing me a large stick. The skin around her brown eyes is bright red, rubbed raw from swiping at tears.

"Thanks, Bea." I grab it and add it to the final layer, using some of the rope Carter grabbed to tie my end together.

She stays close to me while I finish, watching Brayden, Draco, and Everett tie off the other ends. Adler and Carter bend down—one lifting Howard's arms and the other his legs—and carry him to the bed we've made. I step back so they can lower him onto it, grabbing Bea's hand and pulling her back toward the other shifters.

A few move over so we can join them, and I give them a small smile before turning to watch the guys. Carter grabs a bundle of sticks, placing it on top of Howard's stomach, then grabs Jackson's sketchbook and one of Morris's sweaters Layla brought out and places them next to Howard. We couldn't find anything of Lincoln's, so we wrote his name on a piece of paper. Carter sticks that under the sweater. With a slight nod from him, Adler, Everett, Brayden, and Draco drag the raft into the water. The twins stand at the front, water lapping at their stomachs. Carter steps into the river, facing the crowd.

"Howard's combat classes were tough but effective. He cared about his students, even going so far as to give extra lessons to the littlest of shifters." Carter glances at Bea. She sniffs and he continues. "As a pure-blood shifter at Bad Moon, he never treated the rest of us like trash. He was kind, a little protective, and wanted the best for each of us."

"Jackson was a prankster, and a bit of a pain in my ass, but he was a great friend." He pauses. "Too many good people have been taken by Jinx. That stops now." Glancing at Layla, he lifts an eyebrow.

She steps forward, clearing her throat. "I didn't know Morris for more than a handful of weeks, but we arrived here together and since we both lost everything we'd ever known when we were changed, we bonded and got to know one another pretty well—" Her voice cracks, and she looks at the canopy, blinking back tears. "Now he's gone," she says, the words thick with emotion. "And he's not coming back." Blowing out a hard breath, she rubs her hands over her damp face and laughs. "You know, he always talked about finding a way out. I just didn't think he'd leave without me."

Moisture pricks my eyes, and I squeeze Bea's hand, hoping it brings her comfort. Layla is sobbing now, and Penelope rushes to wrap her arms around her, walking her back to us. I reach over and rub her back while the others whisper that it'll be okay. Even though they all know that's a lie, they can't seem to help themselves. I remember how it felt to be told over and over how it would all be okay at Mom and Dad's funerals, and how those words were such a slap in the face. So insincere.

It'll all be okay, Raven. You're in good hands.

Aunt Lou is good, but it wasn't all okay. So I keep my mouth shut but offer her support in the only way I know how right now.

"Lincoln wasn't very kind," Penelope says, surprising me by stepping forward on his behalf. "He was cruel, but even he didn't deserve this. None of us do," she says with a trembling voice. "We deserve more than this."

Shifters murmur in agreement, and Penelope goes back to Layla, wrapping her arm around her shoulder.

"May the moon guide them home." Carter's voice draws my attention, and he lights a match, opening Jackson's notebook and setting the paper on fire. Then he lights another match and holds it to one of the twigs on Howard's chest, letting it burn down to his fingers until the stick on top finally catches and begins to burn.

Brayden and Draco walk the raft out a little farther before swimming it down a ways and letting it go. The waterfall is behind us, so the current is fast enough to take him away as everything begins to catch fire and burn, taking the scent of singed hair with it. The twins stay treading water, watching with the rest of us for a few minutes. Even after the river bends and carries him out of sight, we stare downstream. Part of me wonders if we're not all wishing the same thing:

I wish the river would carry us all away.

∽

ADLER

After Howard disappears from sight, small groups of shifters leave, heading off to the shared sleeping area in the library or off to wander the woods for a bit in their wolf form before going in for the night. Raven stays behind, waiting for me and the guys. We're all drenched, wet clothes clinging to our bodies, but for me, it doesn't matter.

"Raven," I say, pulling her dazed gaze in my direction. "Do you want to talk about what happened earlier?" Walking over to her, I keep my hands open to let her know I'm going to wrap her in my arms.

Her bright green eyes track my movements, and there's a moment where the link surges with panic and I worry she'll run away from me, but I send some of my peace to her. I know all about losing a life you once loved. I was a kid when I was traded for a human, but I lived many years mourning what my family had done and adjusting to my new life. Though no matter how many decades pass, there's still a sting of hurt whenever I recall the look on my mother's face when she saw what I'd done.

"I." Raven stammers, glancing around at the others. "It's complicated."

Reaching her, I pull her against my chest and hold her tight, running one hand over her back and burying the other in her soft hair. She smells like violets and honey, and as her scent fills my nostrils, some of my unease fades. Her reaction to Jinx's request is seared into my mind. Those small hands are still stained red from Howard's blood. I don't think she's noticed or realized it.

"What is more complicated than this?" Brayden asks softly.

She sucks in a sharp breath and presses her forehead into my chest. "My mother," she says then pauses.

"It's okay, we're here to listen. We're pack now, remember?" Everett says as he comes to stand next to me, placing his hand on her arm.

With a heavy sigh, she nods against my chest then pulls out of the hug, stepping back so she can look at us. "My mother tried to bring my dad back to life a few months after he died." She swallows, face scrunching up as she tries to rein in her emotions. "He came back, but he wasn't the same. Imagine Howard times three hundred. Dad's soul wasn't intact, so he was pretty much a zombie, minus the brain eating." Releasing a bitter laugh, she swipes at her cheeks.

"You're not your mother," Carter says.

Raven's eyes flash, and she shakes her head. "There are too many similarities between her and me. Part of me will always be like her."

The link pulses with anger, and I take a step toward her, stopping when she holds her hand up.

"It's okay."

"Raven," I say, searching her face. "Lou told me about your mom. You may share blood and have the same power, but you're nothing like her."

"How do you know?" she asks.

Meeting her gaze and not daring to blink, I say, "Because the woman before me would never leave the people she loves. She's strong, and even when she feels like she's drowning in a sea of darkness, she'll try to save someone else from the same fate by helping them out of the undertow."

She glances away and bites her cheek, eyes filling with tears again. "Ugh, they won't stop," she says as she rubs them away.

Draco is suddenly in front of her, clutching her cheeks in his hands and tipping her head up so she has to stare at him. "Don't hide them." He kisses her cheek, and her eyes flutter closed, tears spilling down her face, and he presses his lips against each eyelid before capturing her lips for a quick kiss.

Linking her hands behind his neck, she hugs him to her body like he's the only thing keeping her from slipping off a ledge. A small pang of jealousy rushes through the link. I scowl at Brayden—who is grimacing—and he quickly shoots soothing vibes in its place. His eyes flit to mine, and he lifts a shoulder to say *I can't help it*. I nod at him in understanding and slide my gaze back to Raven and Draco.

I understand Brayden's jealousy, but we're a unit, so there is no place for competition. The others keep a lid on their emotions, and I suspect Brayden's knee jerk reaction is driven by having always been in competition with his brother more than it is about the hug itself.

Making a decision, I step into their space and put my arms around both of them. Carter and Everett do the same a few seconds later. Brayden hesitates until I scowl at him, then he rolls his eyes and joins our group hug, face softening as he lays his arms over mine and Carter's. The link fills with sunshine the longer we stand there in the embrace, the warmth of it curling around each of us before shooting in the center to Raven.

Our entire world.

Our luna.

CHAPTER 23

RAVEN

Thursday morning I get up before the sun to go make food with Brayden and Draco. I don't think Draco will be doing any cooking, but he's coming to make sure nothing happens. Not that he's able to stop Jinx if she wants to do anything. We've been sticking to *the safety in numbers* rule in hopes that it will deter her from showing up.

This is the first time I've been alone with the twins, and it's a little unnerving. Their mannerisms are so similar: the way they push their hair out of the way, the way they arch one eyebrow when they think something is amusing. Their eyes, though different shades of blue, are not what sets them apart. No, Brayden's are more haunted.

"Since the alpha's men brought some food, we can have eggs, sausage, and toast for breakfast." Brayden sets the eggs on the counter, and I grab a bowl without having to be asked. He hums in appreciation. "You're a quick learner."

"That or she's afraid you'll turn Gordon Ramsey on her," Draco says around a yawn.

Cracking the first egg, I pull the shell apart. "What are you?" I whisper shout at him over my shoulder.

His eyes brighten, and he snorts. "An idiot sandwich."

Brayden laughs as he sets out the sausage in a big pan. "I'm way more attractive than good ol' Ramsey."

"You know what I like about you?" I wink at Draco and glance at his brother who grins.

"Don't tell me. My charming good looks?" Brayden asks.

"No," I reply, cracking another egg and watching the yolk plop into the white of the one in the bowl. "Your humility does it for me."

Draco scoffs. "Yes, he's humble, isn't he?"

We share amused looks.

"I'll have you know it isn't easy." Brayden clacks tongs at us, eyebrows drawing down. "I don't think I like you two ganging up on me. Draco's bad enough on his own."

"Ganging up on you?" I hold an egg above the edge of the bowl and give him a look. "Honey, if you can't handle the heat, get out of the kitchen."

Draco's soft but dark chuckle zings down my spine, making me shiver. Lifting my hand slightly, I get ready to bring it down and hit the shell against the bowl, but Brayden catches my wrist, spinning me around. The egg tumbles out of my hand and lands on the floor with a splat. Before I can worry about the mess, he leans into me, pushing me against the counter and caging me between his arms.

"Let's get one thing clear, Little Red." He growls the nickname, sounding every bit the big bad wolf. "This is my domain. I can handle everything you dish out, but I don't think you're quite ready for what we have in store for you." He runs his thumb over my cheek then draws it across my bottom lip.

Heat pools in my stomach, and I press my legs together to keep from rubbing against him like a cat.

Moons, if you don't fuck him right now, I'll be pissed. Joan's voice cracks like a whip through my head.

We're in the middle of cooking, Joan. Not now!

Spoil sport. She blows a raspberry.

Brayden buries his nose against my neck and inhales, groaning against my skin. "I can smell how wet you are."

"Fuck," Draco curses.

I grab Brayden's pants, ready to rip them off when the swinging door pushes open. The twins growl in unison as Erron pauses, panicked eyes shooting around the room. A current of violence crashes through the room, funneling toward the guy.

"Co-co-coffee?" he manages to ask.

Shoving against Brayden's chest, I push out from under him and go to the coffee machine, grabbing a filter and filling it with scoops of the cheap grounds which come in a can.

"Five minutes," I say, giving him a grin to try and defuse the *murder* vibes my twins are giving off.

Erron dips his head and practically runs from the room.

I try to fight off a laugh, but the two of them look half ready to run after him, and I can't help it. When the first giggle fills the room, it snaps them out of their possessive reaction, and they both shake their heads, giving me curious glances. Smoke rises from the pan behind Brayden, and he sniffs, eyes widening slightly when he realizes he's burning the sausage.

"This isn't finished," he warns.

"No it's not," Draco says, prowling toward me. "You know my favorite part about *Little Red Riding Hood*?"

I shake my head.

He picks up a piece of my hair and tugs on it. "The wolf only wants one thing."

Licking my lips, I clear my throat. "And what's that?"

"To devour Little Red, of course." He pulls on my hair

again, drops the lock, and turns to go finish cracking the eggs I left behind while I try to keep my brain from short circuiting.

These two are dangerous.

I think I like it.

You and me both, Joan whispers.

∽

DRACO

Making her heart skip and flutter is quite possibly my favorite thing to do. Raven stands in shock for a few more seconds. The sweet scent of her arousal wraps around me like a warm hug, and my wolf whines in my head.

She is in need.

She is in the middle of helping with breakfast, I tell him.

That doesn't matter. A zeta fulfills his luna when she needs him.

There is a distinct difference between need and want. Needs are uncontrollable at times. Wants are very deliberate decisions. I will fulfill her every want, but I'm not going to fuck her in the kitchen while other shifters are in the cafeteria.

Pussy.

I growl at him. *Keep talking like that and you won't get to run for three weeks.*

He chuffs but shuts up. Raven would totally be up for a quickie, but there's more to this attraction between us than sex. Half the fun is working her up, making the little organ inside of her chest nearly give out before I give her what she wants and what her body desperately needs. But she'll have to ask first.

CHAPTER 24

RAVEN

After breakfast, those of us who don't have class on Thursdays go for a run. As soon as we hit the trees, people begin to strip. I pause for a moment and glance around, taking in flashes of flesh. It doesn't shock me like it used to, but watching a group of people undress is still wild.

Ahem.

Real subtle, I say to Joan and pull off my shirt. As soon as I'm undressed, we shift, and Joan takes control. We take off, sprinting through the trees, jumping over bushes, yipping into the slight summer breeze. There's a faint bitterness in the air, something I've never smelled before.

Fall is approaching.

Oh, I say. It's almost September now. Two more weeks and the weather will start to change. We're running along on our own in a small clearing, listening to the birds tweet and other wolves barking, when someone crashes into our side, knocking us to the ground.

Releasing a growl, we roll and hop to our feet, baring our teeth.

A dark wolf prowls toward us. The power rolling off of him is stronger than Draco, which means it must be Brayden. His black fur is identical to his twin's.

Snarling, we snap our teeth, though we have no intention of hurting him. He lowers his head, but continues toward us until he's standing at our feet, chin touching the earth. Bowing to us.

Swoon, Joan says on a sigh. *Are we allowed to have favorites?*

No.

Ugh, you suck.

I snort because she's been picking up a lot of random sayings, but that's the first time she's ever sounded like a petulant teenager.

Lowering our nose to him, we sniff his head, licking his nose and playfully biting it. He yips in mock pain, and we snort.

Puh-lease. You know he likes pain, right?

Yeah. I laugh. *Can wolves wrestle?*

With a small warning growl, we pounce on him, tackling him and rolling in the dirt. He snorts in surprise and pushes against us, but he doesn't put up much of a fight. We tumble on the forest floor for a few minutes, making Joan deliriously happy before dropping onto our stomachs and rolling over. Brayden rumbles in approval, laying his head against our stomach and stretching out on his side.

Three wolves come into the small clearing a little while later. Carter, Draco, and Everett didn't have any academy duties today, so they're free to roam. They join us in the literal doggie pile, each warm body finding a place to connect with mine until my heart warms. A soft squawk sounds from the tree above us, and we glance up, spotting Adler's eagle. His head tips back and forth, studying the five of us together.

We yip, trying to call him down, but he chitters and gazes around the forest.

He's protecting us. Joan groans. *Are you sure we can't have favorites?*

No favorites, I say. *He better not poop on us.*

Joan chuffs. *That would be hilarious.*

Maybe for you.

Adler keeps watch while we lie together, soaking up the beams of sunlight filtering through the canopy, and for a few seconds, I can visualize what the future will be like as a pack. He may never join our doggie piles, but he'll find his own ways to be with us.

And I wouldn't want it any other way.

∾

Later that night, we gather around the librarian's desk. Shoulders hang heavy—most of the shifters have already resigned themselves to death. Adler's fae friend hasn't come back yet, and even if he had, I'm not sure he could break through Jinx's demon power again. He couldn't break through the wards when they trapped Adler and me inside, and Adler can't fly out of them. Whatever she did is too powerful for fae magic.

"Why are we even meeting? There's no point. You saw what she did to Howard." A guy I haven't really talked to crosses his arms over his chest. A few shifters frown and nod, agreeing with him.

Every day that we don't have class, we spend it scouring the library in search of information. It hasn't gone well, and while I understand his frustration, he's being a defeatist.

"I refuse to give up. There has to be something in the books that helps—" I start to say, but he growls.

"You're fucking kidding me," he mutters. "You can't find

the answer in these stupid history books." He picks one up and hurls it against the wall. Moving to pick up another, he growls when Carter shoves his chest.

"Don't fucking mess with my books." Carter pushes him back again. "You want to give up? Fine, but leave us out of it."

Moons, he's so hot when he talks about books, Joan whispers.

Oh my god, I know! *Better go stop him before he does something he'll regret.*

Inserting myself between them, I press my hands against their chests and ease them apart. "Listen, no fighting, okay. You," I say to the angry shifter, "go run in the woods and let it out. And you," I turn to Carter, "no beating people up over books."

He snarls, and I narrow my eyes.

"No. You can't rip his head off for throwing a book, no matter how rude," I swing my eyes to the shifter, "it was."

"Whatever. I'm out of here." The shifter takes off, slamming the library door open and storming away. A few other guys follow after him, making their choice clear. They're done helping.

Shaking my head, I scrub my hands over my face and pick up a textbook. "All right, everyone else ready to work? We have one day to figure out how to vanquish the demon."

Bea runs to the desk, picks up a book, and holds it up. "Let's do this."

Hours pass and people slowly begin to fall asleep where they're sitting. It's nearly two in the morning, but my mind is too wired to stop. I'm reading about necromancy, two short paragraphs in an eight-hundred-page book about witchcraft.

Necromancy, the art of bringing the dead to life, is not known to be a naturally occurring power of the witch gene mutation. The earliest account of necromancy traces back to Theodore Thatcher, who was shunned from his coven at age twenty-two. Thatcher practiced blood magic and his relatives suspect he attempted to summon a demon the year before he began using necromancy. It is not known if he was successful, but the necromantic power he used is not witch born.

Other cases of necromancers have been traced throughout history (see a full listing in Appendix C). All of those captured by the Supernatural Force had DNA that matched that of Theodore Thatcher's. Thatcher is known as the Father of Necromancy and was sentenced to death in eighteen fifty-two. Necromancy is illegal and the Supernatural Force actively persecutes those reported to practice it.

I trace a finger over the black and white sketch of a man standing over a grave where a skeletal arm pops out of the dirt. The image hits close to home, since that's exactly what Mom had done for Dad, and I chew on the inside of my cheek and read over the paragraphs again. I'm surprised there isn't more information, but I guess if they outlawed necromancy, it stands to reason they wouldn't want to provide in-depth details on how it works. That or they didn't know. Either way, I am no closer to understanding my abilities. I wish Mom were here, then at least she could fill me in on what she learned over the years.

She never talked about my grandparents, and Aunt Lou hasn't said a whole lot either. I gather there's a story there that neither are keen on telling. Sort of like me not wanting to tell people about my family. The most people need to know about me is Aunt Lou is my aunt and she's my guardian. At school, everyone knew because it was a small town and once one of the nosy neighbors got ahold of the obituary section of the Sunday newspaper, word spread around that Lou lost a sister. No one ever asked me outright what happened, and that was fine by me.

Telling the guys about Mom and Dad, and how Mom tried to revive him is the most trust I've ever placed in a person outside of Aunt Lou, let alone a group of people. Not even the girls I befriended in high school knew about it. It's a relief none of the guys judged my parents, especially Mom, for what happened. While I'm angry at her, the protective part of me wants to keep her safe from anyone else's scrutiny. Kind of messed up considering how much I hate her little visits, but family can make you do strange things.

"Little Red," Brayden's voice brushes over my ear seconds before strong arms wrap around me from behind. "You're sending waves of gloom through the link."

Aw crap. I'm still getting used to them being in tune with my every emotion, and I have yet to work on shielding them from my stronger reactions. I glance at Everett, who's carefully studying my face, holding his hand against his book to keep it from falling closed. Maybe he can help me figure that out.

"Sorry," I say, running my fingers along Brayden's arms. His hold on me tightens, and a low growl rumbles against my skin, and his teeth nip my ear. "Hey, stop that."

His dark chuckle makes my thighs clamp together. "Can I let you in on a little secret?" he asks, lips brushing over my ear. "I've never been good with authority." He catches the lobe of my ear between his teeth again and gently bites me.

With a soft moan, I press my hand against his jaw, holding him still. "We have too much work to do for you to be messing around like this."

"Everyone deserves a break." Draco closes his book and smirks at me. "Isn't that right?"

Adler clears his throat and taps his fingers on the top of the table. "I'm not finding anything useful in these books."

Everett's eyes darken, and he licks his lips. "I can think of something useful to do."

We all turn to glance at Carter, who's frowning and rubbing the bridge of his nose. "The full moon is literally tomorrow and you all want to get your rocks off because reading is boring?" The slight bite to the question makes my chest deflate.

"Well." Brayden huffs. "When you say it like that, it doesn't sound nearly as fun."

Draco snickers and lifts his gaze over my head, eyes locking with Brayden. The two of them together are dangerous. Maybe Brayden should have stayed a phantom, that way I wouldn't have to deal with identical, broody, half-cocked shifters. I assumed me liking Jon Snow was a phase, and that in real life, I'd be more drawn to someone like Everett. As it turns out, I'm wildly indecisive and my type is. . . well, all of them.

Is it wrong to be smug? Joan asks.

Rolling my eyes, I sigh in my head. *Go on, get it out. I know you've been waiting for this moment.*

She chuffs. *I TOLD YOU! Didn't I say, 'Gee, Raven. Wouldn't it be nice to have all the cocks? Why don't you give it a go?' Then you said, 'Ugh, Joan, gross, leave me alone, I don't want endless orgasms.'*

That is not *what I said.*

Please. I distinctly remember you ranting about how much you didn't need or want a harem, yet here we are, a few weeks later and you've fucked them all. Called it.

Ugh, smug Joan is annoying, I say with a laugh.

Don't fuck this up for us. The mating ceremony was epic, but think of all the one-on-one time you'll get to have. Or, oh my moons, a twin mother freaking sandwich. Brayden and Draco's dicks deep inside of you, pounding into you, filling up—

Dear God, Joan, I get it. You're excited for more sex.

With a growl, she snaps her teeth at me. *Of course I fucking am!*

Down, girl. There will be more fun times, but right now, Carter is right. This is our last chance to find something useful to help us tomorrow night.

Dropping my head back to meet Brayden's intense gaze, I grimace. "Carter has a point."

"Damn. I lost to books."

With a laugh, I kiss his chin and glance back at the textbook.

"Get used to it," Carter says, eyes tracing over a page. "Books will always be better than you are."

I snort. "Oh, burn."

Brayden's soft growl doesn't scare me, and I shake my head.

"Come on, cupcake. Sit down and help me read about water witches."

"I thought the wicked witch melted when she got splashed with water," he says on a sigh, plopping into the seat next to me.

"We're not in Kansas anymore, Toto."

"For the last time, I'm not a dog."

Adler throws his head back and laughs. My lips twitch, but I'm caught up in watching his face transform from thoughtful to outright glee. I make a note to make my fae mate laugh more because he's fucking hot as hell when he does it.

"You're drooling," Everett whispers, pushing his foot against my shin.

Lifting a shoulder, I tip my head to the side and meet his eyes. "I think I like having a harem."

Joan is doing a weird version of a wolf fist pump in my head, and I giggle, slapping my hand to my mouth. *Stop it. You're making me look crazy!*

She totally ignores me and continues to do her happy dance.

"For what it's worth, I think we all like being in your harem," Everett says with a megawatt smile.

And despite the looming darkness ahead of us, my heart

sprouts wings and soars off into a *happily ever after* sunset. I don't bother telling her not to get her hopes up, because my heart is already falling for these guys. Slowly but surely, they're becoming my everything.

I think I'm okay with that.

CHAPTER 25

RAVEN

We read well into the night. I'm staring at a book about lower demons, the words blurring together whenever I blink. My head is resting on my hand and I yawn, flipping the page to read about edax animae. Glancing over the picture, my gaze catches on a black shape bent over a human; a white mist floats out of the dead person's mouth and the demon takes it in.

"Oh," I whisper, but no one hears me because they're all snoring.

I set my finger on the caption and read.

Edax Animae, or Soul Eaters, are common lower demons who can be found feeding off of the newly deceased. Their powers are amplified with each soul consumed. They can be parasitic in nature, feeding off of live beings until they die, but the majority of historical accounts link Soul Eaters with the deceased.

"Holy bananas," I mutter, glancing at Carter. "Hey," I whisper before shoving my foot against his leg. "Wake up."

He snaps awake, eyes blazing yellow until he realizes it

was me who woke him. Running his hands through his hair, he yawns. "What is it?"

"I found something." Turning the book, I show him the picture.

Leaning forward, his eyes skate over the page, widening the more he reads.

"This is good, right?"

He nods, jumping up from his seat. "I'll be back."

"Wait, you can't go alone!" I shout, but he runs away with his supe speed before I can stand up. "Damn it." Sighing, I get ready to wake one of the other guys up so they know where we went, but the library door bangs open, and Carter runs back to the table.

"I have two books." He slams them on the table, and Adler jerks awake. "Luckily, they're short."

"Good, I'll take one." Snatching the smaller one, I settle into my seat and turn it so Adler can see.

With a nod, Carter plops into his seat and buries his nose in the book, skimming each page.

Adler and I are halfway through our book, having no luck finding anything about soul eaters when Carter clears his throat.

"I found it," he says in a groggy voice. Lack of sleep is getting to him but there's a small smile on his face. "Soul Eaters are impervious to almost all types of demon magic, except their maker's."

Oh great, Jinx is hard to kill. Why is he smiling? This isn't good news, if the only way to get rid of her is to have her maker take her out, we're screwed. Unless...

Blinking, I glance at Adler. "Wait, who is their maker?"

Carter full on grins. "Death."

∽

Parties usually mean cute dresses, make-up, and hours spent on hair. By the time the clock strikes eight on Friday night, well after classes and dinner have finished, we're gathered in the library as one group. Whatever she has planned, we're doing it together. Even the guys who stormed off last night agreed to stick with the group instead of attempting to stay on their own.

Jinx struts into the library wearing a bright pink bandage dress. Her hair is styled in a ballerina bun and her make-up is over the top smoky eye. Instead of looking cute, she's terrifying. The whites of her eyes seem whiter, if that's even possible, and the bright pink lipstick isn't pretty on her.

"Oh, don't look so unhappy," she says, waving her hands at us. "We're going to party tonight! You should be excited." She whoops and spins.

Is this her first party ever or is she simply delighted she'll end it with a snack?

Thanks to our hours of research, we might be able to defeat her. The plan relies completely on me, so you know, no pressure or anything.

You are going to do great, Joan says. *I have every confidence you'll zap her ass back to the Underworld.*

I laugh in my head. *Thanks, Joan.*

Jinx claps. "Well, what are you waiting for? Follow me!" With a big smile, she spins on her heel and leaves.

Glancing at the group, I nod and we start after her. She's halfway up the first flight of stairs when we make it to the foyer and she squeals, muttering to herself about how spectacular the night will be. She turns down the west wing of the second floor, and my stomach drops.

The ballroom.

Of course that's where she wants to throw her extravaganza of death.

I lead the way down the dusty hallway, batting a loose

cobweb out of the way as I go. The least she could have done was clean.

"I'm scared," Bea whispers from behind me.

Looking over my shoulder, I grimace. "We'll figure it out, Bea. Stay strong."

Layla and Penelope wrap their arms over her small shoulders, and she tips her chin up.

"Okay."

Facing forward, I smash into Jinx's chest. Her freezing hands clench around my wrists and she leans her face toward me.

"Careful, my sweet."

I yank free of her hold, and she giggles, turning around to shove the ballroom doors open.

"Ta-da!" She holds her arms out and swings her gaze to me to check my reaction. "Isn't it marvelous?"

"It's something," I say, taking in the neon boas, fuzzy pom-poms hanging from the ceiling, bright flutes filled with bubbling champagne, and colorful tablecloths. It looks like Lisa Frank threw up on a nineteen-nineties bedroom.

"Take a drink." She waves her hand to the table filled with drinks. "The orange one is for Bea and the yellow one is for Raven. The rest are for everyone else."

Narrowing my eyes, I walk to the table and pick up the yellow glass, which stands next to the orange one. I sniff Bea's, making sure it's non-alcoholic.

"It's just juice," Jinx says. "I'm not that crazy."

Giving her a doubtful look, I lift mine up and inhale. The scent of sickly sweet, fizzy champagne tickles my nostrils, and I chew on the inside of my cheek.

I can't drink this.

High heels clicking across the dance floor, Jinx hops on stage and turns, placing a hand on her hip. "Let's make a toast. To new friends." She snaps her fingers and a flute of champagne magically appears. Lifting it to her lips, she pauses when she realizes no one is going to join her. With a scowl, she points at Penelope, and she collapses to the ground, screaming in agony.

"I said: To new friends!" she shouts, and this time we all drink with her.

Closing my eyes, I fight against the dark whispers urging me to grab another before I've even finished guzzling the first. This is a horrible idea, but I won't stand by and watch anyone else die. I'll play along with her until I find the right moment to strike. Then she's dead.

Penelope has stopped screaming now. Thank the moon Jinx stopped hurting her.

"Good." Jinx's words come from behind me, caressing my ear as she presses into me. I open my eyes and turn my head, staring into her white irises. She reaches her hand up to tip the rest of the alcohol into my mouth. "Drink it all."

A shudder runs through me as the last drop trickles down my throat and my mind is screaming for more. I pinch my eyelids shut again and shake my head.

"No," I say, but the word comes out slurred, which is impossible because it hasn't been long enough for any of the champagne to take effect.

"Now you're ready to dance." Jinx claps her hand, making me start.

Up on the stage, a group of ghosts appear. I furrow my brow when I count six, then twelve, then six again. There had to be more than alcohol in that champagne. Even sober for a year, I'm not this much of a lightweight. The spirits open their mouths and out comes a haunting tune, something you might hear sung at a funeral. She shoves me toward the middle of the dance floor.

"Dance." She yanks on Brayden's arm and pushes him to me.

The room spins, and I stumble, smacking my hand to my head and groaning. I haven't felt like this since the last time I drank. Right before Aunt Lou sent me to rehab. Brayden catches me around the waist before I can fall, swaying a bit on his feet as well. He's so graceful he makes it seem like he'd planned to dance this way all along, but when his glassy eyes clash with mine, I know he's not right either.

"I'm sorry," he whispers, taking lead and dragging me along for a waltz.

Jinx claps when we finish and snaps her fingers. "Again!"

With a soft growl, I try to pull away from Brayden, but as soon as I do, Penelope starts to scream and drops to her knees.

Shit.

Brayden pins me against his body. "I'm sorry," he says again, practically carrying me through the entire dance.

"For what?" I slur the question. Lifting my head to meet his gaze leaves me panting from the exertion.

"Everything," he mumbles, picking up our speed when Jinx complains about how slow we're moving.

The ghosts are still moaning and wailing a creepy song, but even their voices fade into the background until all I can hear is Jinx's foot tapping against the ground. The tempo matches my heartbeat, and when she starts to tap it a little slower, my thudding heart slows as well.

Brayden groans and shoves me away, staggering a few feet from me before he vomits.

"Are you okay?" I ask, trying to get to him, but Jinx appears in front of me.

"Stupid girl." Jinx cackles and shoves me hard enough that I begin to fall, but before I can put my hands out to save face, everything goes black.

The next time I open my eyes, my wrists and ankles are bound, and I'm lying on my side under a cloud-covered sky.

Lightning flashes and thunder rumbles. Some of the angry storm clouds break apart, and the light of the full moon spills through, illuminating the ground. Someone is on the ground in front of me, but I can't tell who because their back is turned to me. It's not my guys, Bea, or Layla. Focusing on the pack link, I search for the men, sighing in relief when I feel them close by. The relief is short lived because the full moon catches my attention. A stone drops into the pit of my stomach.

The full moon.

If you have grand plans to save everyone, now is probably a good time, Joan says.

Joan! Are you okay?

She huffs. *I am for now. The demon spirit is about to kill us all though.*

Lifting my head is a struggle, but I manage to glance around. Everyone is tied up and lying on their sides. Jinx has placed us in a circle, and she stands in the middle of it with her hands raised toward the sky. Her eyes are glowing white like the moon, and she drops her head back, soaking up the moonlight.

I push to my knees, falling on my face when I lose my balance. "Damn it," I mutter, using my shoulder to get off the ground and flexing my abs to keep from slamming into the earth again. Wind whips over the yard, tossing my hair into the air. Whatever Jinx is saying is carried away with the breeze, but there's a deep tugging inside of me, like she's hooked on to my soul and is reeling it toward her.

"Jinx."

"Good. You're awake." Jinx lowers her head to stare at me, her lips drawing back to reveal sharp teeth. Powered by the souls of shifters, Jinx stands completely solid. No more flickering form. Consuming Howard's spirit the other day gave her an extra boost, and now her skin is as real as mine.

"You don't have to do this!" I scream into the wind, spitting out pieces of my hair. "You don't have to listen to the alpha."

"I'm not listening to him." I can barely hear her over the thunder. "This reaping is for me, and it's all thanks to you."

My face wrinkles in confusion. All thanks to me? Because of my powers?

She laughs, still holding her hands toward the sky. "Thanks to you, Raven, I can take from Death himself and become real once more. No more planes separating me from the living. No more flickering in and out. I'll be one-hundred-percent demon in the flesh."

"You're crazy," I say, shaking my head. "He won't let you take from him and go free. He's going to come for you, and he will destroy you. Is that what you want?"

Jinx scowls and glances at me. "Shut up, you're ruining the reaping."

"No. You have to listen. You can't—"

"Don't tell me what I can't do. If you haven't noticed, you're already marked for death. You feel that grip I have on your soul?" The tugging sensation returns, this time harder and more painful. I gasp, sucking in a hard breath. "That's me. You can't escape this time."

No. There has to be a way out of this. I look around, seeing a few people moving, rolling over to see what's happening. They're still alive! For a second, I thought maybe she'd taken them all already, but Bea's gaze finds mine, and she calls my name, face screwing up in fear. Another hard pull inside of me makes me cry out, and Jinx begins to siphon my essence, dragging it into herself.

Fight, Raven! Fight! Joan yells inside my head.

Grasping on to my soul with my mind, where the invisible hook is attached, I grind my teeth and tug. The thread between Jinx's body and mine snaps tight, and I breathe in, yanking again.

"You little bitch." Jinx flashes to me, palm cracking against my cheek.

My head whips to the side, but I refuse to let her take me without a fight. I open my mind to my necromancy, dredging up the oily substance from the depths of my being, calling on Death's darkness to force her back.

Holding on to both my necromantic powers and my soul is hard. Sweat breaks out across my forehead, and I pant, sucking in air so I don't pass out. I strum against the strings of Death's power, taking in more than I ever have and shoving it toward Jinx, shaping it into a tool that will take instead of give. Take her soul, strip her of everything, and get rid of the threat. That's what I need to do.

With a scream, she releases her hold on me; the binds holding my hands and feet fall away. She lifts her hands, and the bodies of my friends float into the air. They collectively scream as Jinx takes from them instead of me.

"No!" I jump to my feet and race toward her, shooting all of the black power I've gathered to my palms, and slam into her, pressing my hands into her chest. "Let them go!" My scream hurts my throat, but I let it all out, pressing her into the grass and reaching inside of her with that black power. There's a small spark of light, a sliver of a soul. Jinx lost her humanity a long time ago when she snuffed out her human side and gave control to the demon.

"You're going to regret this." Her teeth flash white when she smiles and cackles, breaking off when I rip the light from her body and send it through the connection I made with Death. Her milky gaze rounds, and she thrashes against me, but it's too late. Whatever strength she's gained isn't enough to keep her here.

A few people scream behind me, but I stay focused, taking

every ounce of her I can. It's not easy, because it's not just Jinx I'm sending through the connection: there are dozens of souls within her. The spiritual wolves of fallen shifters lift their heads, howling for the last time as I send them to the Underworld where they can finally rest. No more being used for power. No more being held captive with no escape.

No more.

Jinx's reign ends now.

"Bye, bitch," I whisper, snuffing out the last of Jinx's life with a final dredge. Her body vanishes underneath me, and my hands slam into the earth, nails biting into the dirt.

You did it! Joan yips, spinning inside my head. *You killed her!*

Good, I say in my head. Then I drop my forehead to the ground and laugh, letting the soft grass tickle my skin. *She's dead.*

She is, Joan says, voice filling with pride. *I knew you could do it.*

"Raven." Layla says my name around a sob.

I spin around on my knees, expecting to see her hurt or bleeding. Instead, I find her kneeling where Bea was lying, palms spreading over the impression her little body left behind. Glancing from side to side, I search for her. Maybe she moved, went to check on the men. The guys are all standing, staring at Layla and the bare ground. The other shifters are slowly getting to their feet as well, but Bea is nowhere to be found. I dig my fingers into the grass and crawl over to Layla, patting the ground like maybe she's there and I just can't see her. Like maybe I'm still in a daze from facing off with Jinx. My fingers slip through the blades of soft grass.

There is no one there.

A bright spear of lightning bursts across the sky, booming thunder immediately following it. The clouds open and rain pours from the sky in a heavy sheet, drenching me in a matter of seconds.

Bea is gone.

What have I done?

To be continued.

AUTHOR'S NOTE

Hey there. Yes. I know.
Breathe.
Okay.
So, you got answers! Maybe not all of them, but now you're starting to figure things out, right?

What do you think is going to happen next? Need other readers to theorize with? Join Rory's Tainted Readers on FaceBook.
The next book, Bad Moon Academy three, is the final book in Raven's trilogy and will end in a happily ever after.
Thank you for reading. I hope you loved Raven as much as I did. If you did, please consider leaving a review.

To stay updated on book news, make sure you subscribe to my newsletter on my website www.rorymiles.com. There's also a special Enchanted Magic novella being issued through there, so what are you waiting for? Come listen to me ramble <3.

ACKNOWLEDGMENTS

I have a ton of people to thank, first being my family. You guy are always there for me. Thank you for loving me.

Next are my alpha and beta readers. They listen to me ramble, help me adjust things that are a little off, and help fix random typos. Brayden would have been Bradyen, Braden, Brayen, etc. without them. Remind me to never pick that name again.

Jennifer, my amazing editor, puts up with my crap and loves me even though I drop these giant cliffhangers in her lap. Thanks J-Bae. Without you, I'd be lost.

There are more people I'm not mentioning by name, but for every reader in reader groups commenting, squealing, and showing how excited you are for this series. THANK YOU. The idea for Bad Moon Academy came to me right after I finished Blood Mafia, and Raven was begging to be written. She's not as hot headed as Demi, but she's spunky and I love her just as much, so thanks for loving her too!

I have a ton of people to thank, first being my family. You guy are always there for me. Thank you for loving me.

Next are my alpha and beta readers.

ALSO BY RORY MILES

Coming Spring 2022

Pretty Broken Things

The Complete Blood Mafia Series:

Blood Owed

Blood Taken

Blood Bound

Bad Moon Academy Series:

Dead Wolf Walking

Dead Wolf Falling

Dead Wolf Rising

Tainted Power Series:

Her Retribution

Her Reign

Her Resistance

ABOUT THE AUTHOR

Rory Miles is a fantasy romance author. She loves cats, memes, gifs, books, writing, her children and her husband. Especially when he makes fried chicken. She loves writing about romantic shenanigans and does her fair share of reading. Her all time favorite books are: #whychoose.

For new on more adventure filled romance, make sure to follow her on Facebook and Instagram.

Please don't forget to leave a review! Reviews are a huge help to authors and Rory loves to hear from readers.

Facebook Reader Group: Rory's Tainted Readers